SNOWBALL
UNWRAPPED

Books by Kristen McKanagh

SNOWBALL'S CHRISTMAS

THE TWELVE DAYS OF SNOWBALL

HOW SNOWBALL STOLE CHRISTMAS

SNOWBALL UNWRAPPED

Published by Kensington Publishing Corp.

SNOWBALL
UNWRAPPED

Kristen McKanagh

KENSINGTON
PUBLISHING CORP.

www.kensingtonbooks.com

KENSINGTON BOOKS are published by

Kensington Publishing Corp.
119 West 40th Street
New York, NY 10018

Special book excerpts or customized printings can also be created to fit specific needs. For details, write or phone the office of the Kensington Sales Manager: Kensington Publishing Corp., 119 West 40th Street, New York, NY 10018. Attn. Sales Department. Phone: 1-800-221-2647.

The K with book logo Reg US Pat. & TM Off.

ISBN: 978-1-4967-3697-0 (ebook)

ISBN: 978-1-4967-3696-3

First Kensington Trade Paperback Printing: October 2023

10 9 8 7 6 5 4 3 2 1

Printed in the United States of America

To our wonderful friends, the Tribbles
We miss you every day

SNOWBALL UNWRAPPED

Prologue

Snowball

I give a leisurely kitty stretch, kneading my paws in the air, as I wake from a perfect nap in my favorite sunny spot only to frown as I realize I'm alone in Miss Tilly's room. Mr. Muir's too, but I'm still getting used to that since the owner of Weber Haus married her beau. Easier to forget when he's traveling right now, too, and took his birds with him.

Getting to my feet I glance around.

Where did one of my favorite humans and nap partners go anyway?

The door is open out into the hallway of the Victorian house that serves as both my home and as a very popular inn called Weber Haus. Voices float up the stairs to me, not unusual with how many people stay here, but I decide to see if Miss Tilly is there and pad off down the hallway in that direction. The voices lead me down the stairs.

What I'm not expecting as I turn the corner into the formal living room is to find Sophie, who manages the inn and hotel, up on a ladder, her head covered by a large swath of red velvet cloth. Meanwhile, Miss Tilly and Emily, Tilly's great-niece-in-law, are standing at the foot of the ladder looking up, pretending to be helpful. Well, Miss Tilly is pretending.

Emily is holding her adorably precious new baby, so she can't help.

"To the right," Tilly says, batting her hand to the right as if she could make Sophie move by her will alone.

"Are you sure this time?" Sophie sounds . . . strained . . . from under the velvet. "Because my arms are starting to lose feeling."

"I'm sure," Tilly says.

A *pop* like a gunshot sounds, then Sophie steps down.

"Watch out for Snowball," Emily warns, pointing at me.

I scowl at her, offended because she should know better. I am *never* underfoot.

Sophie moves the ladder over a smidge and climbs back up. I blink as what they are doing finally starts to make sense. Is it time for Christmas decorations already? A glance outside at the pristine, snow-covered grounds and mountains beyond and I guess I should have realized sooner that the holiday season was here already.

I study the decorations.

These aren't the usual evergreen garlands that they put up around the house for the holidays. These are, now that I see them, *much* fancier.

"They need to be *perfect*," Miss Tilly tells Sophie. "The crew arrives at the end of the week, and they need everything up in time to start right away."

I tilt my head, ears perked. Start what?

"Don't worry." Sophie comes down to pat Tilly's arm. "Lukas and Daniel are coming tonight, along with Lara and Peter, and we're all going to work very hard to have everything up in plenty of time."

I'm staring at them as if they are speaking gibberish. Maybe they are. Because I've never seen Miss Tilly this worked up over holiday decorations. I mean, she wants Weber Haus to look just right for the guests that stay here through December, but not like this.

And what is she talking about? A crew? What's that?

Maybe Daniel, Sophie's husband, is doing more construction? Weber Haus has been expanded the last few years. When I first arrived here, it was only the house, which was operated as a smaller bed-and-breakfast. There were other buildings on the property, which were all unused. Since then, the barn and a carriage house have been converted into shops and a larger hotel wing was added on. What else could they possible add, though?

"Well, I won't be here. The one year I make plans to spend Christmas elsewhere, and this happens."

What happens? She's going to meet Mr. Muir to visit some friends of his for the holiday.

Miss Tilly is still fretting. "Weber Haus is going to be on national TV, *live*, and I want it to look perfect."

I freeze, except for my tail, which flicks back and forth. On TV? We're going to be on TV? That sounds terrible!

Don't get me wrong. I love all the visitors we have here. But being on TV sounds . . . like a lot of chaos. I mean, are the humans going to seriously expect me to perform on cue now? I'm a cat. Cats don't do that. Besides, for once, I would love to just have a quiet Christmas.

That never seems to happen around here.

Not that I'll do anything to ruin this for Miss Tilly or my other humans who love this place. I sigh. I guess as the official kitty of Weber Haus I'd better make sure I look my best. Because of course they'll want to include me.

I'm adorable. Everyone says so.

In fact, maybe they'll want to include something about how I matchmake all the couples around here. I'm the reason Emily and Lukas are together. And Sophie and Daniel. And even Emily's brother Peter and his fiancée Lara. I'm practically famous for my skills.

Yes. I'd better be ready for this TV situation. They're going to need me.

Chapter 1

Jocelyn Becker was so focused on the microfiche film she was staring at through an ancient machine, it took several rings of her phone before the sound even penetrated. She almost ignored it, too absorbed in her research on film and television legend Barbara Stanwyck to want to stop to chat.

Except the name on the screen read "Ilse" and she never ignored her twin sister.

"Joce?" Ilse said as soon as she answered the phone. "I need your help."

Jocelyn straightened so hard she knocked the table, and her pen rolled off with a clatter. Ilse didn't ask for her help. Ever. Her sister was the one who managed everything. "What's wrong?"

"I don't want to tell you over the phone."

Yup. Definitely bad.

"Can you come to me? I'm at the studio. We're not quite done filming this episode but will be soon."

Jocelyn made a face. She avoided the studio in general. The few times she'd gone, fans kept mistaking her for her sister, so she'd stopped going. "It'll take me a little while. I'm at the archives."

"Oh. Um . . . I could meet you at your apartment. I don't mind waiting there."

Jocelyn's eyebrows tried to crawl right off her face. Ilse wasn't exactly known for her patience.

As the host of *Home & Hearth*, a popular TV show that focused on home and garden and decorating and cooking and whatnot, patience wouldn't have gotten her sister as far as she'd come. Tenacity had done that.

Tenacity and talent.

Two things Jocelyn had not a shred of. Despite being twins they couldn't be more different. Ilse showed the world her best face and shared her homemaking tips, doing anything from baking to singing to crafting, and doing it to perfection. Jocelyn on the other hand couldn't bake, or sing, or craft. Her passion was her job as a film historian.

"Okay. I'll see you there as soon as I can."

They hung up, and immediately, Jocelyn was on her feet, turning off the machine and gathering her things. Her highly independent twin never needed her. Given that she sounded like she'd been crying, this couldn't be good.

She worried all the way home and parked.

"Hi, Bart!" She waved at the apartment manager as she hurried toward her building.

"Hey," he called back. "Did you see what was on TV last night?"

Jocelyn, eager to get to Ilse, shook her head.

"*It's a Wonderful Life.*" The way he beamed, she realized what was happening. Bart liked to test her movie knowledge, particularly movie quotes. Maybe she should focus on him for longer than two seconds. What had he just said?

Right. The movie. Black-and-white. Holiday feel-good story. Sort of. She found that one depressing more than up-lifting. " 'Every time a bell rings, an angel gets his wings,' " she quoted.

He laughed. "You know them all."

She should, given her job.

"I enjoyed it."

Jocelyn gave him a thumbs-up. "I'm glad."

She would have loved to stick around and discuss it more or give him another recommendation, but Ilse needed her. She was sure her sister had been crying. To do that on set . . . that just wasn't Ilse.

Jocelyn hurried all the way up to the apartment she shared with her best friend, let herself in, then stumbled to a halt at the sight of Ilse's face.

Her sister was sitting down on the couch in the small living area and her face was streaked with tears and runny makeup.

"Good grief!" Jocelyn shut the door behind her, dropped all her things on the floor, then hurried over to throw her arms around Ilse's shoulders. "What happened?"

Ilse burrowed into her—also an unusual reaction. "Gregori. Left. Me."

She burst into tears and all Jocelyn could do was hold on as her sister cried and cried. Her mind spun with a truth that seemed so far-fetched she might have laughed if Ilse wasn't so upset. Ilse's longtime boyfriend had left her? Impossible. Gregori Stadnicki-Borch was some kind of Polish count or baron or a descendant of one. Jocelyn wasn't entirely clear. But the man loved Ilse the way puppies loved cuddles and treats.

As her sister kept crying in her arms, Jocelyn tried to make plans in her head. Plans for retribution. How dare he make Ilse miserable like this? He'd clearly shattered her tenacious, strong, but secretly delicate sister's heart. But the worst Jocelyn could come up with was a strongly worded social media post. Given she only had a hundred followers, total, versus Gregori's rabid and plentiful following, she was pretty sure that wouldn't even make a dent.

Eventually, Ilse's tears wound down to a soggy, hiccupping mess of her usually put-together twin. Able to let go, Jocelyn grabbed a box of tissues and plopped it in Ilse's lap. "Talk to me. What is this all about?"

Ilse shook her head as she blew her nose, then looked up, blue eyes dulled. "I don't know. Look at this."

She fiddled with her phone, then handed it over. Jocelyn frowned at the text scrawling down the screen. "He . . ." She was going to post *two* strongly worded social media diatribes. "He broke up with you over *text*?"

Ilse's chin wobbled but she managed to keep it together with a nod. "But he doesn't say why."

Jocelyn scanned through his words again with a growing frown. Ilse was right. He only vaguely said he couldn't keep going the way they were.

"Did you have a fight?"

"No." Ilse mopped at her eyes. "Gregori doesn't fight."

Clearly. He just hid behind the safety of technology. What a passive-aggressive wuss he turned out to be. Jocelyn hadn't spent much time with her sister's boyfriend. The man was a wealthy heir to a jewelry business and fortune and traveled all over the world, jet-setting. But she'd liked him.

Or thought she had.

Ilse straightened, chin jutting out. "I need to see him. In person."

"Good idea. Get some answers." Jocelyn nodded.

"I have to go to the Philippines. Tonight, if there's a flight." Ilse jerked forward to take Jocelyn's hand in hers, her watery gaze imploring. "Which is why I need you."

Jocelyn looked down at their clasped hands then back up into her sister's pleading gaze. "Um . . . I'm still stuck on the Philippines. Is that where he is?"

"Yes. And he's working and can't leave for a week or two."

"Okay. I'm not sure how that involves me though." Jocelyn had never been to the Philippines. "Do you want me to go with you or something?"

Moral support maybe? That would be a first.

Her sister was the most stubbornly independent person Jocelyn knew. Ilse saw the need for emotional anything as weakness. Jocelyn had been sneaking moral support in when Ilse wasn't looking for as long as she could remember.

Ilse's lovely features—even looking like a half-drowned clown—pinched, and Jocelyn's gut said she should run away fast. She knew that expression. Never mind the need for a hug or something. Clearly, Ilse had cooked up some cockamamie plan. Except she usually didn't drag Jocelyn into them.

"The thing is . . . there's a problem with my leaving just now," Ilse said.

This close to the holidays was bread-and-butter season for the TV show Ilse hosted. "I would imagine so."

Ilse gave her arm a little shake. "A bigger problem than usual. We're taking the entire show to this adorable Victorian inn in the mountains. We're going to do five *live* Christmas-themed episodes of *Home & Hearth* from there. Each episode will be all about decorating and cooking for the best holiday season ever." Ilse's sorrow cleared for a second. "Isn't that adorable?"

Not really. It sounded like torture to Jocelyn. Also . . . didn't every show do something similar?

Ilse's face clouded back over. "But there won't be time to fly halfway across the world between shows, let alone convince Gregori to take me back."

"Maybe you can work it out with the showrunners—"

Ilse jumped to her feet. "I can't. There are other things going on, but because it's live, there's no leeway here."

What other things were going on?

"I still don't see what that has to do with me—"

"I need you to stand in for me," Ilse said in a rush.

Given how disastrous that went the last time they tried it, when they were about sixteen, Jocelyn burst out laughing.

Except Ilse wasn't laughing with her. Her chin was wobbling again.

Jocelyn sobered on a horror-filled gasp. "You can't think that's a good idea. I'm *terrible* at all that stuff."

"Everything is already set to go." Ilse dropped back down beside her, taking her hands. "All the crafts are made, and the recipes prepared. I can go all diva and make someone else do the cooking. That way you don't have to do or make anything. You just have to smile at the camera and read the script." Ilse gripped her hands harder, expression pleading in a way that was so unlike her sister, Jocelyn's heart cracked. "The crew sets everything up for you. I'll send my assistant, Margot, to take care of your wardrobe, hair, and makeup. I can give the script to you now, so you have plenty of time to memorize—"

"It won't work." Jocelyn surged to her feet. This was a terrible idea on so many levels. Not only were she and Ilse night-and-day different, but Jocelyn was the opposite of crafty and bake-y. She burned toast and mangled decorations. A five-year-old child could do better.

Ilse grabbed her hand, pulling her up short. "It will. It has to. I *have* to—" The tears welled up in her blue eyes. "I have to," she whispered brokenly.

Jocelyn closed her eyes to block out her sister's distress but seeing her strong sister like this—Ilse was the one who took care of her, not the other way around.

Am I really considering doing this? "All I have to do is memorize lines and say them at the camera?"

That didn't sound too hard. She had a vlog about her film research, so she was used to that, on a much smaller, indie scale of course. But still, she wasn't camera shy.

"That's all." Ilse nodded, hope lighting her eyes.

A painfully desperate hope that Jocelyn found impossible to deny. "I don't have to actually craft or bake anything?"

"I promise. I'll make sure."

Jocelyn shook her head. Then shook it again. "This is possibly the worst idea in the history of ideas. You realize that, don't you?"

After all, it would be Ilse's career—the most important thing to her in the world—on the line. Not that she'd let her sister down if she could help it. But they were talking about pretending to be someone she wasn't for a long time. The odds were against them.

Ilse gasped. "You'll do it?"

Heaven help them both. Jocelyn paused, then nodded, and Ilse threw her arms around her, squeezing tight. "Thank you. Thank you. Thank you. I'll owe you forever." Then, in true Ilse fashion, went straight into doing mode. "We don't have much time to get you ready. Let's start with this."

She pulled a massive diamond ring off her finger and held it out, the gaudy jewelry glinting in the light. It was the first truly extravagant thing her sister had ever bought herself once she landed the show. She never took it off, so of course Jocelyn had to wear it, but something about being responsible for it made the reality of what they were doing strike a cold note inside her.

She swallowed, then reached out, slipping it on her finger. The weight of it threatened to topple her over. "You realize how serious this is, right?" She looked up from the ring.

Ilse winced. "Of course I do. But . . . I have to do this. I . . ." She shrugged, the most helpless Jocelyn had seen her in a while. Or maybe ever. "He's supposed to be my everything."

The thing was, growing up, after their parents had died, Ilse was the one who'd kept it all together, who'd taken care of Jocelyn and made sure they were fine. She never asked Jocelyn for anything. Definitely not for help.

Jocelyn sighed. "I can see that. Just don't get mad when I screw up and get you fired."

Ilse grinned through a new spate of tears. "That won't happen."

Jocelyn wasn't as confident.

"Oh!" Ilse pulled back. "And don't tell Theo."

Chapter 2

"Impossible," Ben Meyer muttered to himself as he rode the glass and chrome elevator up to the executive suites of the studio.

The doors whooshed open with a subtle ding, and he made his way down the hall. He'd been summoned.

"How my agent talked me into doing this show will be a mystery never solved," he muttered under his breath.

Possibly a murder mystery. He could practically hear the death knell for his career with every clack of his feet on the tiled hall. Mike, his agent, had convinced him to act as a temporary cohost of *Home & Hearth* after Ilse Becker's longtime cohost had quit abruptly. Ben had yet to get the explanation for why.

"They'll be appreciative," Mike had said. "They'll reward you for your hard work," he'd said.

Ben had been in this business forever. Early in his career, they'd stuck him on a show with problems, with a directive to "fix it." He was sure, even now, that the studio had expected one of two outcomes: He'd actually succeed, which worked out for everyone. Or he'd fail and they'd fire him and cancel the show. No skin off their backs either way.

He'd succeeded.

Then they'd stuck him on another show with problems, and he'd succeeded again.

And again.

Until he'd gotten the reputation for fixing anything he touched. It didn't matter if he was in front of the camera as cohost or behind it as a producer and showrunner, he could look at a show and see what it needed to turn a corner and attract or re-attract audiences.

But that wasn't happening with *Home & Hearth*. Because of Ilse Becker.

Reaching a set of glass double doors, he walked through into the swish offices of the executives, still chrome and glass with unimaginative black leather added in for good measure. Another door led him into the office of the executive assistant, where Heather, who had to be sixty if she was a day, ruled the roost of the show's executive producer with a velvet-covered iron fist.

"Go on in, Ben," she said with a wave at the closed door to her right, his left. "They're waiting for you."

They? He kept his thoughts hidden behind a polite smile that he pinned in place as he strode straight to the door and right inside.

The three men and two women waiting for him probably expected him to hesitate on the threshold at the sight of them—including his agent—and he silently thanked Heather for the subtle warning she'd given him to expect a crowd.

Instead of hesitating, he strode all the way in, then stopped in the middle of the circle of vultures, hands casually in his pockets, and allowed himself a small but visibly uninterested smile. "What's all this about?"

He directed the question at Herbert Delores.

For such a big man in their industry with a reputation for being ruthless, Herbert's physical person was incredibly deceptive. Average height, he sported a mild face with enough baby fat, even at the age of fifty-some-odd, to make him appear cherubic. Except, at the same time, the rest of him was skinny to the point of emaciation. Ben wasn't entirely sure Herbert wasn't an addict of some sort, except the man's behavior was too consistent to support that theory. He was always sharply present.

"*Home & Hearth*," Herbert answered. Straight to the point as ever.

"I've been on the show a few months," Ben pointed out. "You could hardly expect me to have turned things around by now."

Actually, they could. Usually he had by now.

But they'd landed him a worse predicament than usual, thanks to his cohost. The woman was impossible—haughty, picky, a perfectionist, and inclined not to listen. Actually, it was more than not listening . . . she actively rejected any idea he dared to suggest. No wonder her previous cohost had walked away.

He'd figure it out, but he needed more time.

"It's not that." Herbert waved a negligent hand.

Ben didn't buy it. The man's eyes were glittering with whatever he was about to propose and the only reason he'd have brought Mike in would be to ensure Ben played nice.

"Then what?"

Sure enough, Herbert's dawning smile more closely resembled a weasel than a human. "We want to change the theme of the live shows."

Ben tried not to let them see how he stilled at that. He'd argued for different themes himself on the second day on the job and had been vetoed by Ilse. But they'd been planning for this for a while. It was too late. "Oh?"

"Your proposal to feature a different kind of unique holiday party for each show is perfect."

You've got to be kidding me.

"We leave for Weber Haus, where we'll be filming, tomorrow," Ben pointed out. They couldn't possibly think he could rearrange all new content by then.

"You've done faster changes than that before," Mike pointed out. "And you can repurpose a lot of what's ready to go."

He wasn't wrong, but that didn't make it easy. "Remind me to fire you after this discussion."

His longtime friend just grinned. Probably because Ben threatened to fire him at least once a month and never had.

"The live shows combined with this format will be perfect," Herbert said. "Just the fresh content *Home & Hearth* has been needing."

Actually, Ben wasn't convinced the content was the issue. "And Ilse? She already vetoed this idea."

All five people in the room grimaced. Herbert had had to throw his metaphorical weight around and insist on doing the live shows at all when Ilse had resisted.

"We're giving you full authority over the production. She'll answer to you."

Ben snorted. That was likely to go down about as smoothly as Santa switching to a jet-pack-powered sleigh and retiring his reindeer. "You've already talked to her about this?"

The exchange of glances gave him the answer to that.

"No," Herbert admitted. "We wanted your buy-in first. But we'll be talking to her next. Before you leave."

Ben considered that. If they could get Ilse out of her own way, the show could definitely do better. She was a pro at what she did, but something was off. Maybe she'd gotten too complacent with the same content week-in, week-out, creating a stale feel? He still hadn't pinned down the issue. There was something missing, and the ratings were evidence of that.

However, changing the format on her without her knowledge went against the grain, no matter what a pain in his rear end she could be.

"I mean it." He gave Herbert an uncompromising stare. "You tell her and make sure she understands *and* agrees, or I don't do this, and we stick to the original plan."

Ben could tell that it visibly went against the exec's ingrained sense of self-worth and position to cave in, or to have his word questioned in the first place. But after a gobbling second, Herbert nodded. "Consider it done."

But Ben wasn't done. He directed a pointed stare first at Mike and then at Herbert. "So . . . what's in it for me?"

Which was when Mike finally allowed himself an open grin that told Ben everything he needed to know. His agent had negotiated something good.

"A new contract for *Home & Hearth* that says if the ratings come up by the beginning of next year, the studio will let you name your own show and put it together from top to bottom yourself."

Yup. Mike had known exactly the carrot to dangle—a show of his own from concept to production. Ben narrowed his eyes. "No proposals. No test audiences. From concept to production entirely under my purview."

Mike nodded.

Well, well, well . . . Merry Christmas to me.

Ben rocked back on his feet. "Let's go through it."

An hour later, new contract signed, Ben gave Heather, still behind her desk in the next room, a small salute of thanks, as he left the office heading back toward the bank of elevators. He could hardly contain the excitement pulsing through his blood. Heck, he might even do a jig if he wasn't in a public place. Maybe when he got home.

Finally. *Finally*, he was going to be able to do what he wanted.

No more fixing broken things. No more having to run every idea by someone else for approval. Something from scratch. Something his own. Something that could succeed from the get-go. A thousand different ideas rolled around in his head, because he had been thinking about this for a very, very long time. Now it was time to narrow down his ideas to the one that would be the best to start with. Maybe he could even get some work done on his plans as they were completing the live shows for *Home & Hearth*.

Only one thing could go wrong. The fly in his ointment. The broken spoke in his wheel. The lump of coal in his Christmas stocking.

Ilse Becker.

But he'd been assured she would play nice.

The elevator doors opened, and Ben almost took a step back. Because the person getting off on his floor was the exact person he'd just been thinking about.

Decked out in her usual pristine designer clothes, sunglasses still on despite being indoors, purse held over her elbow with her well-manicured hand held like she was cupping something. Perfect from the top of her golden blond head to the tips of her pointed Jimmy Choos.

"Ilse," he acknowledged.

He waited for her to do the same in the impatient tone of voice she seemed to reserve just for him. That was how they handled each other. Instead, she stared at him like she had no idea who he was, then abruptly smiled.

This time Ben did take a step back. Just a small one, but still a show of weakness that he did not like in himself. But Ilse had never smiled at him like that. Not once. Honestly, he wasn't even sure she smiled like that for the camera. Like she meant it. Like it came from the heart. If she had, her ratings would probably be better than they were.

A smile like that was like looking into pure sunshine or catching a glimpse of Santa as he shimmied down the chimney.

Ben had no idea how to react except with suspicion. Maybe she'd heard about what was going on with the show, the changes they'd just contracted him to make, and was determined to put a stop to it? He narrowed his eyes.

Neither of them moved.

Then the elevator doors tried to push closed. At the same time, they both jumped forward, sticking a hand in between to stop the doors.

"You should probably get off," he said. And the cutting suspicion in his voice was more than he meant to show her. Letting her know that he was wary was not the smartest move. She was smart enough to use it against him.

While he held the door open, Ilse stepped out into the hall, but before he could get in the elevator, she placed a hand on his forearm. A zing shot from her soft touch all the way up his arm and down his spine.

"I'm sure whatever they told you couldn't be as bad as all that."

It took a lot to surprise Ben, so to say he was shocked when she patted his arm in a motherly fashion would be a colossal understatement.

Then she took off the sunglasses and he found himself staring into clear blue eyes that seemed to be completely sincere.

Confusion held him immobile until the elevator started to buzz angrily. With a jerk, Ben backed inside. The last thing he saw was Ilse's blue eyes widen and her eyebrows lift in confusion as the doors closed between them.

"What just happened?" he muttered to himself.

Chapter 3

Holy moly and happy holidays. Wow, Ben Meyer was even better-looking in person than he was on her television, if that was possible.

An impression Jocelyn had formed yesterday at the elevator when he'd acted so strangely. Or maybe she'd been the one acting strangely. She'd been flipping her lid when that elevator door had opened. Not an hour after Ilse had left her, she'd gotten a call on her sister's phone that Ilse was wanted at the studio immediately.

Which meant dressing up, acting the part, and figuring out where the heck she was going while appearing to know exactly where she was going. Taking over her sister's life had come way too fast for her comfort.

And then Ben Meyer was suddenly standing in front of her, and she'd frozen.

Not just because he was nice to look at, which he was, but there was something about him in person. A dynamic aura. Magnetism. He was definitely used to being the man in charge. She suspected if he really let himself take full advantage of his skill set, he could be one of those men who charmed his way past every single woman's defenses, even when said women saw him coming from a mile away.

But the way he'd acted toward her . . . or rather toward

Ilse. . . . Well, Jocelyn got a feeling he wasn't the bad boy, player type of guy, with women lined up on a string ready to be pulled when he had the time or the whim.

He seemed too . . . alone . . . for that to be true. Too self-contained.

She hadn't really had an opportunity to make more of an impression today, either. He'd been seated far away from her on the flight, and when the cars hired to pick up the cast and crew of the show had arrived, he'd sat in the front seat rather than beside her. From where she sat now, behind the driver, she had a decent view of the side of his face. His cut jaw currently was set at an angle that indicated a stubborn insistence on getting his own way. A characteristic she should probably be smart to remember while she was pulling the wool over his eyes.

Shame. Wouldn't it have been nice to meet him as herself?

Not that he was likely to give her a second glance.

"So, you have three boys?" he was asking the driver, whose name was John.

John nodded. "Yes, sir. Ages three, five, and eight."

"Sounds like a handful."

Which was exactly what Jocelyn would have said. She eyed Ben's profile.

The thing was, despite her impression of him as coldly in charge, he also seemed genuinely interested in John the driver. In one short hour, Ben had managed to learn that the driver had grown up in Braunfels, the small mountain town where Weber Haus was located, and was well familiar with the Victorian inn where they were headed to film the live shows. And now Ben was learning all about John's family.

Meanwhile Ilse's cohost seemed set on ignoring her entirely.

Not that Jocelyn should mind that. If anything, she should be incredibly grateful that he wasn't paying her more attention. The fewer people who paid attention to her, the more likely she was to get away with this farce she'd agreed to for her sister's happiness.

For Ilse.

Jocelyn glanced at the ring on her finger. Like carrying around a physical manifestation of her sister and everything she had riding on Jocelyn's doing this right. She had been repeating "for Ilse" to herself over and over ever since arriving at the airport. While trying not to shred whatever she was holding in her hands at any given minute. Including Ilse's Hermès scarf.

Actually, her new mantra had started well before the airport. Just dressing in her sister's clothes and putting on her makeup had been enough to set off a mild panic. Maybe because she'd waited for Theo to leave before she got started, so she'd been in a rush.

Her roommate for the last few years, Theo had grown up with her and Ilse. He was Jocelyn's best friend, but lately he and her sister had been not exactly speaking. So she'd taken the coward's way out, leaving him a note saying she and Ilse were going away together for the holidays. Not an entire lie. They just weren't going to the same places together.

Mental note to call and reassure him. Preferably when she knew he'd be busy, so she could just leave a voicemail.

Because right now, the thought of helping her sister didn't do much to alleviate her reindeer-sized nervous knots. Dancer, Prancer, and Vixen might as well be doing the "Macarena" on her stomach. Theo would definitely be able to tell something was wrong.

At this rate she would lose a lot of weight this Christmas, rather than gain it like she usually did. Because she didn't think she could put a single bite her mouth without spitting it back up. The nerves were taking up all the space.

So she sat quietly, even though she wanted to join the conversation with John. She found him to be just as interesting as Ben seemed to.

But she was painfully aware that her sister only tended to interact with people when the cameras were on. It wasn't that Ilse was antisocial or even the bitch a lot of people thought she was. Her sister was secretly an introvert, and that made it difficult for her to talk to people.

How Ilse had become a host of a show that regularly had guests to set at ease and bring out of their own shells, Jocelyn had never quite figured out. But Ilse could turn it on when she wanted. She just had to pick and choose when, so she didn't drain herself completely.

Sitting with her hands folded primly in her lap, Jocelyn forced herself to stare out her window at the wintry scenery flashing by and try not to worry about her lies or the incredibly expensive cream-colored vicuña coat her sister had lent her. In fact, any of the incredibly expensive clothes currently in her luggage were a problem. It would take a month of her wages to replace just one of these items if she stained it or ripped it or ruined it in any way. Given her tendency to trip all over her feet—or worse, get stuff all over herself—meant one of those outcomes was highly likely.

Nothing you can do about it.

She had to look the part.

They were traveling along a road covered in a fresh fall of snow, the tires crunching as John drove them down a two-lane, tree-lined street. Here the mountains were more like rolling hills, though she knew if she turned to look behind them, sharper peaks rose into the sky. She'd heard a boutique ski resort was not even an hour's drive away. Thank heavens skiing was not one of the shows. She'd break something trying that.

They had already passed through the town of Braunfels, adorable with a lone main street of shops lined with buildings all from various bygone ages, erected over time. She knew, as they passed through, that historically this town would have seen wars, but it was so picturesquely lovely, she could hardly picture that now.

Suddenly the trees broke open into a field, and John almost immediately turned the SUV off the road and onto a long gravel drive.

And Jocelyn couldn't help herself, her jaw dropped.

This had to be Weber Haus. The pictures and descriptions hadn't done it justice. It was classical Victorian architecture—probably three stories tall but also with a full-sized attic and basement, white wooden siding, black shutters, and a porch that wrapped around at least the front and sides. In the bright sunlight reflecting off the snowy ground, the Christmas decorations popped against the scene, with strings of lights, green garlands, and red and gold bows that looked picture-book perfect against the pristine house.

It was, in a word, idyllic.

At least, it was until she caught sight of Ben canting his head in her direction, eyeing her like he worried about what she was going to do or say.

Immediately Jocelyn snapped her gaping mouth shut and tried to assume a serene expression behind the large sunglasses that she thought made her look more like a bug. Again, Ilse's fashion sense, not hers. She prayed she got her sister's uncaring, supremely confident expression right.

"What do you think?" Ben asked, clearly directing the question at her and not at Margot, Ilse's personal assistant who was riding beside Jocelyn in the back seat.

What did she think?

If she was answering for herself, she would have said that she'd never seen something so ideal for the holidays in all her life. That clearly Santa would want to use this place as a replacement for the North Pole, or maybe his retirement home, because it was so perfect.

But Ilse was never one to gush like that. So she kept herself to a reserved, "It's lovely."

Ben grunted a sound that could either have been an agreement or disappointment.

"Just wait until you see the shops around back," John said. "You've certainly chosen a wonderful place to film your show."

Jocelyn agreed wholeheartedly with that comment but kept that to herself. She was tempted to turn around and see the other SUVs carrying the rest of the crew. What did they think of it, finally seeing this place in person after what she understood had been a lot of time spent researching and scouting?

No doubt they were looking at it with different eyes. Which made sense. They had problems to solve and issues to think through, like where they would place the cameras or the lights and so forth.

Even so, how anyone could take one look at this house and not want to curl up on a couch in front of the fire, with a steaming cup of wassail, and Christmas carols playing on an old-fashioned stereo, was beyond her. In fact, maybe she could do exactly that tonight.

Although that wasn't something Ilse would do. So maybe not.

As soon as they came to a stop out front, Jocelyn slipped out of the car and moved to the side so Margot could get out too. She stared up at the house, taking it all in.

"I think this is going to be better than you were expecting," Margot murmured quietly beside her.

Jocelyn was suddenly glad that she hadn't exclaimed over the beauty of the location the way she naturally would have. She couldn't make a mistake on the very first day.

Or second day. Meeting with the executives within hours of agreeing to stand in for Ilse had been the most nerve-racking hour of her life. Because Ilse had already left. Jocelyn had barely heard the words the men and women had directed her way, happily telling them that she'd go along with whatever Ben said needed to happen on the show. Vaguely she'd thought they'd seemed surprised. Maybe because they also had said something about Ilse objecting to these shows being filmed live in the first place, and had been overruled. But clearly her sister had rethought that idea, because she'd seemed enthusiastic enough when she'd gone over the setup and plans for each show.

And as far as Jocelyn was concerned, thank the high heavens that Ben was around to make the decisions. That took a lot of pressure off her.

She answered Margot's comment with a vague hum of what could be agreement or disagreement, hoping she sounded like her sister. Or at least generic enough to be interpreted either way.

At the click of the SUV trunk being opened, she grabbed on to the opportunity of a distraction and moved around to the back of the vehicle to find John pulling out the luggage. Jocelyn reached for the handle of one of the smaller cases at the exact same time Ben did, their hands meeting on the handle.

The man had surprisingly nice hands—big, strong, capable, but also well kept.

"What kind of lotion do you use?" The question was out of her mouth before she could stop to reconsider, and Jocelyn almost made it way worse by slapping a hand over her mouth.

Only she didn't, and thankfully Ben only gave her single sidelong glance before saying, "I've got the luggage. You just go inside and wait."

Part of Jocelyn wanted to argue that she wasn't helpless and could be just as useful as the rest. But she was pretty sure that wasn't something Ilse would say, so after having already made one gaffe, she wasn't about to make another.

She still couldn't stop herself from picking up her smallest bag. "Thank you. I'll just take this with me and save you a trip." Then she turned and headed up the stairs with Margot right behind her.

A bell tinkled as she opened one of the double front doors that led into the house. There she found a wooden podium situated in the foyer with a woman standing behind it—pale blond hair pulled back in an elegant twist, professionally dressed, and a polite but warm smile pinned into place.

"Welcome to Weber Haus," the woman said. "My name is Sophie, and I'm the manager of the inn and hotel here. You must be part of the production crew for *Home & Hearth*?"

Jocelyn smiled back, liking Sophie already. "Yes, I'm—"

"This is Ilse Becker." Margot stepped in front of her, handing Sophie a packet of papers that probably had the details of their booking.

That's efficient. I should get a personal assistant just to handle my life. Not that I can afford it.

"Excellent. I have reservations for . . ." Sophie named the number of rooms and guests. "I have Ilse Becker and Ben Meyer both booked here in the house, as requested. Everyone else is set to stay in the hotel wing all on the same floor with the conference rooms." She glanced up at that. "It's easier if anyone who will be staying in the hotel takes their luggage around the back of the house and then follows the path that crosses behind what looks like a barn but is actually the shops. I'm sorry there's not parking closer."

Margot nodded, not looking too happy. But what could she do?

Sophie continued. "A continental breakfast will be served between six and ten in the morning. If you want lunch or dinner here, you'll need to book it with us at least a day in advance. Although based on the shows you're doing, I know things will be different for your group. Including having your own access to the kitchen, dining room, and other spaces within the house at specific times."

"When the house will be off-limits to your other guests," Margot tacked on in a tone of voice that had Jocelyn smiling at Sophie just to take out the sting. No need to be rude to the woman.

"Of course. Did I miss anything?" Sophie addressed the question to Margot, though she flicked Jocelyn a quick glance.

Did she recognize her sister from the show?

A thought that managed to re-remind Jocelyn that she was not here on a normal vacation. She was here to work. In front of cameras. While pretending to be her sister.

All of which she forgot all over again the instant she spotted the tiniest, fluffiest white cat she'd ever seen. The adorable pet was lying in a pool of sun on a maroon, velvet-covered chair in what appeared to be a formal living room off to the right of the foyer.

Even if Ilse herself had been standing right there with a neon sign that read, "Stop," Jocelyn couldn't have stopped herself from hurrying straight to the cat with a cry of, "Oh, aren't you the most precious thing I have ever seen in my life."

She didn't pick the cat up, but she ran a hand over her silky soft fur. The sweet creature was small, but obviously not a kitten. Big blue eyes stared at Jocelyn unblinking, and the cat tipped her head as if trying to decide if she was going to like this new human or not.

Jocelyn smiled and petted her some more, scratching her under her chin and at the base of her ears, and not giving up until a contented little purr erupted from the tiny body.

Ilse was being . . . very *not* Ilse.

Ben couldn't put his finger on it. In the car ride up here, she'd said very little, keeping her sunglasses-covered gaze turned away, obviously uninterested in talking to their driver, John, who was a nice guy. That was the Ilse he knew. But then she'd stared at the Victorian house where they were filming like she'd found heaven and never intended to leave. Top that off with trying to actually help unload the luggage . . . and something was up.

Mike had said she'd agreed to giving Ben full control while they were here for the live shows. Not a single argument, in fact.

Ilse never just agreed with anything. Especially when he was involved. He'd come to the realization early on that she intended to argue with every word out of his mouth, even if he said something that was in agreement with her.

She had to be up to something.

The question was . . . what? She wouldn't dare sabotage her own show and her career. *Home & Hearth* meant more to her than anything. Only her upper-crust boyfriend seemed to manage to trump the show. Sometimes. So she wouldn't do anything to hurt the show. But he *could* see her trying to sabotage him and his career. They weren't exactly best buddies.

Understatement.

He'd have to watch her closely until this was over.

Hefting her three massive suitcases up the steps, he left them outside and let himself into the house, only to stumble to a halt at the sight of Ilse scooping up a fluffy white cat and cooing as she sat back down with the small creature in her lap. In her perfectly styled, expensively clad lap.

Her coat was cream colored, but the top-end-label suit underneath was black. She was really risking white cat fur all over her couture clothes? He'd once seen Ilse slap her assistant's hand away when she got too close with a securely lidded cup of coffee.

Before he could comment, a ruckus that sounded like a cross between an angry elf and a dying pig along with an impressive amount of hissing sounded behind him. Ben lifted his gaze to the decorative foyer ceiling, searching for patience there.

Isaac, the animal handler for the show, was bringing the show's resident cat in. The thing hadn't shut up the entire plane ride here. He knew because of all the glares Isaac got as they'd deplaned. Thank goodness he hadn't had to sit in the same car with the thing.

Isaac set the carrier down with a thump. "Is it okay if I take Angel out?" he asked the blonde watching with wide eyes from behind the console in the foyer, clearly part of the inn's staff. "She'll calm down once she's out of the carrier," Isaac assured her.

"I don't—"

Before the woman could finish responding, three things happened all at once: An older woman entered the foyer from the back hallway, Isaac unzipped the top of the cat carrier, and the cat flew out of its enclosure like the Ghost of Christmas Past rising from the grave.

"Oh no—" Ilse exclaimed behind him.

A streak of white from the corner of his eye was Ben's only warning of impending doom. Angel took one look at the white cat Ilse had been cooing over, which was now running over with a happy little meow to say hello, and went berserk.

She arched her back so fast, looking like she'd been plugged into an electric socket the way her fur went up, he was surprised she didn't snap her spine. With a hiss she swiped her claws at the other cat, who hopped back, blinking in shock. In an instant, the hotel cat transformed from sweet and curious to banshee, snarling and hissing and mimicking Angel's posture.

But Angel didn't back off. Like an abominable snowcat, she went into a frenzy and the two white cats went at it, hissing and biting and scratching at each other in a melee that looked like a blur of white fur, fangs and claws.

"Snowball, stop that!" the older woman cried out, hurrying forward with the obvious intention of breaking up the fight.

Without thinking it through first, Ben stooped over and grabbed the inn's cat, only she went wild in his grasp, going after his hands and arms, trying to get away. At the same time, Angel attacked his ankles trying to get to Snowball.

Gritting his teeth, he managed not to drop one or kick the other. "A little help, please."

Isaac lunged for Angel, managing to grab her before she tried to climb Ben like a tree.

"Oh my goodness." Ilse rushed over. Not to take Snowball, who stopped fighting and was now clinging to his brand-new jacket with her claws sunk in through the material and down to the skin . . . but to *pet* her. "Poor baby," Ilse murmured soothingly.

Me or the cat?

"You're shivering," she said.

So the cat. Never mind the maimed human.

Thankfully, the cat calmed at her touch, retracting her claws. A string of swearwords poured from Isaac at Ilse's back as he tried to corral Angel. A cat, incidentally, that looked exactly like the one Ben was holding. All white, big blue eyes, just a tiny bit larger. He might have assumed the two cats had come from the same litter if he didn't know better.

Every detail of which abandoned him when Ilse raised her own blue-eyed gaze to his—eyes sparkling with a gratefulness that hit him right in the solar plexus. "You saved her," she whispered.

Like he was suddenly hero material in her eyes.

Ben had no idea what to do with *this* Ilse.

All he could do was stare right back. Flummoxed. Maybe she was buttering him up so that he'd listen to her ideas more? If she'd bothered to collaborate with him from the beginning, she would have learned that he always listened to other ideas. Unlike her.

Ben cleared his throat. "All I did was save the studio from a lawsuit."

With a screech to wake the dead, Angel was shoved unceremoniously back into the cat carrier.

"Got her, Isaac?" he asked.

"Yeah, boss."

Ben looked pointedly at the blonde who he hoped was the manager of the inn. Her nametag read "Sophie." Without being told, she immediately handed over a key to the cat wrangler. "Why don't you take her to your room? It's in the separate hotel wing and will probably be safer to let her loose to calm down in there."

Grumbling, Isaac took the key and left.

"I'm so sorry about that," the older woman who'd come in as Angel had been released hurried to say, looking at him. The inn's owner perhaps? "Snowball is never like that."

"I'm pretty sure that was all Angel's fault," he assured her. "She can be a little temperamental." The official *Home & Hearth* kitty was not a favorite with the cast or crew, though he'd never seen her lose it quite so spectacularly.

"Oh . . ." The woman glanced around, then seemed to collect herself and offered her hand with a smile. "I'm Tilly Weber-Muir, the owner of Weber Haus. You can all call me Miss Tilly."

After a quick shake, Ben eyed her. Surreptitiously. His producer instincts were going off. He could see the potential. This adorable woman would be perfect for the show. Maybe a small segment in each episode, with her showing off a different aspect of the house and grounds or sharing history or stories of visitors?

"Unfortunately, I already had plans to spend this month with my beau." She used the word "beau" like it was still in vogue and he smiled until her words sank in.

"Oh? You won't be here?"

She shook her head. "I wish I was, but I'll be watching from his house each week. If you need anything at all, Sophie will be able to help. My great-nephew Lukas will too. He and his wife, Emily, are expecting."

As if that were her cue, Sophie glanced around the gathered group, then efficiently started handing out keys and room assignments.

"Am I allowed to hold her a little longer?" Ilse asked Sophie, scooping the cat off of him to cuddle her close.

Sophie grinned. "You can take her to your room if you want. She stays in the house mainly, but Snowball likes to think she rules the entire grounds of Weber Haus. A rare people-friendly kitty."

With a chuckle, Ilse grabbed the handle of one of her suitcases—the largest one—and started wheeling it toward the stairs with one hand while still holding the cat with the other.

"We can bring your luggage up," Sophie called.

"I'll just get this one." Ilse didn't even turn to answer. Then proceeded to lug the thing up one clunking, red-carpet-muffled stair at a time. The entire while chatting away to the cat in her arms.

Things like . . . "Did that horrid other kitty scare you?" and "How naughty of her to attack you in your own home." And "I imagine she was frightened from all the travel."

Ben stared after her departing back with a growing frown.

"Is there anything else I can get you?" Sophie asked.

He blinked, focusing on her. Then cleared his throat for the second time since stepping into the foyer as he realized he was standing alone with her, everyone else having cleared out to go to their rooms. "Uh . . . no, thanks."

I'm still shaken up after that cat fight.

Miss Tilly scolded me. *Me.* Then she apologized for me. I didn't do anything wrong, though.

I was going over to the new cat just to say hello to her. She's the one who started the hissing and clawing. All I did was defend myself. Is that so wrong? Sheesh, I didn't realize another cat could be so mean. The cats who hang around here haven't been.

No way is she on Santa's nice list with an attitude like that.

And what human thought Angel would be a good name for her? I really hope they keep her locked in a room far away from me.

Chapter 4

Jocelyn sat on the beautiful four-poster bed in her room. The dark wood was carved into a swirl on each post, and the thing protested loudly every time she climbed off and on. But she didn't care, because it was so beautiful. Like going back in time. No one made houses or furniture the way they used to.

Tapping out a quick text to Theo, she let him know she'd arrived safely, was settled at the place she was staying, and was off to play tourist.

Hopefully he wouldn't call.

She gazed out a single, wide window that looked out over the snow-covered front lawn and gave a blissful sigh as she ran her hand over Snowball's soft fur. The little cat had curled right up on the cream and blue toile quilt—handmade and no doubt almost as old as the house, though in pristine condition. At least Snowball had stopped shaking. That encounter with Angel had really bothered her.

At a quiet knock at the door, Jocelyn got up to answer it to find two people standing outside, only one she recognized. Margot. The other was a handsome man with dark hair, blue eyes, and an easygoing grin.

"Hi," the man said. "I'm Lukas Weber, Tilly's nephew and the muscle around here." He pointed at all her luggage.

On a chuckle, Sophie swung the door back and ushered

him in. She didn't help bring in the cases though. Not after her hand had twitched in that direction and Margot had frowned at her. Instead she moved to the dressing table where she'd left her cream-colored Chanel purse that matched her coat—Ilse's of course—and riffled through the wallet for a tip.

By the time she turned around, though, Lukas was already at the door and Margot was handing over a bill, which he waved off. "I'm one of the owners," he said. "And this isn't my regular job. I am a photographer and have a studio and exhibition room in the shops here."

"Oh." Margot dropped her hand to the side. "How nice."

Jocelyn frowned at the other woman's back. She'd never met Margot before this, as Ilse tended to go through assistants like Jocelyn went through bags of chocolates. But she'd sounded cold. Dismissive.

Lukas didn't seem to notice, grinning as he rocked back on his heels. "We like it. It lets me be here to help, and my wife, Emily, owns and runs a bakery right next door. All in the family, so to speak."

Before Margot could give another dismissive nothing of a response, Jocelyn stepped into the doorway. "That sounds lovely. And what an idyllic place to live. I'm jealous."

Kind eyes twinkled back. "It is."

"I'll have to come look around the shops as soon as I'm settled," she said next.

She ignored the way Margot was looking at her, pretending to herself that Margot's frown was really a smile.

It wasn't like Jocelyn didn't have time today. The cast and crew of the show had all been essentially left on their own for the rest of the afternoon and evening, allowing them to get settled in. She needed to feed herself, and stretching her legs after the flight and car ride would be lovely. Maybe she could get a little Christmas gift shopping done at the same time.

Lukas left but Margot stayed. Not the most comfortable

experience having the dour-faced assistant do all the unpacking for her—as much as the limited space to put clothing allowed at least. But then Margot left her on her own.

That's what she really needed. A moment to just be Jocelyn, without being seen by anyone who cared.

A change of clothes was definitely needed, so Jocelyn pulled on the antique handle of the wardrobe only to frown. "I should have paid more attention to what Margot packed and unpacked," she muttered, partly to herself and partly to Snowball. The little cat, now awake and watching curiously, tipped her head sideways and actually seemed to study the contents with Jocelyn. "Not a single sneaker or pair of jeans."

In the end, she changed into black leggings she was pretty sure were real leather—the supple, thin kind that cost a fortune and didn't squeak when she walked—a black-and-white blouse that was probably silk, and calf-length boots that at least had a low heel.

Then, pausing at corners to check that she was alone, she made it around the back of the house and into the area where the shops were. Having read up on the place out of curiosity, she knew that the Webers had converted what had originally been a barn and a carriage house behind the main house into individual shops.

Smart. A way to entertain folks staying at the inn as well as bring business out their way, since they were out of the city limits.

Everything in the shops, including a gazebo in the center of the thoroughfare between the two buildings, matched the house—white with red roofing and ornate iron details. In addition the entire area had been decorated for the holidays— all evergreen wreaths and garlands with red and gold bows and white twinkling lights. With the snow and the mountains and the trees all around them, she revised her earlier descriptor of "idyllic" to "holiday-tastic." She could practically hear the jingle bells from Santa's sleigh.

"A yuletide wonderland suitable for Santa and his elves," she murmured to herself. And smiled.

"That seems a little fanciful," a deep voice sounded behind her.

Blinking, Jocelyn turned to find Ben, then blinked again to find he'd changed into jeans and sneakers like a normal human. And standing not two feet from her. How was it possible for him to seem even more handsome wearing a hooded sweatshirt with a bulky jacket over it? If she'd have worn something like that, she'd look like a shapeless blob, but on him the broadness of his shoulders and leanness of the rest of him was emphasized.

Must be nice.

On a sigh, she pulled her gaze up to his, only to blink a third time. Hands stuffed in his pockets, Ben was eyeing her narrowly, like he was trying to solve the mystery of how Santa got down a stovepipe chimney.

What did I say? She scraped her mind. The thing about Santa and elves? Uh-oh. Ilse definitely would never say something like that.

Forcing what she hoped was a breezy expression to her face—the acting gene wasn't one she'd picked up—Jocelyn managed a shrug that felt more awkward than casual. "What? You don't like the shops?"

Without moving any other part of himself, Ben glanced around. "I like it fine. I'm just not the type to wax lyrical about it."

He cut his very serious, very intense gaze back to her and tipped his head, message clear. She wasn't the type either. Or rather, her sister wasn't.

I'm going to have to be more careful even when I'm alone. "Well . . . enjoy your shopping."

On a self-conscious little wave, she walked straight into the nearest shop, which was a toy store. She stopped suddenly just inside the door as she realized what she was looking at. Ilse wouldn't be caught dead in this shop.

"Problem?" Again that deep voice was behind her.

Why had he followed her? She glanced over her shoulder.

Ben raised his surprisingly thick eyebrows slowly. Eyebrows with personality. "You're blocking the door."

Oh.

Forcing her feet to move, she stepped further inside and pretended to be looking around, meanwhile scouring her mind for any excuse about Ilse coming in here. Until she got distracted by the space itself.

Trying not to let her mouth hang open, Jocelyn took a closer look around. Not at the toys, many of which were lovely, handcrafted concoctions, but at the shop itself. The main part of the store was set up to look like Santa's toy shop, with elves all over. An arched entryway, with massive doors covered in glitter, led to the next room.

Inside the second space, the area was set up to look like the North Pole, with snow, including glittering flakes hanging from the ceiling. The ceilings in this shop, once part of the Weber Haus barn, went up to the second story, and in one corner was what looked like a real, floor-to-ceiling Christmas tree with its limbs hanging out, the piney branches covered in bright colored lights, ornaments, and what appeared to be fluffy white snow that actually seemed to sparkle.

Wow. This place is amazing.

At least this time she managed to keep her thoughts in her head. She flicked a glance at Ben, who was across the room leaning over a four-foot dinosaur that appeared to be a puzzle.

Maybe he wasn't suspicious.

Turning away she found herself in the books section of the shop and naturally gravitated to a shelf that included some classics, including a beautiful hardback, gold embossed and illustrated version of *Little Women*. It was in her hands, and she was flipping through it in a heartbeat.

"I didn't peg you as a reader."

Jocelyn paused mid-flip and did her best to hide a sigh. She'd let her guard down again. Although, there was nothing in here Ilse would be interested in anyway.

Lie. Tell him a big fat whopper and then leave.

She was a terrible liar. "It's for a gift."

"For who?"

How did he manage to make two short words sound so skeptical? Or was she just being sensitive?

She closed the book. "No one you know." Mostly because she was about to buy a book for no one she knew either. She'd pay for it with Ilse's credit card, too. Her sister owed her big-time. It could be an early Christmas present.

Ben crossed his arms. "I didn't peg you as a toy shop person either."

There really was only one way she could see to handle this. Lying wasn't it. She pinned a smile to her face. "Do you need help picking something out? I'm a terrific gift giver."

There went his eyebrows again in a doubtful arc that she found . . . kind of adorable. In an annoying, superiorly suspicious way. "You had Margot do your Christmas shopping already."

Jocelyn lowered her lashes, staring at Ben's sneakers. How very disappointing of her sister, though she'd suspected that might be the case for years.

"Why are you suddenly interested in my shopping habits anyway?" Okay, so maybe a little of her hurt crept into her tone.

Ben stiffened. Not a lot, because he'd learned to hide his reactions long ago. In this business he had to. Why was he bothering to follow Ilse around asking her questions anyway?

Because she was acting strangely, that's why.

But why did he care? "No reason," he said after a pause. "You just surprised me."

What surprised him more than Ilse coming into a toy shop and buying a copy of *Little Women* for some unidentified person was the flash of hurt in her eyes right before she'd lowered her lashes. What had he said to cause that?

Crystal-blue eyes raised to meet his gaze, and her smile was perfunctory. "I guess we don't spend much time together."

He couldn't put his finger on what about that felt off. "True." Then . . . "I'm scoping out shops for the shows. Things to highlight or that might be good for our parties. Do you want to join me?"

Now why in the name of flying reindeer had he gone and offered that? *Can't take it back now.*

"Oh! Um . . ." Ilse's eyes darted to the right and left of him like she was choosing the best route of escape. "I trust anything you decide."

Those words coming out of her mouth were the only reason she was able to step around him. Because he was in shock.

Turning on his heel, he joined her in line to check out. "Okay . . . what's going on with you?"

She stiffened so hard, she suddenly reminded him of the two cats earlier today, arching their backs as they hissed at each other. Ilse didn't bother to turn around, facing forward and only canting her head a little to the side so he had a view of her profile. A lovely profile with a dainty nose and lips that he just realized right this instant were surprisingly plush.

"What do you mean?"

Her question snapped him out of thoughts that had no business in his head. "I mean, my lovely cohost, that you haven't trusted me an inch since day one on this show."

The corner of her lips he could see drew down. "I'm sure that's not true."

An odd way to word that. "It's true. And you haven't

agreed to anything I've ever suggested. Not once. So why, all of a sudden, are you so . . . agreeable?"

"Well . . ." She wrinkled her nose. " 'This is Christmas. The season of perpetual hope.' "

What? Ben frowned. "Why does that sound familiar?"

Ilse brightened. "It's a quote from the movie *Home Alone.*"

True. But . . . "You're quoting movies at me now?" He crossed his arms. "I asked a serious question."

She snapped her head forward so he couldn't see her expression at all. Then her shoulders rose and fell sharply. Twice. Like she was having to take deep breaths. "Look—" She cut herself off and shook her head. Then spun to face him so abruptly he didn't have time to back up, and in the small space in line and in the store with so many toys and people, the move pressed her right up against him.

Close enough for him to catch the small hitch in her breathing.

Serious blue eyes trained on his chin, or thereabouts. "This isn't the place to get into it. Let's just say I'm having some . . . personal issues. Okay?"

Personal issues? He couldn't even begin to imagine this woman with a personal life, family, friends, or otherwise.

She whirled back around, clearly having said all she intended to.

The person ahead of Ilse moved forward, and he and Ilse stepped together at the same time. Then Ben bent his head closer to her ear so he could lower his voice and still be heard, and had to ignore the whiff of vanilla. She smelled of vanilla. Did he know that before now?

Not important. "Are these personal issues going to affect filming?"

If he hadn't been standing so close, he wouldn't have caught the way she ducked her head. "Not if I can help it," she muttered.

The words were confident. Her tone and the way she held her body were anything but. Suddenly to him she felt small. Had she always been this tiny up close? They sat side by side or stood side by side frequently on set, and he'd never really noticed before.

"Hey . . ." Ben put a hand to the small of her back, stepping in closer. "I can handle everything as long as you show up ready to work."

Suddenly, despite the crowds and the yelling kids and the noise of toys and the Christmas music and standing in line in the middle of a crowded store, it felt like he and Ilse were totally and utterly alone. Just the two of them.

She hesitated. He knew because in the next second she leaned back into his touch. Only slightly, but to him it felt as if Ilse Becker had finally given in. "I can do that," she said.

What on earth had Herbert and Mike said to her? Or maybe she was giving in because the personal issue was enough of a burden. Either way, by giving him her trust, she'd just made his job a thousand times easier.

Satisfaction thrummed through him. "Trust me. I'll handle it."

Ilse suddenly half turned, her shoulder pressing into him. Not that she seemed to notice as she looked up at him, studying his face. "Do you think of yourself as a good person, Ben?"

The satisfaction dimmed. Had she been stringing him along just now?

He searched her gaze. "Yes."

"Even in this cutthroat industry?"

What on earth was she getting at? He tried to find any hint of ill humor, but her eyes remained clear and bright. "Yes. Even in this industry."

She gave a tiny little nod, as if she liked that response. "Okay . . . just don't . . ." She grimaced. "Don't surprise me with anything."

Ben stared at her.

Color bloomed over her cheeks and she glanced away. "I'm not good with surprises," she muttered at her feet.

"Next," the cashier called out.

Ilse lifted her head and he saw the moment she deliberately chased away whatever worries she was struggling with and pinned a bright smile in place. Then she turned away from him to step up to the register.

Ben stepped off to the side, out of the way and watched out the window at the shoppers hurrying by. Then huffed a sharp laugh that he immediately swallowed.

If anyone would have told him even an hour ago that he'd have to fight back the urge to hug Ilse Becker and tell her everything would be all right, he would have laid odds at Vegas that they'd be wrong.

He'd have lost.

"Mrrrrowww . . ." A tiny little cat sound caught his attention a second before something brushed against his ankles.

He glanced down to find the tiny white cat from the house winding figure eights around his feet as she rubbed up against him. "Hey there."

She looked up with big blue eyes, the same blue as Ilse's, and he swore the little thing smiled.

"What are you doing out here, Snowball?" Ilse's exclamation came a heartbeat before she also brushed against him, on another subtle wave of vanilla, and scooped the cat up against her chest, crooning to her.

He stared at the cool blonde in her leather pants and silk blouse under a black wool jacket, who didn't seem to care at all about cat fur—though Margot would probably care a lot. He knew Ilse's assistant handled all her dry cleaning. Ilse's smile for the cat—for the blasted cat—was this side of heaven. And Ben suddenly wanted to hug her again for completely different reasons than before.

Which was why he just stood there and wondered when it was, exactly, that he'd lost his marbles.

*   *   *

I settle into my new friend's arms. She knows all the best ways to cuddle a kitty. After so many years around humans all the time, I can tell which ones are true cat people, and she is. So I decide I like her a lot.

Mid-purr I glance over at the man I was rubbing against. He'd been standing in Lara's toy shop staring at my new friend like Santa had forgotten to deliver his toys on Christmas Day, and so I gave him a good kitty rub. But the second I see his face now . . . see the way he's looking at the woman holding me . . . my matchmaking kitty instincts kick in hard.

She's not paying him a lick of attention, her focus on me. But him . . . his focus is *entirely* on her.

I smile to myself. I haven't helped any humans find their true love since last Christmas with Emily's brother Peter and his fiancée Lara. I was just thinking I needed something to entertain me.

Now I know what I'm going to do. I'm going to help these two humans fall in love.

Chapter 5

Crash.

The sound came from the direction of the kitchen, followed by a string of swearwords, and Jocelyn hurried through the swinging door from the hallway to find the room packed with several members of the crew all now facing a flour-covered director. Meanwhile, a fluffy white cat sat in the middle of more flour all over the floor and casually bathed its back leg with its tongue like she wasn't at the center of the disaster.

"Someone get this darn animal out of here." Walter was visibly holding himself in check.

Without a second thought, Jocelyn moved into the room and scooped the animal up. "Where's Isaac?" She looked around for Angel's owner and trainer.

"That's not Angel. That's the inn's cat."

Oh. She looked closer.

"Snowball, you naughty thing." She tickled the cat under her chin.

Immediately the cat blinked at her with large crystal-clear blue eyes, then butted her chin with her head, setting up a loud purr. The rest of the crew just stood and stared.

"What happened in here?" a deep male voice asked from the doorway where she'd just been standing.

Jocelyn glanced up to find Ben propping the door open

with one hand and surveying the room. His gaze landed on her and descended into a frown. Why? She was just holding a cat.

Then he opened his mouth. "Did you make this mess?"

In her entire life, Jocelyn had never been so tempted to sweep flour off a floor and into a bowl just so she could dump it on another human being's head. Why in heaven's name would he even think that at all, let alone first thing? Even Ilse wasn't prone to fits where she doused people in flour. Apparently, the guy from last night was gone, replaced by mistrustful Ben the "professional."

She aimed a smile at his hard heart. "Good morning to you too, sunshine. And no, the cat made this mess as far as I can tell. I wasn't in the room when it happened."

His eyebrows practically flew off his face.

Whoops. The sunshine bit was probably too much.

"Uh-huh." His gaze traveled from her head to her toes. "You're getting flour all over your sweater."

Jocelyn glanced down and winced. She'd forgotten she'd worn a dark green cowl-necked sweater. Cashmere too. Although, to be fair, *all* of her sister's clothes were made of some ridiculously expensive material.

Sorry, Ilse.

Nothing she could do about it now, so she shrugged. "I'll take it to the dry cleaners."

But when she glanced up again, it was impossible to miss another round of raised brows in the room. Because Ilse *was* fastidious about her clothes. She bought a lot of them and paid out the nose, but she kept them in pristine condition too. The product of living an early life where the next meal wasn't always a guarantee, let alone nice things.

Ben was still frowning. She really needed to get him not frowning . . . or not paying attention to her at all. That would be even better. "What did she do?" she asked Walter.

Wrong question to ask.

"That cat"—Walter pointed an accusatory finger at poor Snowball—"is a menace. She's been underfoot in every place we've gone to measure and scout."

Ben tilted his head. "So what are you going to do to handle it?"

He didn't use an accusing tone or even a forceful tone. If anything, he put it kindly, but the blunt words sent red surging into Walter's already ruddy cheeks. Because he was right. It was the crew's job, but as far as Jocelyn was concerned there was duty and then there was consideration.

"I'm not doing anything. I can take her."

Rather than try to move past Ben, who still crowded the doorway to the hall, she headed for the back set of stairs that led up to the bedrooms on the second floor. She didn't get far. Moving as quick as a cat, Ben snagged her by the elbow, gently plucked Snowball from her, and dumped the cat in the arms of a man who looked not much past boyhood. Very handsome, but a babyface. She was pretty sure he was the intern. She was still getting faces and names straight.

"Are you going to talk to the owners about her too?" Ben asked her.

Oh.

Jocelyn tipped up her chin. "Why not? Miss Tilly is a sweetheart. I'm sure she'll understand."

"A sweetheart?" Ben was frowning again. "Really?"

Deliberately misunderstanding that the frown was about the word choice for Ilse, not about Tilly, Jocelyn blinked at him with wide eyes. "You don't think so? That lovely older lady who owns this house?" She tipped her head. "Maybe you caught a different vibe than I did."

Someone in the room sniggered. The intern, she was pretty sure.

Ben's lips flattened. "That's not what I meant."

"Oh." *Get out of here before you say something really out of character for Ilse.* "Well . . . I'm glad we're on the same page there."

She glanced around for anything, any change of topic, and caught the intern—Kyle, that was his name—staring at her clothes. Following his gaze, she caught sight of her flour-covered sweater. Perfect excuse. "I'd better go change."

And hide the thing from Margot, who might get as upset as Ilse about the state it was in. Jocelyn was up the stairs and in her room probably before Ben even had a chance to move. She stood there after changing, debating just camping out in here the rest of the day.

Was hiding cowardly? Probably. It was also smart.

They didn't need her today. Not really. The crew were figuring out exactly the spaces and shots and lighting and other technical stuff. Tomorrow they would discuss the schedule and any—hopefully minor—changes, depending on how today went.

But just sitting in her room seemed so . . . boring. She was in a Christmassy paradise. When else was she going to get this chance?

Sneaking back down the front stairs, she got a small taste of how Ilse must feel when she was avoiding paparazzi. No Ben in sight, so she scooted into the dining room where a continental breakfast was laid out for cast and crew. Part of the deal with Weber Haus.

Dishing up fluffy scrambled eggs, crisp bacon that smelled heavenly, and a piece of toast that she slathered with butter and what appeared to be homemade blackberry preserves, Jocelyn sat down, happily took a big bite, then smiled. She could get used to this part. No cooking. No burnt-toast breakfasts or a breakfast bar. Which was what she tended to eat, since she couldn't cook worth anything.

This was soooo much better.

"You're back, Ms. Becker!"

She glanced up to find Kyle—that was his name, right?—standing in the doorway that led to the kitchen. She really hoped so.

"Is Ilse in there?" she heard Margot call from the kitchen.

Kyle called "Yes" back to her. Then turned nicely blue eyes her way again. Jocelyn slowed in her chewing because . . . well . . . he was staring. "Is the cat okay?" she asked. Just for something to break the moment.

"She's fine." He grinned before thankfully moving to dish up his own breakfast.

The swinging door that led from the kitchen to the dining room opened and Margot backed in. "I have your breakfast smoothie." She turned around only to stumble to a halt at the sight of Jocelyn's plate of food. "Oh," she said after a second. Then looked down at the green liquid concoction in a pristine glass—she'd even added a sprig of mint and a slice of orange on the rim—then back at Jocelyn's plate.

Right. Ilse was on a diet. Perpetually.

Nope. Hard line. Jocelyn would do a lot for her sister. Not eating all the goodies at Christmas was *not* one of those things.

Channel Ilse. Be Ilse. And Ilse never explained herself. "You can put it here." Jocelyn tapped the table. "But don't make any tomorrow."

Not going on to explain why or give some lame excuse had Jocelyn almost biting her tongue off. Especially when her assistant's face fell a little.

"Okay," Margot said slowly. But she put the cup down, then helped herself to a plate and sat across the way. Kyle took the seat beside Jocelyn, his broad shoulders crowding her a bit. A few other crew members joined them, each of whom glanced at Jocelyn's plate but said nothing.

Strike two and it was only eight in the morning.

At least Ben wasn't here.

"Maybe I should switch the third and fifth episode schedule," Ben mumbled to himself. Ending on the traditional holiday party instead of the stocking stuffer party might wrap things up more satisfactorily.

"What do you think?" He glanced to his left where Snowball was curled up beside him on his bed. She'd followed him into the room when he'd come up after dinner.

The little cat lifted her head, ears flickering like she'd heard and was thinking about it seriously. "*Meow.*"

"Keep it the way I have it? Are you sure?"

"*Meow.*" He swore she nodded her head.

Ben huffed a laugh at himself. "You're the boss."

Snowball laid her head back down on her paws, her tail flicking around to hide her paws and face, transforming her into her namesake. A literal ball of white fluff.

Now he was talking to cats. This job was going to break him.

Ben sighed, staring at his computer screen. He hadn't shown Ilse any of these changes yet. And yes, he was deliberately waiting until the last second, in front of the crew, where she would have no time to argue with him and be less likely to make a scene. He knew he'd be creating extra work for her, although he'd tried to incorporate many of the foods and crafts she'd already planned and prepped. Hopefully the bigger changes were all doable at such short notice. He'd find out tomorrow in their production meeting and adjust accordingly if he had to.

If she made him.

"As long as Ilse keeps being easy to work with," he said more to himself. She really was the biggest potential problem.

Snowball's ears twitched at Ilse's name and her eyes opened to pin him with all sorts of questions.

"She's acting strange," Ben explained. "Not herself at all."

Look at this morning. Ilse ate bread. Not just bread . . . but bread with butter and preserves. He'd watched her slather it on with his own eyes from his vantage point in the foyer, and he wouldn't have believed it if he hadn't witnessed it personally. All of that after picking up a flour-covered cat and offering to do the crew's job dealing with the owner. She'd even smiled at Kyle, and usually Ilse didn't give the intern the time of day.

Something was definitely going on with his cohost.

Giving him carte blanche, as it were, cuddling Snowball three times that he knew of so far, and the smiles.

"When did Ilse Becker become a smiler?"

All of the warmth he'd felt for her last night in the shops was melting under a heat lamp of his own suspicion. Was she doing this on purpose just to mess with him? Drawing him in and letting him think he'd won, only to turn it around at the last minute? Usually she was more direct than that—never one to keep her thoughts to herself.

On a small growl of frustration, Ben picked up his cell phone and dialed.

"Do you know what time it is where I am?" Mike grumbled in a sleep-laden voice.

"I don't know where you are so . . . no." Ben glanced at the clock on his computer screen and winced. It wasn't exactly a decent hour here, actually.

Mike grunted and Ben could make out the rustle of sheets followed by the click of a lamp being turned on. "Really, really . . ." Mike sighed gustily. "Really . . . early in the morning. That's what time it is. This better be important."

"What did Herbert say to Ilse exactly?"

The length of Mike's pause told him a lot. "Mike?"

"Not much, actually. He told her that you were going to

take point on the live shoots, and he expected her to partner with you, go along with your production plans, and to make it work."

Ben frowned at a spot on the fancy, patterned wallpaper across from him. "That's it? Nothing else?"

"That's it."

Not exactly specific. Herbert was such a weasel. "Nothing about changing the format or the feature of each show?"

Another pause, then more slowly, "Now that I think about it . . . no."

Uh-huh. Which meant Herbert "told" Ilse the bad news without actually telling her the worst of it. For an executive producer, the man could be a coward when it came to conflict with his stars.

"And what did she say?"

"Why?" Another rustle of sheets, probably Mike sitting up straighter. "Is she making trouble for you?"

"What did she say?"

"Umm . . . She looked at him, smiled, and said she'd do her best to work with you."

More smiles from her. What was with the smiles all of a sudden? Ben blinked, frown deepening until he could see the tips of his eyebrows at the top of his vision. "She actually said those words?"

"Verbatim. Is she causing problems already? Do I need to call her agent?"

Ben thought about it. Maybe she was being easy to deal with now because she really didn't know how much was going to be changing? Except Ilse wasn't easily fooled. She was smart enough to know a warning from the big boss meant something more than just "toe the line and don't make your cohost's life difficult."

Wasn't she? But why hadn't she asked any questions? He would have, by this point.

"Ben?" Mike asked.

Running a hand through his hair, Ben made a face. "No. She's been fine."

Mike huffed a laugh. "Really? That's unexpected."

Exactly. Ben didn't trust it. Even if her smiles were starting to make him want to smile back.

She had a boyfriend. Some kind of European royalty with more money than brains or heart. Until all the smiles, he'd thought of Baron Von What's-His-Name as perfect for Ilse. All about status, like her clothes and her car, that gawdawful monster of a diamond ring she wore, and probably her house.

"*Meow.*" Snowball made a chirrup of sound and bounded off the bed to go paw at the door.

"What?" Ben asked as he set his computer aside and got out of bed. "I'm not good enough to snuggle with?"

"*Meow.*"

He opened the door and Snowball ran out of the room without a backward glance.

Ben sighed. Maybe cats couldn't be trusted either.

I wait until Ben closes his door, then I slink off down the hallway toward the back stairs down to the kitchen. Something has my kitty senses tingling. I know it's not vermin. After the rat that went after Mr. Muir's birds, Sophie and Miss Tilly had this place checked and treated and checked some more. The exterminators never found anything, but I still patrol at night just the same. A year later, I haven't found anything either.

But I don't think this is any kind of vermin.

As quiet as a Christmas ghost, I pad carefully down the stairs. No sounds alert me to anyone or anything in the kitchen. Just the same, I'm cautious about poking my head into the room, sniffing the air.

Cat.

I smell that other cat. The one with the nasty temperament. They named that devil cat Angel, I overheard. One of my humans would probably call that ironic, though I haven't figured out what they mean by that entirely. Funny, maybe. Regardless, she shouldn't be in the house. She's staying in the hotel wing with her owner.

Except she's not in there now.

Rather than go through either of the swinging doors that lead to the hall and the dining room, and tend to squeak when opened, I go back up the back stairs and over to the grander main stairs that lead down to the foyer. I peek over the landing down to the ground floor.

There.

I catch the flash of a fluffy white tail disappearing into the hall underneath where I'm perched.

Ghost cat in the moonlight. Is that what I look like wandering the halls? A shiver chases its tail down my spine. Angel can't be up to any good, to my way of thinking.

She should *not* be here. Especially without her humans.

As quick as I can while maintaining stealth mode, I'm down the stairs and following in her wake. I check the small sitting room off the hallway first. It takes a second, because I want to make sure she's not hiding in the Christmas tree. Sophie puts those trees in every commonly shared room in Weber Haus, each decorated specifically for the room.

Angel is not in here.

I'm out and down to Sophie's office, which is tucked in the back of the house, but the door is impossible to open. A while back Lukas installed a lock on it that's a panel with a key code to unlock it and that automatically locks itself a few minutes after being opened. I've memorized the code, but my kitty paws can't press them correctly. Although I have figured out how to trigger the automatic lock, which is fun.

I can open a lot of doors in Weber Haus, but not that one. The doors to the basement and the attic and the cleaning closet for the cleaning crew that comes in are all the same.

Next, I check the small half-bath at the end of the hallway. Not there either.

How in the name of elf magic could I have missed her? Other than the kitchen with its creaky door, there's no other—

A small noise inside the kitchen has me pausing, one paw raised mid-step, ears flicking. That was definitely from the kitchen. How did she get in there? I should have heard the creaky door.

Ghost devil cat.

I shake off the silly thought.

Should I follow? She'll hear me for sure. But she shouldn't be here, and if she does catch me, I'll just warn her off. This is *my* house after all.

Another noise in the kitchen coming from the direction of the sink at one end makes up my mind for me. As carefully as I can, I nose the door open just a crack. *Squeeeeaaaakkkk.* I go still and wince. But she doesn't show her face. The door is cracked open just wide enough for me to slip inside without any more noise.

But when I jump into the open . . . she's gone.

Not hide nor hair of the white cat ever having been here in evidence, though I can still smell her.

There's only one place she could have gone from here, because the back door that leads outside is also locked at night.

I sprint up the stairs, determined to track her down.

But I get to the top and . . . still no sign of her.

How could I have lost her? This is *my* house. My territory. No other creature, human, cat, or otherwise, knows the ins and outs of this place as well as I do.

I sit my rump down, my tail curling around my feet as I stare, narrow-eyed, down the quiet hallway.

So . . . Angel the devil ghost cat can get out of her room, out of the hotel wing, and into and out of my house without a trace. And she's darn tricky to follow. And the humans clearly have no idea.

She can't be up to any good. That's for sure. The thing is, there's not much I can do other than remain vigilant.

So that's what I intend to do.

I curl up on the carpet where I am. The best place to hear anything happening from both sets of stairs. I close my eyes. My kitty senses will warn me if she comes back.

Chapter 6

Jocelyn stared at the words on her phone. **Where are you staying?**

Theo wasn't happy with her sudden disappearing act with Ilse and was asking for details. Why? So he could join them? He didn't have family, and normally she would have invited him on a trip. She'd tried texting that Ilse had felt bad and needed sister bonding time, so he wouldn't feel left out.

With a sigh, she switched back to the video she'd been watching, not answering Theo. She'd have to do that later when she thought something up.

The tap at her door a few minutes later wasn't unexpected.

"Come in," she called around the bobby pin clenched between her teeth as she attempted one of Ilse's "simpler" hairstyles. TikTok had shown her the easy way to recreate the look.

Easy.

Ha!

She wanted to reach through her phone and strangle the woman smiling as she so effortlessly made her hair do what she wanted it to do, in seconds. Seconds. Meanwhile Jocelyn was left looking like Cousin Itt from *The Addams Family* after an hour of trying.

"Oh!" Margot said as she opened the door. "You're up."

Ilse wasn't exactly an early riser.

"Uh-huh," Jocelyn agreed. Then yelped as the bobby pin in her fingers sprang out of her hand and across the room to smack Margot right in the face.

Jocelyn jumped up. "I'm so sorry."

Only Margot waved her off. "I barely felt it."

Except there was a small red welt on her cheek. "Are you sure? I can get some ice."

"Here." Margot moved further into the room, setting the large bags she always had with her in a chair as she did. "Let me."

After a small hesitation—maybe she should apologize again?—Jocelyn gratefully handed over the torture devices and sank back down on the small chair in front of the vanity. Then proceeded to hide her awe as Margot whipped her hair into something even more complicated than the video . . . and picture-perfect.

Skills. That's what Margot had.

Only Ilse already knew this and wasn't a gusher. So Jocelyn was forced to keep it to a sedate, "Much better. Thank you."

Margot offered a perfunctory smile, then moved to her bags and whipped out the planner Jocelyn was already well familiar with after only a single day of travel. Clearly both Margot and Ilse lived and breathed by the planner.

"Today all of the cast and crew are gathering in the conference room in the hotel wing to discuss the order of the shows, locations, challenges, and so forth and to start prepping for the first show."

Jocelyn nodded as she rifled through the cases of jewelry. She was wearing slate-blue slacks with an adorable slim belt, a cream-colored blouse, and a peach-colored suit jacket over the top that was long, almost to her knees. She already knew the schedule and had tried to find something both business professional and at least a tad comfortable to wear today. Understated jewelry would work, right?

"These." Margot reached over her and picked up silver triangle-shaped earrings. Ilse's assistant stood back, tipping her head to study the outfit, then turned and riffled through the wardrobe. "With these shoes and handbag." She produced peach-colored snakeskin heels and a matching clutch. Jocelyn was tempted to lean around her, because she didn't remember those things being in there. Maybe the wardrobe was enchanted, like Santa's bag of gifts, or the gateway to Narnia, or Mary Poppins's carpetbag?

Then she focused more solidly on the shoes. Three-inch heels. Jocelyn tried not to wince. "Perfect."

"We'd better get going."

Right. As quickly as she could, Jocelyn transferred things from yesterday's handbag—um, who needed matching handbags on vacation?—to the new one. Why did it matter today if her handbag matched? "Do I need anything else?"

Margot's quick frown was smoothed out almost as fast. "No."

By the time they made their way downstairs, out the back door, followed the already shoveled path between the house and shops to the side entrance of the hotel wing and down the long hallway to the first-floor conference room, Jocelyn's feet were already screaming. The shoes had pointed toes and she was pretty sure by the end of the day her pinky toe was going to have grown into the one beside it from pure pressure. They'd have to be surgically separated. Trying not to hobble, she sank gratefully into a seat farthest away from Ben.

Who raised his eyebrows at her. "It's better if you sit over here," he said. Then nodded his head at the empty chair beside him.

Great.

Don't limp. Don't limp. Don't limp.

She made it around to where he was and sat down. Immediately, Margot appeared at her side with a neat binder of papers. One she was intimately familiar with. The show plans she'd been memorizing.

Looking up, she caught Ben's glancing gaze.

What now?

Before she could ask—not that she wanted to—he stood up. "Ready, Walter?"

He was addressing the director, who then stood, clearing his throat. "Right. As you all know, we have some last-minute changes."

Changes?

She glanced around the faces at the table. Not a single one was looking surprised. But Jocelyn didn't remember being informed about any changes.

Maybe they were all small changes?

As she flipped open Ilse's notebook, a tiny click sounded, and an image popped up on a TV screen mounted to the wall. "We've discussed much of this with you individually, but let's run through the new episode themes."

Wait . . . *what?!*

Walter was still talking, but his words weren't computing. "Management wanted a different direction . . ."

They did? A vague recollection surfaced, of sitting in that office with a bunch of Ilse's bigwigs. All she really remembered was being in a state of panic and trying to make sure they didn't notice.

But now words like "I'm sure you can do it" and "You're a true professional" were spinning around in her head. What had she agreed to?

"Ben came up with a fantastic idea to make each show

about a different holiday-themed party." Walter clicked a button, and a new slide came up on the screen listing each new episode.

Parties. Oh God. Oh God. Oh God. Her chest tightened as she stared at the words on the screen.

"We're going to feature various similar elements, all themed for each specific type of party—elements like the food, the music, alcoholic and nonalcoholic cocktails, parting gifts, et cetera."

A murmuring of interest and smiles and nods passed around the room.

Jocelyn barely computed. They wanted her to set up parties? Her. Jocelyn. Not knowing that she wasn't her sister.

Ilse did parties.

Big, elaborate, themed parties with decorations and entertainment and Cordon Bleu food made to seem like it was simpler than it was. Jocelyn did beer and chips at a local pub. If she was really feeling it, she'd buy some balloons, or those cheap paper decorations she could get at the market.

This isn't happening.

All those scripts she'd memorized. And Ilse had prepared everything in advance. Jocelyn wasn't supposed to have to do *anything* except speak. But if they were starting from scratch, then they'd expect her to do it all. Wouldn't they?

Walter was still talking. Ben was sitting beside her, turned slightly away, completely oblivious to how on the verge of hyperventilating she was. "I know this is last-minute," Ben spoke up, turning to face the table. "But I also know this crew now, and with both my and Ilse's support—"

Now he looked directly at her.

Jocelyn was pretty sure that the smile she forced her lips to form came off more like a grimace of pain, because Ben paused. She wasn't sure, though, because she wasn't looking him in the eyes. Couldn't look him in the eyes. Or anyone else, for that matter.

She was too busy freaking out.

Beside her Ben cleared his throat. "The first show is going to be a caroling party—"

Caroling.

The word rang like a clanging bell inside her head. That was even worse. This was a complete and utter disaster. Ilse often sang on the show. Despite never having taken a single singing lesson, she was a natural. They might be twins, but the similarities stopped at their looks. Jocelyn couldn't hold a tune to save Christmas from the abominable snowman.

I'm going to be sick.

Never mind the bile creeping up her throat in a slow burn. Her stomach was heaving.

Jocelyn went to push back from the table, hoping she could exit with some dignity and go throw up the lovely breakfast she'd indulged in this morning. That French toast with cream cheese filling and all the syrup and strawberries wasn't sitting so great now.

"Oh geez," someone muttered.

And Jocelyn actually flinched.

"Um . . . Ilse . . . have you seen this?"

Jocelyn froze. Seen what? The new plans. No. No she definitely had not. She started shaking her head. If she opened her mouth, she'd vomit.

One of the assistants—Bitsy, Jocelyn was pretty sure that was the woman's name—held up a tablet.

Her phone. Jocelyn tried to focus. Were the plans on the phone?

"Seen what?" Ben asked.

Which was when Jocelyn realized Bitsy—or maybe Betsy?—wasn't talking about the show changes. Ben held a hand out for the device, which the woman handed over with a reluctantly concerned look in Jocelyn's direction.

After a glance that involved a descending frown, Ben peered over the top of the tablet right at her.

Heaven help me. What now?

In what felt like slow motion to her, Ben handed the thing over, which she took with hands that shook slightly, then bowed her head to stare down at it. It took a solid chunk of time for her to focus enough to see that she was looking at an article with pictures splashed all over it.

Gregori Stadnicki-Borch.

Ilse's boyfriend. He was with a stunning brunette. Most of the pictures were innocuous, the two of them laughing or talking. But the one of her in his lap was impossible to ignore or excuse. As well as the headlines which read, POLISH COUNT TRADES IN AMERICAN TV HOST FOR A PRINCESS.

Somehow the tabloid had dredged up some old picture of Ilse crying and looking haggard, and stuck it right between all the glamorous, long camera shots of her cheating jerk of an ex-boyfriend.

Jocelyn's heart sank. *Oh, Ilse.*

"It's only in that one tabloid so far," Betsy said. She must be involved in the PR of the show. Jocelyn honestly couldn't remember.

Ben nudged her with his elbow. "You're going to want to get ahead of it," he murmured softly. Almost like he was only speaking to her and not their entire crew.

Jocelyn wasn't sure what she did in another life to deserve this, but either way she was going to have to deal with it.

On a long, calming breath, she lifted her head and her gaze collided with dark eyes that weren't concerned. More like . . . shrewdly calculating in a helpful way. Like Ben was already thinking through the ways to "get ahead of it," as he'd said.

Which somehow managed to infuse some starch into her

own spine. "I'll work with my agent on this," she said. "But I already knew."

A murmuring passed around the table like an ocean wave in a bottle.

Ben tipped his head, searching her face with a sharpening gaze. "You knew?"

Jocelyn nodded. "I broke up with him a few weeks ago."

"You did!" Kyle's excited exclamation was immediately shushed by the woman sitting next to him.

At the same time, the room filled with indignation on Ilse's behalf, and it was nice to see that the crew cared. And Jocelyn tried not to droop in her chair. At least they'd believed her. It was the truth after all. Or sort of the truth. Close enough.

Gregori had done the breaking up, but Ilse should have, in Jocelyn's opinion. If her sister managed to fix that relationship—though given the pictures, that seemed doubtful and ill-advised—Ilse could tell the crew they'd patched things up. Right now, Jocelyn had much bigger, more immediate issues.

Like getting out of singing.

Hand going to the back of her chair, Ben leaned over and lowered his voice. "Are you okay?"

Jocelyn scooted away, folding her hands in her lap, hoping like anything that he didn't see how much she was shaking. "I'm fine."

"We can delay the meeting if you need to deal with this."

Hopping to her feet, she shook her head. "No. You go ahead without me. I'll catch up when I get back." Clearing her throat, she spoke louder for the rest of the room. "Excuse me. Continue with this while I make a few calls."

Then she rushed out of the room, heels clacking with every hurried step, headed she had no idea where. Somewhere she could have a full-on meltdown without anyone seeing.

*   *   *

I happen to be standing in the upstairs hallway in the house when I catch the rapid patter of human feet coming up the back stairs. A second later, Ilse appears, hurrying toward me. Only she doesn't seem to see me. And her face is all pinched and pale. And she's breathing funny.

I spin to watch as she runs by, seeming to pause at each door as if she might go into the room beyond, but changes her mind each time. When she gets to the end of the hallway, she bolts up the stairs to the top floor.

As a kitty with naturally heightened senses, I can feel more than humans ever could, and I know she's very upset. I can't just leave her like that. So I follow, reaching the third floor just in time to see her try the attic door—but it's locked with one of those coded panels Lukas installed—then backtrack and rush into one of the two unoccupied bedrooms up here. Only she closes the door before I can follow her inside.

Not good.

I have learned that it's not good when humans go hide away in some unused space. Sure enough, a sound like harsh breathing reaches me through the door.

Definitely not good.

I'd better go find another human to help her.

She broke it off with the boyfriend? When? Why?

Actually, the why seemed pretty obvious now. Those pictures didn't exactly paint the Red Baron in a good light. The comments on the breakup below the article seemed to agree that Ilse was way prettier than her ex's new girl—which she was, but Ben had always had a thing for blondes.

Ben had watched Ilse walk out of the room, toddling a bit on her sky-high heels as if she wasn't as steady on her feet as she wanted everyone to think.

Only, just before that, he'd been close enough to see the flash of worry in her eyes.

Or maybe that had been pride. After all, no one liked a breakup, even if you were the one doing the breaking up. But definitely not when the other person shoved it down your throat with an open display in the tabloids with another woman so soon afterward. No matter what he thought of Ilse, her ex was a first-rate jerk.

And maybe Ilse's behavior all these months had all stemmed from a relationship headed downhill fast. That was certainly possible. It would explain the difference in her lately. Easier to be around, more relaxed, friendlier.

"Can't say I didn't see that one coming," Margot murmured as soon as the door closed behind Ilse.

Curiosity chased across every face in the room. Some more than others. Before anyone could voice a question though, Ben stood up. "Let's get into the first party."

With a click of the button, he pulled up the details he'd already worked through, including an image board for inspiration, all signed off on by Walter, of course. "Here's what we're thinking . . ."

Except a solid thirty minutes later, Ilse hadn't returned, and she really needed to be part of the discussion and planning. The cast were all on board, but if she put a spanner in the works then they'd have to start all over. "Let's break for a minute," he said. "Grab a donut, check your messages. I'll be right back."

Only Ilse wasn't in the hotel. Or her room. Or the kitchen. Or anywhere downstairs in the house. Standing in the foyer, hands on his hips, Ben tried to think of where she could possibly have gone. She wouldn't go to the shops, would she?

"*Meow.*"

Ben looked up to find Snowball standing at the far end of the hallway, prancing around like a reindeer ready to fly.

"Where's your owner?" he asked. Miss Tilly had left this morning, but Emily and Lukas were still around. And Sophie. He looked around like one of them might jump out of the woodwork where they were hiding.

"*Meow.*"

Snowball ran in the opposite direction a couple steps then turned to see if he was following. Ben shook his head. It only appeared that's what the cat was doing. Right? She probably wanted to be fed or maybe couldn't get to her litterbox or something. He'd help, but he needed to find Ilse first.

He half turned away, taking a single step away.

"*Meow. Meow.*"

Now the little cat seemed to be griping at him. If he spoke cat, he'd translate those meows as "Where are you going? I told you to follow me."

Maybe I need to get more sleep.

But the cat meowed again, then pranced a few more steps in the direction she was headed.

"Okay. I'll help you first." Then he'd find Ilse.

As soon as he moved in her direction, Snowball took off toward another set of stairs leading up to the next level. She paused every so often to make sure he was following. Until she got to a closed door, where she stopped. Then pawed at the door twice before looking over at him.

"What's in here?" he asked as he caught up to her.

Snowball pawed again.

Ben studied the door. Probably a bedroom? It had a label on it calling it the LITTLE PRINCE'S ROOM.

"*Meow.*" Snowball pawed some more.

The little cat was very insistent. "Is this your room?"

A small squawk of sound came from behind the door. Not a cat noise, but a human one.

Um . . .

Another squeak, or maybe. . . . That sounded awfully familiar. Ben wasn't about to just walk in, so he knocked.

The noise stopped.

"Hello?" he called, then knocked again. "Are you okay?" Silence.

He raised his hand to knock again, then . . . "Ben?"

Ilse. That was Ilse.

He opened the door and walked in to find the room empty. A bedroom all done up in blues of all shades and antique furniture, similar to his room. Totally empty. Or at least at first glance. "Ilse?"

A rasping gasp was followed by, "Over . . . here."

He rounded the bed to find her sitting on the floor, knees drawn up to her chest, her back to the bed. And she was clearly struggling to breathe. Wide blue eyes trained to his as she battled, sucking in too fast, the air a rasp of noise in and out of her throat.

"Do you have asthma?"

She shook her head.

Right. No inhaler needed. She must be having a panic attack. He doubted he'd find a paper bag anywhere handy.

Ben sat down in front of her. "I want you to purse your lips like this." And he demonstrated.

Ilse blinked at him, might have even huffed a laugh, which was a good sign, then did as he asked.

"Now," he said. "Breathe in, two, three. Out, two, three, four, five, six." Then repeated.

She kept having to stop to suck in as he counted, though, so on the next inhale he said, "Now stop and hold your breath, two, three, four, five, six, seven, eight, nine, ten. Now out . . ."

But she was still struggling.

Without a thought beyond helping her, he took her hand and pressed her palm over his heart. "With me." Then kept going. In. Hold. Out. In. Hold. Out.

As he did, he talked between instructions. "Did I ever tell you I had asthma as a kid?"

She shook her head.

"Yeah. Bad, too. My mom made sure the staff had inhalers stashed everywhere . . . practically every room of the house, my backpacks, the glove box of every car. And she made sure they cleaned everything like crazy. Dust was not allowed to exist in our house."

"No . . . pets?"

She was talking. Good sign, and her breathing was starting to ease, the panic too, her shoulders not so tense.

"Definitely not. And I couldn't spend the night at any friends' houses if they had pets."

"Wow."

"Yeah. I also wasn't allowed to do outdoor sports."

"That had . . . to be . . . hard."

"That was harder than the no-pets rule. I wanted to play football and tennis. My best friend was on the football team, and he got all the girls."

Ilse's lips twitched. "I'm . . . sure . . . the girls . . . gravitated to . . . you."

She was talking more, breathing almost back to normal.

Ben still grinned. "Are you telling me you think I'm good-looking?"

The way her eyes widened again, color surging into her cheeks, he immediately wanted to take it back. But she didn't start hyperventilating again, so instead he just held his smile.

To which she narrowed her eyes. Then chuckled. "You know you're . . . good-looking."

"Don't worry. I won't let it go to my head."

"Too late."

He chuckled along with her. Then, with his free hand, reached out to tuck a strand of her honey-blond hair behind her ear. He'd never seen her so disheveled. "All better?"

She took a deep breath. In then out. Then nodded slowly. "Thank you."

Ilse Becker had the bluest eyes he'd ever seen. Deep ocean

blue. Calm-evening-sky blue. A man could drown in eyes like those and be happy to go down with the ship.

Which is when it hit him that he was sitting close enough to smell the vanilla scent of her shampoo, her hand held over his heart warming his skin, as they stared into each other's eyes.

Clearing his throat, he backed up, letting her hand go. Time to get back to their usual footing. "Want to tell me what triggered that?"

Chapter 7

Staring into kind green eyes, the remaining tension from Jocelyn's earlier panic receded, leaving her unexpectedly . . . calm. Exhausted, but calm. Because of Ben Meyer. The man would be very easy to like, if she let herself.

Except you're lying to him. He thinks you're Ilse.

She shouldn't let herself get close. Of anyone on the show, Ben was the one Ilse wanted her to stay away from the most. He was also the most likely to realize the bait and switch, except for maybe Margot. Those two worked in the closest proximity to her sister.

He ducked his head, leaning closer again. "Ilse? Why the panic? Was it the boyfriend? Or the bad press? Or—"

"I can't sing." The words blurted from her lips before her brain could call them back.

"Can't . . ." Ben's frown was slow, and all colors of confused.

Oh no! He'll know now. Think, Jocelyn Becker. Think.

"I've heard you sing a dozen times. You're great. Do you have stage fright or—"

Her mind made a desperate grab for an excuse. Any excuse. "Nodules."

"What?"

"I have nodules." She winced inwardly. *Sorry, Ilse.*

The thing was, her sister was dead-serious worried about nodules, always careful to warm up properly and not strain her voice, talking about how they'd be career ending. Which made no sense to Jocelyn, since Ilse didn't actually sing for a living, just every so often on the show. But her sister was a bit of a perfectionist. If she did anything, she did it to the tune of all the over-performer clichés. Above and beyond. A hundred and ten percent. To perfection.

The problem was, nodules also didn't just go away on their own. Ilse would have to figure her way out of this later if she wanted to ever sing on the show again.

"Nodules," Ben repeated. Did he sound doubtful? Suspicious?

Jocelyn nodded and tried to remember anything she knew about the condition, mostly from the movie *Pitch Perfect*. "They happen when your vocal cords rub together and can be painful."

"I know what nodules are."

Well . . . then why was he staring at her that way? He looked so confused.

"When did you get diagnosed?" was his next question.

The trouble was, Jocelyn was way behind on watching *Home & Hearth*. She usually kept up with Ilse's shows religiously, but she'd had a project she'd been obsessing about at work, and so had a backlog saved to watch. Worse, the shows were taped well ahead of when they were aired.

Which means I have no idea what she's been doing . . . or more specifically singing . . . at work.

But if Ilse really did have nodules, she would have informed the studio immediately so they could work around it while she healed her voice. Which meant this needed to be recent.

"Last week. I was going to tell you and . . ." She suddenly

couldn't remember the name of the man she'd talked to before coming here. The executive producer guy. Good grief, what happened to her brain? It was short-circuiting.

"Last week?" Ben asked. "When?"

What day did Ilse not film? "Monday."

"And the doctors said not to sing?"

"Exactly."

Hopefully they didn't do anything beyond that for nodules initially. All she knew for sure was that the singer Adele had surgery to fix them, successfully, and Julie Andrews had as well, not so successfully. She thought. She couldn't remember for sure because thoughts were flying around in her mind like a pinball machine.

"Then why did you sing so well on Wednesday when we taped? You should have said something."

Oh. My. Father. Christmas.

Jocelyn opened her mouth. Then closed it again when she drew a complete blank. Nothing coming to her. Zero. Zip. Zilch. Nada.

She opened her mouth again, hoping against hope words that made sense would magically pour out, but had to close it again, because otherwise she'd just squeak ineffectually. Meanwhile, Ben was eyeing her more and more narrowly, his gaze starting at the top of her head and moving slowly downward.

Maybe she could have another panic attack and he'd forget about this. Although her acting skills were worse than her lying skills.

Before she could try to breathe in hard and give a plausible excuse one last try, Ben suddenly straightened, eyes flashing to hers. "Oh my God . . ." He studied her so hard, he probably had her freckles memorized. "You're not Ilse."

Lie! Jocelyn could hear her sister's voice . . . the same as hers really, but this was definitely Ilse in her head. *Lie until Santa permanently crosses you off the "nice" list.*

"Of course I'm—"

His expression hardened, going so dark she swallowed the rest of her words. "Don't even think of finishing that thought," he warned. Not angry. Not loud. But quiet. Apparently, Ben Meyer had a temper under all that calm control.

Run.

"Ilse has a twin sister." Ben was inspecting her again. He didn't even need a microscope. "Doesn't she?"

"Well . . . yes, I do . . . but I'm not—"

"I can't believe I didn't see the difference sooner."

Oh God. Oh God. Oh God. She could really use some holiday magic about now.

Ben's gaze snapped to hers, sparks practically shooting out of his eyes. He was definitely angry. "Where is she?"

Deliberately she misunderstood. "My sister Jocelyn is back home probably in her hole of a research room looking at some gawdawful old film that—"

"Stop it." Again, he spoke with a leashed sort of quiet. Forceful.

Jocelyn stopped, biting her lip.

He glared first at her lip, so she stopped doing that too, then at her. "I'm only going to ask this one more time. Where. Is. Ilse?"

Jocelyn's heart was pounding so hard she couldn't even hear him now. But she had no problem making out the words he was saying. The jig was up.

I'm so sorry, Ilse.

This switching-places gambit really had been a foolish idea with a high likelihood of failure from the get-go. At least she hadn't been caught in front of everyone.

Jocelyn deflated like kids the day after too much excitement and sugar at Christmas. She glanced away, because she couldn't hold eye contact while confessing. "She's in the Philippines."

*   *   *

"The Philippines—" Ben fisted his hands at his sides as he stared at the exact replica of Ilse Becker who wasn't really Ilse. What name had she mentioned?

Jocelyn.

He stared at her. It fit.

More approachable than her sister.

He was an idiot not to have seen it way sooner. It explained *everything*. The way Ilse had been acting so strange . . . kinder, helpful, less . . . hard. And all the cooperating. No wonder.

And the way you react to her.

He shoved that thought under anger that incinerated it. Ben breathed through his nose, searching for calm that was not coming. "What, if I may ask, could she possibly—"

Jocelyn winced.

He cleared his throat and tried to soften his tone. "What is Ilse doing in the Philippines?"

Another wince. Apparently, he didn't soften it enough. Jocelyn still answered though. "She's trying to win her boyfriend back."

Baron Bad Boyfriend who just today Ilse . . . no, not Ilse . . . who *Jocelyn* had just told the entire crew Ilse was the one who'd done the breaking up with. That boyfriend?

"So let me get this straight . . . Ilse ran off and left her twin sister in her place on her TV show like a bad version of *The Parent Trap*, right in time for the show to be filmed live all month long."

"Not for *all* the episodes. Hopefully." Jocelyn leaned forward, putting her hand on his arm. "She was desperate. You know Ilse. She's a professional and the show means everything to her."

He wasn't so sure about the professionalism, given this not-so-little stunt, but the show did mean everything to Ilse.

That much he knew. But still . . . "Then she should have figured out another way."

Jocelyn's blue eyes were imploring him to understand. "If you had seen her. . . . She was heartbroken, Ben. Please understand—"

"*Don't* ask me to understand."

Jocelyn froze, then slowly lifted her hand, leaving his arm cold, a sensation that spread to his heart as she visibly shrunk in front of his eyes. She dropped her gaze. "What are you going to do?"

Which left him suddenly feeling like he'd kicked a puppy.

When did he turn into the one in the wrong here?

Ben dropped back to sit on the floor in front of Jocelyn. Funny how, now that he'd figured it out, his mind easily accepted who the woman in front of him truly was—the differences becoming more obvious. Like the small freckle under her right eye. Ilse didn't have that. And Jocelyn's skin was paler and smoother. Her word choices different. Her smile easier . . . and a tiny bit off center. Ben leaned against the wall under the window, facing her, and propped his elbows on his bent knees.

And just stared at her.

She looked back at him with wide, wary blue eyes, though after a few seconds her gaze skittered away like a frightened bunny rabbit.

"Please," she said in the soft voice of someone who knew what she was asking was impossible. "*Please* don't tell anyone."

She wasn't looking at him as she asked for this monumental favor.

Ben ran his hands through his hair, blowing out a long breath.

If this had happened as recently as last week, and if it had been Ilse sitting in front of him instead of Jocelyn, he would have said no before she'd even finished asking the question.

Possibly even taken some level of pleasure in outing her. Payback for months of difficulty.

But the woman in front of him wasn't to blame. Not really.

Someone who could risk hyperventilating and panic attacks clearly was only doing something she hated because she loved her sister that much. Ben wasn't convinced Ilse deserved that kind of devotion, but who knew . . . maybe for her twin, Ilse turned into the good fairy of sweetness and light.

He almost snorted an unamused laugh at that mental image. "When does Ilse get back?"

Still not looking at him, Jocelyn nibbled at her lower lip.

Not a good sign. "She didn't tell you?" he demanded.

After a brief hesitation Jocelyn shook her head, then shook it again. "She was going to surprise him, then see how it went from there."

In other words, Ilse was going to *ambush* her ex.

"She was hoping she'd only miss the first show at most."

Ilse clearly was delusional about this situation. The travel time alone would make that difficult. Besides, what if it went well, and she and the Baron got back together? Ben couldn't see her coming back in time to do any of the shows if it got romantic. Or maybe the Baron had broken it off because he wanted more of Ilse's attention on him and less on the show. She'd have to prove herself. Or . . .

No use thinking through all the "or else"s of this scenario. Regardless, even if Ilse hopped on a plane today, she wouldn't be back in time for the first filming.

This is a disaster.

Jocelyn cleared her throat. "I get the impression that Ilse has not been the easiest cohost to work with."

Ben glanced up to find Jocelyn finally making eye contact again, this time with a spark of— Was that hope in her eyes? Where did she get off having any hope in this situation?

And where was she going with that question? "What tipped you off?"

Jocelyn's lips twitched.

Of the two sisters, she was definitely the smiler, especially given that she could find anything to smile about right now.

"I honestly didn't pay that much attention to what the studio guy was saying when I went into his office before we came here," she confessed with a rueful lilt in her voice. "I was too busy being terrified that he would see I wasn't Ilse. But based on the changes you're making and some of the words I remember him saying, I get the impression it's unusual for you to be in charge of the show content. Am I wrong?"

It actually took Ben a solid ten seconds of picturing a shaking Jocelyn standing in front of Herbert—who was intimidating on a good day—before he managed to refocus his mind and figure out where she was headed with this topic. He'd give it to the nicer twin, she was quick on the uptake. But had they told her what was really in it for him? The show of his own? "What are you offering?"

Jocelyn visibly swallowed. "I'll give you full control of the shows."

"I already have that," he pointed out. "*That's* what Herbert was telling you that day."

"Oh." She grimaced, but also straightened. Then adjusted to sit with her legs crisscrossed so she could lean toward him. "Okay, but if I was really Ilse instead of me, she'd be making it . . . difficult . . . for you to do that. Am I right?"

She wasn't wrong. Ben's gaze narrowed. "Are you threatening me?"

Waving a hand like she was batting away that suspicion, Jocelyn leaned even closer, her other hand flashing out to lay on his arm again. She was a smiler and a toucher. "Not at all. But without Ilse here, you do kind of need me. And I can be *very* helpful. All I ask is that you help us keep this a secret."

Ben said nothing.

"Please, Ben. I'll do anything you ask."

His own career was on the line here. Either way he approached this, he was damned if he did and damned if he didn't. But he was more damned if he outed her and they had to cancel the shows. That was for sure.

He glanced down at the hand, then back up to her. Which was when he got tangled up in the hopeful, desperate, bottomless blue of Jocelyn's eyes. Without the harder edge of Ilse's personality, those astonishing eyes became something else. Deeper. Warmer. Kinder.

More compelling.

I'm in trouble.

"Anything I ask?" He blinked. The words had come out before he'd even decided to say them.

She gave an eager nod, then held up three fingers like she was making a pledge. "Anything. Promise."

"*Anything* is a dangerous word to throw around lightly." And now it sounded like he was flirting. Why had his voice dropped on those words?

As if she couldn't help herself, Jocelyn's lips trembled into a smile. One that reached her eyes and right into his chest where his heart gave an extra hard thump.

"Well . . ." She grinned, then rushed into speech. "I'll admit you're getting the short end of this deal. I can't sing. I can't cook. And I can't craft."

She grimaced, then the words poured out even faster. "I think I'll be okay on camera, so that's helpful. I mean, I already do, with a vlog. Though to be fair it's about something I'm very familiar with and I'm passionate about. So I could talk about that all day long and still not run out of things to say. And I only have like two or three viewers who bother to come on. And they don't do very much interacting. It's certainly not a national show."

Her eyes widened as she seemed to recognize that maybe

she shouldn't have confessed all that while trying to convince him to help her. "I mean you could go all Clark Gable and say something like, 'Frankly, my dear, I don't give a damn,' but hear me out—"

Ben leaned forward and put his hands on either side of her face, cutting her off from what was quickly turning into a babbling downward spiral that could lead to another panic attack. "Breathe."

To his surprise, she took in one long breath, then let it out slowly. Then, trusting gaze on his, she wrapped her hands around his wrist and gently tugged them away. "Thanks."

He didn't know where to put his hands now.

Jocelyn offered him another sunny smile, only this one didn't reach her eyes, so he knew she was faking a confidence she was far from feeling. "So . . . do we have a deal?"

The trouble was, Ben didn't see any way around it.

Ilse wouldn't be back in time, no matter what, and the studio had nothing else to fill the slots for these live shows on such short notice. Holiday shows. Ones they'd been advertising like crazy already. They would be furious if this project got canceled so late in the game. This situation impacted his job just as much as it did Ilse's. The Becker sisters, apparently, had painted him into a corner while his back was turned.

I can't believe I'm agreeing to this.

"Is there anything else you can't do?" he asked her.

Jocelyn gave a little bounce. "We have a deal?"

She held out her hand as if she trusted him to keep his end of the bargain if they shook on it.

Ben grasped her hand in his, giving it a firm shake, and trying not to notice how delicate her bones were, or how soft her skin was. "We have a deal."

The humans haven't noticed at all that I'm up on the bed looking over them. I ran in right behind Ben and jumped up here in case I could also be of help. It is a scientifically proven fact that cuddling a kitty like me when upset makes humans feel much better.

But Ben managed to help Ilse—or not Ilse—calm down.

I still can't believe she's not who she said she was. What a twist! I guess her name is Jocelyn and she's the real Ilse's twin sister? I heard the whole thing, and it seems overly complicated to me. Humans really do know how to mess things up in the strangest ways.

Look at these two now. Messing it up even more.

I shake my head at them. I was planning on matchmaking Ben and Ilse . . . or Jocelyn . . . which usually involves pushing them together or bringing them together in little ways. I find if humans just spend time together, they figure out their feelings faster.

But these two already spend time together. And there have been lies between them. And Ben doesn't seem to like Jocelyn's sister very much. Actually the sister seems to come with a lot of drama.

I tip my head, studying them. The thing is, my kitty senses—and I'm never wrong—are telling me that Ben and Jocelyn are meant to be together.

Can I help them see around the lies and the sister and everything else?

Either way, they definitely need my help.

Chapter 8

Jocelyn sat on her bed, feeling much better than she had earlier. No more panic attacks, thank goodness.

She'd gone back to the meeting with Ben, who'd explained to everyone that, after talking it over, they thought the best first show would be the Stocking Stuffer–themed show. Saint Nicholas Day was coming up, and many people celebrated that holiday with stockings. She'd been the one to point out that detail, catching a small nod from him.

A small nod that had put a warm fluttering in her stomach.

Why? Because he'd approved of her?

At least she wasn't all alone in figuring out how to get through this now. The problem was going to be—

The ring of her cell phone jolted her out of her thoughts. Jocelyn glanced at where it sat charging on her bedside table, next to the diamond ring that she took off at night.

Not Theo. Not Theo. Not Theo.

It wasn't. But it was almost as bad. She winced at the sight of her sister's name.

Time to fess up.

After pressing a button, she put the phone to her ear. "Ilse?"

"Hi, Joce."

Jocelyn straightened. Her sister only called her Joce when she wasn't feeling well. "Honey, are you okay?"

Silence, then a small sniff. "Not really."

Heart squeezing, Jocelyn wished she could travel right through the phone and give Ilse a hug. Her sister might act tough and hard on the outside, but she was a marshmallow on the inside and her feelings were easily hurt. She just hid it better than others, usually behind annoyance and a pair of dark sunglasses.

"What happened?"

"He . . ." A tiny sound squeaked down the line. "He . . ." Then a sound suspiciously like a sob. "He won't even see me," Ilse wailed. "His assistant refused to let me anywhere near him."

Jocelyn bounced to her feet, the bed creaking a protest at her sudden action. "No way. What a jerk. I'm going to give him . . ." Except there wasn't anything she could do to him.

A watery chuckle reached her. "I know. I will give it to him too. As soon as I can talk to him."

Wait. "So . . . you're not coming back yet?"

"No." Ilse sniffed, then suddenly sounded more like herself. "I'm going to stay and make him face me in person. Even if the result is the same, I'm not letting him get away with breaking up via a text. Someone has to teach him some manners."

That sounded more like her sister—determined to face the hard things head-on. Except in the next second, Ilse's voice went all wobbly again. "How are things going there?"

Jocelyn swallowed, staring out the window at the darkened snowy vista beyond. She *should* tell Ilse that Ben knew now and was helping them. After all, this was Ilse's life and career on the line. But right this second, she just couldn't make herself pile on. "Everything is going fine. We're filming the first episode tomorrow."

"You have everything you need?"

Ilse still thought they were filming her original plan, too. *Something else I should probably tell her about. But it will only upset her, and she can't do anything way over there in the Philippines.*

"All set," Jocelyn assured her, proud of how confident her voice came out.

"Is Ben being his usual self? Meddling and trying to do things that are likely to turn out sloppy or rushed?"

That was an impossible question to answer. Because Ben was changing all sorts of things. And now even more things to fit Jocelyn's limitations. But as far as she could tell, not in a bad way. Why was Ilse so dead set against the man and his ideas, anyway?

Now's not the time to ask.

"He's been . . ." What? Fine? Trying to make changes? Justifiably and yet adorably angry while still helpful? What answer would her sister accept?

Ilse heaved a big sigh. "He's being a pain, just like usual, it sounds like. I don't know why he's so determined to force things on this show. I think he might be trying to oust me and take it over."

Jocelyn opened her mouth only to shut it again. That didn't sound like what she'd seen, but what did she know.

"I'm sorry you have to deal with that."

"It's fine."

Silence followed by muffled voices told her Ilse had been interrupted. Then her sister popped back on. "I have to go."

"Okay. Give the Baron hell and a black eye from me, yeah?"

Ilse gave an elegant little snort. "As if you'd ever give any-one a black eye."

True.

"And Jocelyn . . ."

"Mmm?"

"Just don't let Ben change anything big for the shows I

planned. Okay? I can't handle anything else new in my life right now."

A knock at Jocelyn's door had her swinging around. Who could that be? Going to the door, she swung it open to find Margot standing there with several outfits slung over one shoulder.

"Um . . . I have to go. Ma . . . my assistant is here with a wardrobe check."

"Wardrobe check?" Ilse's voice carried a wealth of pique. "Why? I picked the perfect outfits for each show already."

"That's right. I'd better make sure they fit. Bye, honey." Then she hung up on her sister mid-protest.

Margot raised her perfectly tweezed brows in question.

Jocelyn glanced at the phone in her hand then back to her sister's assistant. Had she heard any of Ilse's side of that? "Just a friend from home."

Margot shrugged, clearly not caring, and walked into the room where she proceeded to lay the outfits across the bed. She pointed to a black dress with a red plaid trim, a belt, and a little flounce at the bottom of the skirt. "I think this would work best given the decorations for this scene will be all sorts of colors."

Which was a good point, but Jocelyn pointed at the pale blue pants and sweater that were more casual. "I'll be able to move easier in these without worrying about keeping my knees closed."

The second the words were out of her mouth she wanted to swallow them right back down. No matter the mode of dress or situation, Ilse always kept her knees closed. Perfect posture too. Given the way they'd grown up, Jocelyn had no idea where Ilse had learned any of that. She almost pulled her shoulders back right at that moment just thinking about it.

Margot, meanwhile, was frowning. Again.

At least this time she was still studying the outfit. "You're probably right. You'll be moving from station to station, sitting and standing." She lifted her head. "I'll let wardrobe know so that they can coordinate Ben's outfit."

"Thank you."

Margot hung the blue outfit up in the wardrobe, taking the other two items with her. The poor woman's hotel room must be filled with racks of clothes, but that was the job. Or Jocelyn assumed so.

Jocelyn opened the door for Margot, only to jump a little because Ben stood on the other side, hand raised to knock and Snowball dancing around his ankles.

I run into Jocelyn's bedroom. I had just missed getting inside when Jocelyn's helper lady, Margot, showed up. But Ben arriving is even better. Maybe I can take this opportunity to work some kitty matchmaker magic between them. Really get that ball of yarn rolling.

Except he doesn't come in. He just stands there in the hallway.

Clearly the man needs prompting, so I meow and run back out to him, circle his feet, then run back into the room with Jocelyn. Surely, he'll get the hint to come inside.

Ben slowly lowered his hand, suddenly feeling all kinds of awkward. Did it look suspicious that he was stopping by Jocelyn-slash-Ilse's room so late at night?

No.

He straightened. Margot was here clearly for business, too, based on the hanging clothes in her hands. She'd assume he was here for the same purposes.

Wouldn't she?

The thing was, if this had really been Ilse, he probably wouldn't have gone near her bedroom. Not even with a ten-foot pole. An idiom that he was just now realizing didn't make a lot of sense. Who carried those around for measuring things?

But "Ilse" had been easier to work with today, so maybe the crew would assume things were finally changing for the better.

Snowball, who he'd been vaguely aware of, made a sound like a snit, then ran back out to circle his feet, then with a *meow* ran back inside a third time. Clearly wanting him to follow. Except Margot was still standing there frowning and glancing between him and Jocelyn. Was that suspicion written across her face? Hard to tell with Margot. She didn't . . . emote much.

And it was highly likely he was seeing things not there. Guilt and lies did that to a person, made them question everything and everyone around them. Subterfuge was clearly not his style, and they'd barely got started on this twin-swap co-host situation. This business was going to stress him into an early grave. Definitely ruin Christmas for him.

"I'll leave you two to it," Margot said, and scooted past him into the hallway just as Snowball did her meow and ankle-running-pass again.

Ben was not prone to being self-conscious, so the horrible awareness of Margot walking away down the hall, no doubt listening to what he was saying to Jocelyn—as Ilse, which he was still wrapping his mind around—didn't feel that great.

"I thought of something for tomorrow's show I wanted to discuss," he said in an overly loud voice.

Jocelyn raised a finger to her lips, and in a hushed voice said, "People are sleeping."

Right. But he'd wanted to make sure Margot heard that. Not that he could say so to Jocelyn right now. Because Margot would hear that too.

See? This was already too complicated. Maybe he should put a stop to it all here?

Jocelyn stuck her head out in the hallway, peering down the hall in the direction Margot had gone. He couldn't tell if she was listening or looking, but either way she was clearly checking. Then she straightened and waved him inside. It wasn't until the door closed behind him with a soft click and he turned around to face her that it struck him that not only was he in her bedroom, but she was in her pajamas already.

Black silk pajamas with lacy trim across the top. At least she was wearing a matching wrap and the bottoms were long pants with the same lace at the cuffs, her bare, sparkly red-and green-painted toes peeking out from underneath.

Christmas colors. Jocelyn had painted her toenails Christmas colors and with glitter. How Ilse thought her sister was going to fool anyone for long was beyond him.

"Are those yours or Ilse's?" He waved a hand at her attire.

Jocelyn glanced down what she was wearing, then gave a little groan, which was this side of adorable, and belted the wrap tighter around her. "I'll give you two guesses," she muttered.

Which suddenly made him want to smile. Why did he want to smile? This was not a smiling situation. His career was teetering at a precipice with an avalanche barreling toward him, ready to push him off the edge and then bury him.

"I tend to be more of a T-shirts with funny sayings and boxers to bed kind of girl." Jocelyn rubbed her hands over her arms. "Though I'll admit the silk feels nice."

I should look away.

He should definitely look away given the interest stirring through him. Unsuitable, unwanted, incredibly ill-timed interest.

Her blue eyes flashed to his and went wide. Then she slapped a hand over her mouth. "Sorry. That was totally inappropriate."

Ben wasn't sure if he wanted to laugh or shuffle his feet. He ended up doing a little of both. "No more inappropriate than my comment. Sorry."

She lowered her hand slowly, shoulders losing some tension. "I guess the situation we find ourselves in makes for awkward at every turn."

A peace offering? Did she think he was still angry about everything? Because he was.

Mostly that he was caught up in it, as well as the way Ilse, in a myopically selfish move, had put both him and Jocelyn in this position. But looking at Jocelyn, in clothes that didn't quite match her personality—and how he hadn't seen that sooner with her other clothes, he had no idea—and her worried expression, and her Christmas-colored toes, Ben just couldn't find it in himself to stay angry. Not with her at least. "We'll figure this out together. Okay?"

"Yeah." Jocelyn blew out a sharp breath, then tipped her head to the side, studying him with an odd little expression. "You know . . . you are not what I expected, Ben Meyer."

"*Meow.*" Snowball jumped up onto the bed and proceeded to knead at the blanket with her paws before sitting and looking right at Jocelyn.

He ignored the cat. "I can only guess. What exactly did Ilse tell you about me?"

He kind of expected her to get embarrassed, because no doubt anything Ilse had said hadn't been kind, but instead she chuckled. "Nothing bad. Just that you were a non-listening, uncompromising, arrogant control freak who wanted to come in and change every single aspect of the show."

Ouch. "That's *not* bad?"

"*Meow.*" Snowball was getting more insistent, clearly wanting Jocelyn to sit on the bed with her.

Jocelyn chuckled again. "You forget that I speak Ilse."

Only she didn't go on to translate any of that into a softer wording, and the smile lingering around her mouth told him she was getting a kick out of whatever his reaction was. Which meant he was visibly reacting. Something he didn't do. Ben schooled his features into a bland nothing. "The show is losing ratings and losing viewers. I was brought in to help fix that."

"And you told Ilse that? That you were there to help?" The words weren't couched as an accusation. More like curiosity.

So why did guilt pinch behind his eyes. "*I* didn't. Herbert was supposed to."

"I'm pretty sure if she had been informed, Ilse would have reacted to you quite differently. And she definitely would have told me about the studio telling her something like that. She talks about the show nonstop."

Ben's hands crept up to rest on his hips. "You're telling me she didn't know this entire time that I was hired to help?"

"*Meow.*" What was going on with the cat?

Jocelyn shrugged. "I can't say for sure. But I do know that my sister pays attention to the numbers, and she's talked about them going down, so she figured that out on her own. If anything, it's made her work harder. Try to be more . . ."

He could see that.

Jocelyn shrugged. "I'm pretty sure nobody at the studio had a conversation with her about why you were brought in. I can absolutely tell you—because these are her direct words— that she thinks you are there to take over the show completely and kick her off after viewers have gotten used to seeing you."

Well . . . hell. Herbert had a lot to answer for, it seemed. How could the man be in his position and still be so . . . spineless?

Ben frowned as another thought struck. "So she thought running off to get her boyfriend back in the middle of these very important and timely live shows, meanwhile leaving her twin here to secretly hold down the fort, was a good idea?"

Another shrug, this one accompanied by nibbling of the bottom lip. A nervous habit of hers it seemed. A distracting habit to his point of view. "That's the only reason I agreed.

Because her behavior was so against the norm, it should tell you just how much he means to her. I've never seen her like this with anyone."

"*Meow.*" If Snowball got any louder, she'd wake the entire house.

Jocelyn dropped back to sit on the bed, propping her heels on the edge of the wooden slat, the part of the bed frame that ran along the box spring. Then she pulled the little cat onto her lap, running an absent-minded hand over her fur. "What you have to understand about Ilse is that she's had to fight very hard for everything she has in life; and everything I have, I owe to her."

That was a pretty big statement. Part of him wasn't interested in what made Ilse the way she was, but a bigger part was interested in how Jocelyn was the complete opposite. "Why?"

She flicked him a glance that seemed to be a quick check of whether she should tell him more or not. Then she grimaced. "We have no family. Our parents were killed in a car crash when we were six and we went into the system. Twice we were adopted, but to separate families. No one wanted twins. Apparently two were too many."

They'd been separated? Twice? That must have been awful for them both. To lose their parents and then each other that way.

"Both times, Ilse pitched a fit loud enough and for long enough, and was badly enough behaved, that they brought us back together in the children's home. She would tell me that we didn't need parents or a home of our own. That she would take care of us."

Ben could easily picture a young Ilse, pitching fits of legendary proportions. So that's where she learned that that technique worked to get her way.

Jocelyn wasn't done. "And when we aged out of the system finally, she insisted on getting a job to put me through school, because, as she put it, I was the 'brains' of the two of us. She had to work three jobs as it turned out, in addition to my one job, because that's what we had to do. She just happened to get one of those jobs as an assistant on the studio lot, and eventually translated that into where she is today. To her, this show proved that she was right. That she could get us both through life without help from anyone. Ever. It's her safety blanket. Other than my degree, it's the thing that she's most proud of. And it's how she never has to be hungry again. Which I know sounds very Scarlett O'Hara, but we were hungry. A lot. For years."

Snowball, who'd been enjoying Jocelyn's petting, hopped off her lap to sit beside her on the bed, then looked directly at him and proceeded to meow again.

He was *not* sitting on the bed with a silk-and-lace-pajama-clad Jocelyn in the dead of night.

Ben dropped his gaze to his feet, trying to picture Ilse—the epitome of high-end labeled clothing, bourgeois cars, and only the best of everything—ever being poor, working three jobs, and just trying to feed and house herself and her sister.

Jocelyn was right. It explained a lot.

After the last six months with Ilse behaving the way she had, he still couldn't quite bring himself to forgive her or warm to her, but at least he could understand her a little better. When she got back, he'd sit her down and explain the situation. The show was hers, he was just helping the ratings and viewership, and then he'd go away and get his own show. Her job was in no danger from him.

"What did you want to tell me about tomorrow?"

Jocelyn's question brought his head up. "I wanted to make sure you were good with the script and the plan."

Another nibble of the bottom lip, which said she wasn't entirely, but she sent him a sunny smile. "As ready as I'll ever be."

"No questions."

She shook her head.

"Then I guess I'll see you in the morning."

"Okay." She got up and walked him to the door and he swore Snowball gave him a perturbed look. That little cat was an oddball, that was for sure. Or the stress of the situation was making him see things, like earlier with Margot.

He was only one step down the hall when Jocelyn stage-whispered, "Hey, Ben."

He paused and turned to find her haloed by the soft light coming from behind her, blond hair spilling over her shoulders, and Christmassy toes sparkling. "Thanks for checking."

If ever there was a time and a place and a woman he shouldn't want to kiss, it was here, now, and this woman.

Which was an issue. Because he wanted to.

Ben cleared his throat. "No problem."

On a smile, she closed the door. And for whatever reason, his feet didn't want to move away, so he just stood there, lost in his thoughts. Which was why he caught her voice through the door when she said, "Snowball . . . how am I not going to mess this up royally?"

Ben turned right back around and knocked on her door. When she opened it with visible confusion, he jumped right in. "Why don't we rehearse the full show a few times now while everyone else is asleep."

Chapter 9

Deck the halls with cows and collies, as Jocelyn's slightly quirky coworker would say. Even classic Hollywood movie-makers would be impressed. The entire formal living room and dining room of Weber Haus had been both decorated in the "Stocking Stuffer" theme for the party as well as transformed into a TV studio set. Wires, lights, cameras, and all sorts of paraphernalia were . . . everywhere.

The crew had taken over like Santa's elves. She'd gone to bed in a normal house-slash-inn and woken up to a TV wonderland. Well . . . not woken up to it. She'd been up for a while—fed in her room on a tray, then in makeup and wardrobe, also in her room, with Margot.

Two things struck her now. The room was blindingly bright . . . and very hot. *What if I get sweat stains in my pits and everyone in the entire world sees?*

Which was silly. The show was popular, but not at that level. Besides, what she was wearing wouldn't show sweat stains.

But now I'm going to have to say stuff. On camera. *Why did I say yes to Ilse? What was I thinking?*

"There you are." Ben's voice came from behind her, so she tabled the panic attack that wanted to sideline her in order to could face him.

Maybe she didn't do a great job with the tabling though, because he frowned, then took her by the arms to scoot them both around so that his shoulders blocked her from view of the crew. He opened his mouth to speak, but paused, glancing around them. Too many people, even if they couldn't see her.

"The wardrobe choice works, I think," he said instead.

What had he been going to say? She nodded, then in a low voice murmured, "Where do you need me?"

"They're still setting up and will be for a while. Why don't we do one more run-through, just the two of us?"

Another run-through. They'd gone over everything several times last night. He'd pointed out things like camera location, how loud to speak, how to follow his lead. It had helped, but not enough. The rocks piling up in her stomach told her a thousand times wouldn't have been enough. Now they'd be doing this in front of everyone, including the audience watching live from their homes. If she messed up there was no reset, no cut, no fade to black, and no way to fix it.

Jocelyn swallowed, her hands curling around her script. "Sounds good."

For the live shows they hadn't gone as originally scripted, as they usually did. Ben's choice, partly given the late change to the show content, and partly, she suspected, so that she wasn't having to memorize things, though they had a prompter, computerized, that Kyle operated with the monitor situated just under and to the right of the main camera.

Jocelyn wasn't sure which would be worse. Memorizing and being all stiff and worrying about forgetting her lines. Or coming up with anything to say about . . . well . . . anything.

She was more of a chatterer than Ilse, though. So maybe she'd be okay . . .

Picking up a packet of papers that looked much less written-on and dog-eared than hers, Ben walked her over to where two wingback chairs were set up in the living room now, with a camera directly in front. In the exact spot he'd said it would be last night.

He sat them both down. Still speaking in a low voice, he said, "Just like we talked about, we'll film a lot of the show from here. We now have a two-camera setup."

He must have caught her immediate flare of panic because he pointed. "One in locked position there, like we practiced. The other will be a handheld for mobility."

Two cameras? He hadn't said anything about that last night. "Am I allowed to move?"

"Only if I do."

Right. "How do I know where to look?"

"Follow my lead. I've set it up so that I speak or turn first every time."

Ilse was not going to like that, because it would make her secondary to him all the time, but Jocelyn just didn't care in this moment. It was going to take a full-blown, Rudolph's shiny nose in the fog, Christmas-style miracle to get her through one show, let alone five.

"You can do this."

She ducked her head. "I think I'm going to be sick. Is it hot in here?" The glaring lights were killing her already. "Maybe my clothes *are* going to show sweat. I should change."

She went to get up, but Ben tugged at her hand. "Hey."

Oh God. Oh God. Oh God. This was easily the most foolish thing she'd ever done in her life. Guaranteed humiliation.

"Look at me."

She forced her gaze up to meet Ben's. Which was steady. Her entire world narrowed down to a pair of surprisingly warm green eyes that didn't waver. Steady. She focused and steadied in return.

Moss green. The color struck her. A really pretty color.

"Don't worry about any of it. Follow my lead and just talk to me like we're having a chat."

Just talk to him. He made it sound so easy. "The script—"

"I'll keep us to that. Pretend I'm a close friend of Il . . . your sister, even." Close call. Good thing they weren't miked yet. Ben had warned her about that last night, too.

She huffed a laugh. "What I have to say about stocking stuffers and what my sister would say are two very different things."

His eyes crinkled at the corners. Not a big smile. Just enough that her muscles, which were practically twitching with tension, eased a tiny bit.

"Better," he murmured.

Warmth spread from her chest all the way out to her fingers and toes. Because Ben smiled and told her she was doing better.

What am I thinking?

Focus on the issue. He can help you, but what if he doesn't know you need help? The problem was if she ran into trouble, she couldn't tell him so in the middle of filming. "I think we need a signal."

His eyes crinkled even more. "What, like a bat signal?"

She thought for a minute. "How about if I do this . . ." She laid her hand on his forearm, Ilse's massive diamond twinkling at her from her middle finger. A casual touch that would look like she was just connecting with her cohost. "If I do that, I'm in trouble."

Ben glanced down at her hand on his arm. Or more accurately on the gray sport coat he was wearing over a blue button-down shirt, no tie, that complemented her outfit. Then he glanced up, first to her, then over her shoulder before he leaned back, pulling his arm subtly out from under her touch.

"Margot saw that," he murmured under his breath.

Oh. Very deliberately, Jocelyn straightened, and then pointed randomly at the script in his lap. In a raised voice said, "I should be the one to say this. It's more something I would say."

Ben frowned and glanced at where she was pointing, which

was a blank spot on the page. Then cleared his throat and sent that frown in her direction. "Changing it now will just interrupt our rhythm."

He caught that she was making them sound like Ilse and Ben on purpose. Good.

"Like we have a rhythm."

He choked, although she suspected it was more of a laugh than surprise. She had to try hard not to wince as she whispered, "Too much?"

"Nope. Spot-on."

Oh, Ilse.

Her sister wasn't really that bad, was she? Did she have sharp edges to her? Yes. But she wasn't deliberately cruel. Maybe more was going on with Ilse than Jocelyn had realized.

Almost two hours later, Walter clapped his hands. "Let's do a soft run-through. If we have time we'll run it twice, break for a late lunch, and touch-ups, then we roll live at five p.m. Got it?"

No. No one had said anything about running through a rehearsal.

This is a good thing. A chance to practice with everyone watching, but not *everyone* everyone, before they did it for real. Just the crew. The people who knew Ilse best and were most likely to notice that this was not their Ilse about to host *Home & Hearth*.

Fifteen minutes later, miked and touched up and checked on by at least four different people, Jocelyn pinned a smile into place that felt about as plastic as a doll's.

Following Ben's lead she looked directly into the lens of the camera in front of them, the one in locked position, as Ben pretended to open the show. She was so focused on trying to look comfortable, that she missed her cue.

"Don't you think, Ilse?"

Ben's voice pulled her back. She flashed him a smile, back

to the camera and somehow managed to pull from the dregs of her brain her opening line. Although it helped to have the monitor with her cues in her line of sight. "I do, Ben." She aimed what she hoped was an appropriately excited grin at the camera. "We all know I love to throw a fabulous party and now we get to do that five times this holiday season."

I sound like a robot. Relax. Relax. Relax.

"Stop," Walter called out. "Let's try that again."

"My fault," Jocelyn called out with a wave of her hand. Then immediately wondered if Ilse would have ever claimed anything as her fault. Probably not.

"No." Walter waved Tony, the sound tech, over. "Your mic has a problem."

Oh. Maybe they missed that spaced-out, freaked-out pause, or the way she sounded off?

She stood so that Tony could fiddle with the pack that was attached to the waist of her pants, under her sweater at her back. Ben had given her some long spiel with technical details about getting the right sound, especially live, but having a backup plan if anything went wrong. Jocelyn didn't remember a word after he'd told her to watch what she said because once the mic was on her, Tony could and would hear every single word they exchanged.

He leaned closer. "Remember that trick we talked about."

Trick? They'd talked about a hundred different tricks. Sit slightly sideways to the camera rather than straight on. Speak from the diaphragm. Tilt her head, but only slightly. Lean toward Ben. If she got stuck, bring Ben into it with a question. As if she was going to be able think of a question in that moment.

"Pick a spot just barely to the side of the lens and pretend it's your best friend and talk to them." The memory of his words managed to wiggle through all the other noise in her head.

"Got it," she said to Ben about the same time that Tony

finished fiddling with her mic pack. Then she was seated again, and Walter was cueing Ben to start.

This time, Jocelyn shifted her gaze to the cue screen. Not the entire thing, just the upper corner nearest the lens, and pictured not Ilse's face . . . but Ben's. This time, she didn't need prompting and she managed to get the words out. Stilted, but better.

The rest of what ended up being two soft run-throughs went, if not well, at least without disaster. Granted, she'd caught several frowns directed her way, but no one was screaming, "Imposter."

That's the best I can do.

At least she was actually feeling a little steadier. The two-camera thing was tricky, but with Ben's direction, she did okay. She had stopped rushing or stumbling over words by the time they finished. She was also exhausted.

And had yet to actually film any of it.

But she had no choice. They still had to do this for real.

Faster than she expected, they stopped and ate. Not that she ate. She couldn't force even a morsel into her stomach. Margot brought her some hot tea, and that was the most she could manage. Then she had her makeup and hair touched up and they were in front of the cameras for real this time.

Don't choke. Don't choke. Don't say something ridiculous or choke.

Walter counted down, the last few numbers silent, and then pointed at Jocelyn and Ben. The red light on the camera showed it was hot, and Ben immediately launched into the introduction. Jocelyn managed to play her part without stuttering, but definitely stiffer than in rehearsal. A wooden puppet in the toy store in the shops showed more emotion than she did.

They said that during a traumatic event, humans did one of four things—fight, flight, freeze, or fawn. Freeze was clearly her go-to. Jocelyn was . . . numb . . . even as her heart was beating so hard, she was terrified the mic pack would pick up the sound.

Breathe. Breathe. For goodness' sake, don't pass out on live TV. Breathe.

"—looking forward to, Ilse?"

What? Oh no. She'd concentrated so hard on slowing her heart rate, she missed her cue again.

Where were they? Something about the music selection? Or maybe they were still talking about what a Stocking Stuffer Party was? They definitely couldn't have moved on to the food and drinks yet.

Without thinking she put her hand on Ben's arm.

But she missed and landed on his hand. Skin to skin. Immediately, his warmth seeped in through that small contact, and her heart steadied all on its own.

Not tensing when Jocelyn's hand landed on his was maybe the hardest thing Ben had ever had to do on camera.

Was that the signal? Wasn't she supposed to grab his arm?

He took a shot, rephrasing the question he'd just asked. "Didn't you say seeing Angel's reaction to all the goodies was what you were looking forward to?"

The relief in her eyes a blink before she smiled told him he got that right, and he silently blew out a long breath.

"Absolutely!" Her voice was almost an octave too high. She cleared her throat. "I love how at Christmas, kitties think all the boxes and the wrapping paper is for them. Don't you?"

"Not as much as you, I suspect." He remembered to smile. "Maybe we should bring Angel out and see what she thinks before our guests arrive?"

Jocelyn glanced around at the beautiful setup they had going on. "How about we provide her with a distraction, just in case."

Then she reached behind their chairs to pick up a box full

of crinkled wrapping paper and showed it to the camera with a cheeky grin. "I just happen to have this available."

Ben chuckled. "I wonder who put that there."

Without a beat, she opened her eyes wide. "Santa's elves. Duh."

That wasn't in the script.

She shook her head at him, suddenly able to tease, then set the cat distraction down on the love seat to her right, which was where their scheduled guests would sit later. Then clapped her hands and looked off camera. "Send in the real star of *Home & Hearth*!"

From off to the side in the foyer, Isaac set down the cat he'd been holding. Angel stood there, off camera, all fluffed and primped and wearing an elf hat. She tipped her head and didn't move a paw.

Ben gave Jocelyn a nudge. "The treat."

She startled, but not enough that anyone at home probably noticed, then grabbed the small treat where it was hidden under a tray and lowered it so that the coffee table blocked her hand from the camera. "Here kitty, kitty . . ."

Immediately, Angel started trotting over, and the tiny bell on the tip of her elf hat tinkled and rang with each prancing step. Paul, manning the handheld camera, moved to track the cat's progress.

Angel might have been difficult with Snowball, and not happy about traveling, but she was a professional when the cameras were rolling. That was . . . until Angel was within about a foot from Jocelyn. Then the cat suddenly stopped, blue eyes narrowing ominously. She sniffed the air and then, with a kitty scream the likes of which the winter winds would be jealous, launched herself, claws unsheathed, right at Jocelyn's face.

With a yelp, Jocelyn managed to get her hands up in time to protect herself, but the cat latched on to her arms. From where he sat, it seemed to Ben that time slowed down as he watched those claws sink in.

"Help!" Jocelyn bolted up from her chair so fast and hard, she knocked the chair over, which fell into the wall behind her, but thanks to momentum reversed course and knocked right back into her.

Still battling with the attacking cat, Jocelyn windmilled one arm, trying not to tumble right into one of the tables all set up for the stocking stuffing events.

Ben grabbed for her, managing to latch on to one elbow, but his grip swung her around in his direction.

"Careful of the cat!" she yelped as they both went over.

By some miracle they missed furniture and displays as they hit the floor with an *oomph*, Ben flat on his back and the air knocked from his lungs, Jocelyn right on top of him. Angel jumped mid-fall, also clearing the tables and chairs to land unharmed.

"Oh my gosh, are you okay?" Jocelyn's frantic voice came from right by his left ear.

Before he could respond, she was pushing against his chest, scrambling to get off him. And his senses returned at the same time. Having a female cohost laid out over the prone male cohost on live TV was not a good look. Not on their kind of show.

Somehow, they both managed to get to their feet without further incident. Then Ben got a look at Jocelyn's arm because the sleeve had pushed up to the elbow. Without a second thought, he grabbed her hand. "You're bleeding."

Claw marks were all over her.

Jocelyn laughed and reached up to push his hair back from his forehead. "And you're all disheveled."

He glanced up to find her laughing eyes sparkling at him. The most relaxed she'd been this entire day.

Ben grinned right back. "You're not exactly your well-put-together self at the moment either."

And then it hit him where they were.

A quick glance showed him they were still filming. Why on earth had Walter not gone to commercial? He leaned forward to whisper in her ear, "We're still rolling."

After a slight hesitation, she pulled back. "I think we were lucky."

"Lucky? How exactly?"

She held up one finger. "We managed to avoid the tables and chairs on the way down. Party disaster averted. Miracle number one." Then put a second finger up. "Miracle number two . . . Angel didn't come in for round two."

Ben's eyes went wide as he checked the room for the cat, but she was nowhere to be seen.

Jocelyn put a third finger up. "And we managed not to hurt her through all of that. I would have felt terrible. Miracle number three." Then she cocked her head at him. "Doesn't that qualify one of us for sainthood?"

Surprise had him huffing a laugh. "What?"

She nodded, turning to face the camera. "I seem to remember from the Val Kilmer movie *The Saint* that three recorded miracles means sainthood."

Ilse had probably not watched that movie. Not ever. But who cared? Somehow Jocelyn, even despite never having been on TV before in her life, managed to turn the moment into something lighthearted.

"Well, folks," Jocelyn said, still addressing the camera, "I think that goes to show that maybe pets shouldn't always be introduced during your parties. Depending on how they are with new surroundings, the number of guests, and the items out, which could be too much temptation or overwhelming to them, sometimes it's better to put them safely in a closed room."

And now she was giving party advice about pets. Who was this woman?

She turned to face him. "Shall we get cleaned up?"

"I think so." His turn to stare directly into the camera. "We'll be right back after this commercial break."

A second later Walter said, "And we're out."

Followed by a pause of dead silence. Probably the crew waiting for Hurricane Ilse to blow through. Because no way would the real host of *Home & Hearth* have let that incident slide.

Jocelyn said nothing though.

Ben glanced around, waiting for someone to question why.

Instead, Walter set the handheld camera down. "Where on earth did *that* chemistry come from?"

Chemistry?

"There's no chemistry," both Ben and Jocelyn said in unison.

Even so, heat flared in his face. He didn't dare glance at her. Jocelyn, meanwhile, walked away, calling out, "Can someone clean me up, please? And check on poor Angel."

Poor Angel, my back left foot.

I was right last night. She's a devil cat. Any creature that could attack Jocelyn is not a good kitty. She's a very bad kitty.

Why would she do that anyway? Isn't she supposed to be a professional actor cat?

Still . . . I tip my head . . . she did do something helpful.

I saw the entire thing from my hiding spot up in the Christmas tree. Lukas tried to stuff me in Miss Tilly's room, warning me that they were filming today, and that the devil cat would be here, and I wasn't to show my face until it was over.

Like Miss Tilly's room has ever kept me contained. Ha! But I did hide, just somewhere more interesting.

And what I saw between Ben and Jocelyn was magic. Angel forced the two of them to help each other. Even if they did fall over in a tangle of limbs. And the way they glance at each other when they think the other isn't watching tells me all I need to know.

Even the humans noticed the sparks, and humans are oblivious creatures.

This might be my easiest matchmaking job yet!

Chapter 10

I trot into the kitchen because I need a midnight drink of water and that's where my water bowl is. Only I stop mid-trot, lift my adorable nose, and give a good sniff.

Something is off in here. It smells like . . .

A whisp of movement catches my eye and a kitty gasp might actually escape my throat. Not that there is such a thing. Kitties don't gasp.

But seriously, if anything would make me, this would be it.

Angel is up on the counter again. This time, though, I've caught her red-pawed. She's standing on the stove and has managed to turn on the gas. Not the flame, just the gas. And she's sniffing at the fumes coming out.

I don't know much, but I've learned to stay away from the stove. Sometimes it's cold, but sometimes it can singe the fur right off a cat. Number-one rule of kitty survival . . . don't mess with the hot things. The stove, or while I'm at it, the oven or fireplace.

With a snarl of a sound, I run right for her, leaping up to the counter in one graceful bound. Only as I go up, she jumps down and sprints for the back stairs. I glance between her and the stove, which is still turned on, and I don't know how to turn it off. Because I've been avoiding it all this time.

My safety rule just backfired on me.

The problem is, I know the gas is still on. I can smell it and hear the faint hiss of it leaking. What if it turns to fire any second?

Before I can decide what to do, the sound of human footsteps treading down the back stairs reaches me a few seconds before Ben appears in the doorway. Did he see Angel as he came down? He should have.

Except he takes one look at me, stops, and sniffs the air like I did. Then . . . "Snowball, you bad kitty!"

Wait! What did I do?!

He's across the room and turning a dial on the stove and immediately that hissing noise stops. Thank heavens for that, at least.

Except he's still scowling at me.

He picks me up and sets me on the floor, gently at least, then wags a finger in my face. "Bad, bad kitty."

I look between him and the back stairs where Angel disappeared. Then I roll my eyes. Humans are blind as bats but without sonar, I swear. They couldn't find a real culprit with two hands, and a sign flashing, "the real bad kitty."

No wonder they've never figured out where Santa's home in the North Pole actually is.

Ben cracked open the window over the kitchen sink and waved a hand ineffectually in the air, hoping to dispel the scent of gas. They were lucky the darn cat hadn't exploded the house, or at the very least caused a fire.

Did she do this often? Were Lukas and Emily aware?

Also, if they had a fire and it burned the whole place down, where would they film any of the food preparation segments for the shows? Not to mention feed the crew breakfast and bake things for the parties? He should definitely say something to the owners. Between the two cats over the last few days, he was all kittied out.

I don't need this. I have enough of a looming disaster with Jocelyn standing in for Ilse.

Satisfied that the gas had dissipated, he got himself the glass of water he'd come down here for, then closed the window again and went to head back to bed. He put one foot on the bottom stair when a loud guffaw reached him. He paused.

Who was down here at this hour?

He should probably leave them to it and return upstairs. But the water had just been an excuse because he couldn't seem to settle. His brain was too filled with the show's problems and trying to solve them.

Problems like a non-cooking, non-singing, non-crafting woman pretending to be his cohost.

He found himself walking through the door that led to the to the hallway beyond. From the small sitting room off the hall, a blue flickering light told him where to go. Sure enough, as soon as he stood in the doorway, there was Jocelyn.

She was sitting on the couch, her computer balanced on her crisscrossed legs, earphones in, and totally absorbed by whatever she was watching.

"Hey," Ben whispered. Quietly. No need to wake up the rest of the house.

She didn't even look up though, totally oblivious that she wasn't alone.

So he moved until he was standing pretty much directly in front of her. She still didn't notice. So he waved a hand between her face and the screen.

"Ah!" Jocelyn softly screeched, arms and legs flailing.

As she jumped to her feet, computer tumbling off her lap, one hand batted upward, right into Ben's hand. The one holding the glass. Water went everywhere, the computer by some miracle landed on the couch, and Jocelyn and Ben stared at each other with less than a foot of space between them, but a little damper than they had been a second ago.

Her eyes went wide, then she yanked one of her earbuds out. "Benjamin. Whatever Your Middle Name Is. Meyer. What on earth were you thinking, sneaking up on me that way?"

"Me?" Ben goggled at her. She was blaming him? "I called your name several times and even stood right in front of you before I waved."

"Clearly I didn't see you." Her beetled brow made her look fierce in the darkness. Whatever she had been watching was still playing, flickering light over her features. One side of her hair was wet and now stuck to her cheek.

Ben had to pinch his lips around a laugh at the sight, because he was pretty sure she wouldn't appreciate that about now. "Sorry," he caved. Then blinked. He never was the one to cave. He'd learned the hard way that being the one to apologize usually ended with him in a position of weakness. "Let me go get a towel. Is your computer okay?"

"My computer!" Arms flailed again as she rushed to scoop the device off the couch to check it.

Ben left her to it as he returned to the kitchen where he fished out two hand towels—one for him and one for her—then padded his way back to Jocelyn.

"No water got on it," she said as soon as he showed his face.

"Miracle number four?"

Now I'm teasing her. What is wrong with me?

She wrinkled her nose at him, then returned to the couch to settle back down. Ben really should go back to his bed, but strangely he was reluctant to leave. He found himself dropping to sit beside her, leaning a tad closer to see her screen. "What are you watching?"

"*Christmas in Connecticut.*" She waved at the paused image.

"Barbara Stanwyck. She's one of my favorites."

In the act of putting her earbuds back in, Jocelyn paused to swing her gaze his way, mouth slightly agape.

Ben tried not to let his own gaze wander to her lips. If Ilse had tried that expression, she would have looked accusing, but on her sister, it came off . . . cute.

Ilse was put together, perfect, and cold. Jocelyn was real and just darn cute. How could the same face do that?

"You know who Barbara Stanwyck is?" The incredulity in her voice made him smile.

"My mother was a huge fan of the classics." He glanced at the screen showing the black-and-white film paused on an image of what appeared to be an idyllic country farmhouse in the snow. Or at least classic Hollywood's version of it. "I've only seen one or two of hers, but not this one."

He glanced back at Jocelyn in time to catch her little bounce and the way she sort of lit up. She pulled one of the earbuds out and offered it to him. "Want to watch with me? I'm only about ten minutes in and don't mind starting over."

Go back to your room. This has "bad idea" written all over it.

"Sure."

He sat and took the earbud, popping it in, connected to her now by the small wire leading to the other half in her ear. Settling back together, Jocelyn scooted the computer over so it was on both their legs, then started the movie.

She leaned closer to whisper, "I just couldn't help it. Being in this place made me think of this film. There's just something magical about watching campy holiday films at Christmas. Happy endings, snow, and shenanigans."

"Oh, there's shenanigans?" Ben pulled his earbud out, pretending to hand it back. "I don't know if I can handle shenanigans."

Jocelyn blinked for half a second, then seemed to clue in that he was joking. Her low chuckle shot straight through his chest and wrapped around something inside him that might be his heart.

"Just watch." She pointed like a strict schoolteacher.

It took Ben a solid ten minutes to watch the screen without sneaking peeks at Jocelyn, because she was entranced. Something about watching her joy was addictive. Which meant he was a tiny bit lost by the time the main character made it to a farmhouse somewhere in Connecticut. He thought she wasn't married, but her fiancé owned the house. What was happening?

Jocelyn leaned close again. "Did you know that house isn't real. They filmed it entirely on a sound stage."

"Impressive."

"Wait till you see the inside. If I could afford to pay someone to recreate that house, I would."

He had to admit, as the movie continued, the place was impressive in a very classic Hollywood overblown-version-of-reality kind of way. But beautiful.

His leaned closer. "Why would the hero be interested in a married woman who would flirt with him like that?" Especially in that era?

To his surprise, Jocelyn paused the film to turn to him with a disgruntled face that was so like Ilse, he braced himself for whatever he did wrong.

"I know."

It took a second for him to realize she agreed. "You know?"

She nodded. "It's my least favorite part of the plot. I really wish they'd had him figure it out before this point and either give her a hard time or be in on it with her. So I like to pretend that's what's happening."

Ben stared. This woman pretended people were better than actually portrayed, just to enjoy a film. How on earth could she be Ilse's sister?

She lifted her eyebrows, a clear signal he'd been thinking and staring too long.

"I guess I can do that too," he hurried to say, then waved at the screen.

* * *

If Ben wanted to get into acting rather than hosting, Jocelyn was sure he had a career as the leading man, heartthrob type. He even reminded her a little bit of Dennis Morgan, the lead actor in the movie. It was tempting to think Ben was watching her the same way the leading man on the screen watched the lead actress, as if he was taking in all the details about her that others missed. She shouldn't give in to the flight of fancy, but her heart fluttered all the same.

Which was ridiculous. He wasn't interested. She was just the thorn in his side until Ilse got back. Besides, he was probably trying to figure her out.

She gave herself a mental shake and pointed. "All of that is plastic snow."

"Black-and-white film covers all manner of sins, I guess," he whispered back.

Which made her chuckle again. "I'm not ruining it for you, am I? I tend to spew factoids."

He glanced at her, then quickly back to the screen, and shook his head. "It's interesting."

Jocelyn stared at a spot on her keyboard and missed the next ten minutes entirely. Interesting. Here was a man who knew who Barbara Stanwyck was, was willing to watch an old film with her, and found her factoids interesting.

Where has he been all my life?

The answer was immediately obvious. He was doing a show with Ilse. Or at least that's where he'd been the last six months. It really wasn't fair.

Despite being supremely conscious of the man beside her, Jocelyn still got lost in the ending. When the hero teased the heroine into revealing her lies, which he already knew about, though not soon enough for Jocelyn's liking, it left her with a happy, contented little glow.

As the credits rolled, she clicked out of the app, shut her

computer lid, then held a hand out for the other half of her earbuds. "What did you think?"

"Mmmm . . . My mother no doubt loves it. Romantic comedies are her favorites."

"But not yours?"

Ben shook his head, eyes twinkling in the glow of the lights on the Christmas tree. "Not mine."

Jocelyn laughed to cover a pinch of disappointment. "You should have said so. You didn't have to watch the whole thing."

He shook his head. "I enjoyed it. You're right. It fits this house."

She glanced around the small room with its antique furniture, beautifully detailed woodwork, built-in bookshelves, all decked out for the season of course. "There's a movie for every place I go. Usually more than one."

"How'd you get into the classics?"

"It started with *Oklahoma!*"

"The musical?"

The way Ben made a face had her laughing. "Let me guess. Not into musicals?"

"Not really."

She shrugged. "Like pretty much every guy I ever dated." She paused, trying not to wince. Because she wasn't dating Ben. This wasn't a date. "Um . . ."

Say something or don't say something?

He saved her from herself. "What did guys you dated do when you said you liked musicals?"

Jocelyn blew out a silent breath. Ben was a good guy under all that scary efficiency. "At least two of them wanted to watch *Romancing the Stone* on an at-home date."

"That's not a musical."

"I know." Her tone turned dry as dust.

Ben laughed. He had a nice laugh. Deep and honest. Not overloud but not soft either. Just . . . nice. Really nice.

"Anyway . . . musicals led to watching movie classics on TV, and that turned into the love of a lifetime." She turned her head to find him watching her with what appeared to be genuine interest. "I'm a film historian now."

"Wow. So you took a passion and found a way to make it a job."

"One that barely pays the bills, which is why I have a roommate, but yes."

"And sort of in the same industry as your sister. Keeping it in the family?"

She snorted, then covered her nose with her hand because the sound was so loud. "Sorry."

Ben chuckled.

"Not really. Ilse wouldn't be caught dead watching the stuff I watch."

"Good point."

"Although . . ." she mused. "I'd love to be one of the hosts for TCM someday. It's why I started doing my vlog."

She blinked at herself. She hadn't even told Ilse about that particular little dream.

Ben didn't laugh this time, which she appreciated. "Once you warmed up, you did fine the other day. And that was live. Too bad you can't send them that as an audition tape."

Jocelyn's stomach flipped over at the mere thought of doing that again. And she still had four more shows to get through. She'd been a wreck, hence the not sleeping and watching movies late into the night. "I think I might be happier behind the scenes."

Ben slowly leaned in closer, looking into her eyes like he could figure out all her secrets. Like he wanted to. "You sure about that?"

His voice dropped, drawing her in, and all Jocelyn could seem to do was stare back.

The man was even better looking up close—eyes crinkling at the corners like he smiled a lot, warm and friendly. He was smart and talented too. Did he have to add mind reader to the list? "Mostly," she allowed in a voice that had turned into a husky whisper somewhere along the line. "A girl can dream."

The crinkles around his eyes deepened along with his smile. "I thought so."

Jocelyn's heart was beating so hard she could hear each heavy thud. *I should look away.*

She didn't though. *Maybe I'm still affected by the movie.* The ending was swoon-worthy. Ben was kind of swoon-worthy too.

His gaze dropped slowly from her eyes, trailing over the features of her face, to stop at her lips. And Jocelyn held her breath. Waiting. Part of her willing him to lean just a little closer.

"This is a bad idea," he whispered.

She didn't bother to ask what "this" was. It was pretty darn obvious, and she happened to agree. Terrible idea. She still didn't move. Not when he continued to look at her like that, not when he leaned slowly—achingly slowly—closer. His gaze flicked up to hers, as if asking permission. In answer Jocelyn tipped her head, making it easier. He may have smiled as he pressed his lips to hers, but she was too immediately lost to wonder.

Ben's kiss was . . . bliss.

A soft brush against hers, a pause as his eyes flicked open, checking with her again, then another soft brush. Then more. Lips pressed to lips, apart. The sweetest kiss she'd had probably in all her life. Gentle. And hot at the same time. Jocelyn gave herself over to the moment, and the sensation, and Ben. Her fluttering hands landed and settled on his chest, and he brought one hand up to cup her jaw and the back of her neck, anchoring her to him.

"Oh! Excuse me. I'll just—"

Jocelyn jumped guiltily back from Ben, aware that he also

hastily put distance between them as they both faced Ilse's personal assistant.

Jocelyn blinked. Margot was frowning as she glanced back and forth between them. Clearly not happy. Why? Beyond this being awkward, and . . .

Well, now she'll have to keep it a secret, Jocelyn realized.

For once, she had no idea what to do. Or say. She glanced at Ben, who appeared to be equally at a loss for words or actions.

What could either of them say, anyway? Something like "It's not what it looks like" wouldn't work. It was exactly what it looked like. Kissing. Something that would never, should never, happen again. They had enough to contend with getting Jocelyn through this time playing Ilse on live TV.

What was I thinking?

And how cliché could she get? Just like a rom-com where the heroine just sort of lets things happen to her. Jocelyn had always thought she was smarter than that. Or at least had more self-control.

Clearly not.

Only a few seconds passed for her to think all that. Before she or Ben could come up with something to say, Margot's expression suddenly shifted to a conspiratorial grin. "Don't worry. This will be our secret until you're ready to tell the cast yourself." She mimed zipping her lips.

"Oh, but we're not—"

Ben reached over to take Jocelyn's hand so abruptly, she cut herself off. "Thank you, Margot."

Ilse's assistant smiled broader. "I guess you just needed to get rid of the boyfriend for the chemistry to ignite."

"I—" Jocelyn cut off her protest mid-squeak after a warning squeeze from Ben.

"Night, you two." Margot wiggled her fingers in a wave, her smirk this side of aggravating, and left them to it.

They both sat in silence for a long beat. Then Jocelyn slowly turned her head, eyes wide, to find Ben watching her. "Why did you let her think that we're . . ." She couldn't finish the thought.

"She wouldn't believe any protests we make. It seemed . . . easier . . . to ask her to keep it a secret."

"Oh."

Disappointment shouldn't be her response to that explanation. That perfectly rational explanation.

"Well . . ." *Do something.* Jocelyn hopped to her feet and gathered her computer and paraphernalia. All without looking at Ben. "Um . . . g'night."

Then she hurried out of the room and up the stairs, not stopping until she closed the door to her room. Then fell back against it, closing her eyes on a groan.

How am I going to face him tomorrow?

Chapter 11

Ben had no choice but to sit next to Jocelyn at breakfast because it was the only seat available. Given her awkward glances, first at him then at Margot, he kept it to a cordial nod. Neither of them spoke.

Which was probably worse.

Was it worse? Middle school was probably the last time he'd debated like this over how to approach a girl.

Actually, there was no debate. He needed to work closely with Jocelyn to prepare for the next show—a Toy Drive Party. Make sure everything was set up for her to not really do anything on the show except talk. Then rehearse and practice in secret. That was it. No more kissing.

Ben glanced at Jocelyn's plate and actually had to stop himself from smiling. This morning, she had limited herself to egg whites and toast with only a miniscule pat of butter, along with the shake that Margot apparently still insisted on making for her, even though she'd said not to.

Should I say anything? Make plans at least. He paused. *No, later. In private.*

Then he actually shook his head at himself before realizing what he was doing. Then stopped when he caught Jocelyn's side-eyed glance. Was she regretting that kiss? He should be.

He didn't dare look directly at her. If he did, he knew he would look at her lips.

So soft last night. And she'd tasted like peppermint and hot chocolate. That kiss had been . . .

Stop.

He shouldn't be thinking about kissing his temporary co-host, and archnemesis's twin sister, who was pretending to be Ilse on live TV.

Ben probably wouldn't have noticed the person who came in the front door with a jingle of bells and stopped to ask Sophie, who happened to be in the hallway, if he could talk to the manager. Except Jocelyn jerked her head up at the sound of the man's voice to stare in his direction.

"What on earth?" Ben caught her whispered mumble.

He leaned closer. "What's going on?"

"Um . . ."

In that moment, the man in the foyer turned his head, only to still as he locked eyes with Jocelyn. Then without looking away, he said to Sophie, "Never mind. I found her."

Before the man took a single step in any direction, Jocelyn pushed back from the table so fast her chair tipped over. Ben flashed out a hand, catching it before it hit the sidebar table. The antique, in perfect condition, and probably worth a mint sidebar table.

Jocelyn didn't even seem to notice as she hurried out of the dining room, straight to the man who she grabbed by the hand and dragged up the stairs without a word spoken.

Every person seated at the table stared after her.

"She doesn't already have a new boyfriend, does she?" Kyle broke the silence.

The kid looked like Santa had just taken away his favorite toy. Everyone else at the table just shrugged. Meanwhile Ben had no idea what to do.

Maybe I should go up there and see what that was all about.

Unless that guy was here for Ilse for some reason, in which case Ben was better off out of it. Except the man definitely hadn't looked like some uber-wealthy European baron. He'd been wearing jeans and a sweatshirt underneath a thick coat that had seen better days. And his dark blond hair was worn in an overlong, unkempt style that Ben would never be able to pull off; his hair was so thick it would just stand straight up off his head.

"Maybe Ilse owes money to the mafia?" Walter said with a big grin that clearly showed he wasn't serious. And everyone laughed.

Except Ben.

And, when he looked up from his eggs that were starting to get cold, Kyle wasn't laughing either. He was looking off in the direction Jocelyn had disappeared, with a concerned frown. The kid obviously had it bad for Ilse and had no clue he was pining after the wrong woman.

Kyle moved to get up, but Ben beat him to it. "I'll go check."

He moved with purpose into the foyer and up the stairs. Jocelyn had come up this way, but that's all he knew. His best guess was she was either in her room, or maybe had gone back to that currently unbooked room where she'd had her panic attack, for more privacy. He tried her room first. After his knock, there was a long enough wait that he knocked again. A few seconds later, the door cracked open, and Jocelyn peeked out with one eye, blinked, then opened the door wider so he could see the rest of her. "Oh. It's just you."

Ben wasn't thrilled with the "just you" bit, but at least her tone was one of relief. Meanwhile he was busy looking over her shoulder at the Viking crowding her room. The man had to be six foot four, if he was an inch, and broadly lean. And he was eyeing Ben with deep mistrust while not remotely bothering to hide that fact.

Jocelyn grabbed Ben by the wrist and tugged him inside, closing door behind him.

"Who are you?" the Viking asked in a tone that matched his doubting face.

"Who are you?" Ben shot right back. Why did he have to be the one to explain things? This was his show, his production, his career. He and Jocelyn were here on business.

Jocelyn rolled her eyes. "Theo, this is Ben Meyer. He is my cohost on the show."

"You mean Ilse's cohost," Theo pointed out.

So . . . the other man knew she was Jocelyn, not Ilse. Then what was he doing here? Had Jocelyn called him?

She ignored the interruption. "Ben, this is Theo Lange. He is—"

"We live together," Theo supplied.

What was this now?

Ben glanced back and forth between them, not entirely sure where to go from that. The statement was clearly a challenge to him, although he didn't know why. Finally he settled his gaze on Jocelyn and raised his eyebrows, figuring she would understand that there were about a hundred questions that needed answering and she should start talking.

Except Theo did the same thing. "You owe me an explanation, Joce."

"Watch your tone." Ben might've been dragged into this, but he didn't like the way the other man talked to Jocelyn. After all, she'd been dragged into this too. Anyone who knew both women would know this was all Ilse's doing.

For his efforts he got an unimpressed look from Theo. "I've known Jocelyn since we were kids. You've known her what, a few days? I'll talk to her any way I see fit."

"Heaven save me from men and testosterone," Jocelyn

muttered. Then took a deep breath. "Theo, Ben is helping me do Ilse's job while she's in the Philippines and—"

"The Phili—!" Theo straightened. "The Philippines? Are you messing with me right now?"

Pretty much exactly Ben's reaction when she'd confessed to him.

Jocelyn kept going. "Ben is the only one who knows that I'm not Ilse."

Theo's face started to turn red like he was a teakettle about to blow steam. "You couldn't even pull off being Ilse when we were kids. How do you think you're going to do it on live TV?"

Jocelyn ducked her head. "How did you know about that?"

Theo ran a hand over his face and then settled a look on her that reminded Ben of the time he'd been ten and had "borrowed" cash from his father's wallet only to have his dad stop him going out the door. One of the few times his father had bothered to notice him. But that was this look—fatherly disappointment combined with stern disagreement.

"*Live* TV, Jocelyn," Theo said. "I watched the most recent episode. Live."

That had aired only a few days ago . . . which meant the guy had immediately put his life on hold, found out where the show was being filmed and where Weber Haus was, then hopped the soonest flight here.

"Are you her boyfriend or something?" The question wasn't going to be stopped.

"We live together," Theo stubbornly repeated.

Only to get a funny look from Jocelyn. "He's my roommate . . . and my best friend."

Theo was being weird. Why did he bring up living together, or at least word it that way? Not that she blamed him for being upset with her. She hadn't expected him to track her down.

Then again, she hadn't thought about him catching her via the TV either.

Theo turned his brown-eyed gaze to her, hard now instead of the usual whiskey warmth, clearly done explaining things to Ben. "So this is you spending time with Ilse for the holidays?"

"Um . . ." She glanced at Ben, who was no help.

"I thought there was something fishy about that note," Theo muttered.

Time to confess. "You would have talked me out of doing this."

He took a step toward her. "Damn straight I would."

Theo was not her sister's biggest admirer at the moment. To his way of thinking, Ilse had gone off to bigger and better things and dropped the people who loved her the second she'd achieved success. Jocelyn wasn't about to argue him out of that opinion; she'd already tried. Long experience told her not to bother anymore. Meanwhile, she was horribly uncomfortable with the fact that Ben was standing there listening to all their back-and-forth, eyebrows crawling into his hairline.

She cleared her throat. "Honestly, I didn't have time to think about it. It all happened pretty fast."

Theo crossed arms. "That's how Ilse sucks you in. She gives you no time to think about the actual consequences. Like *live* TV."

"Ilse never asks me for help. You know that. And you didn't see her. She was desperate."

Theo frowned. "But you can't do anything she can do."

Blunt as usual. Jocelyn crossed her own arms and stared right back at her best friend. "Well, it's too late to put the cookie back in the jar now. We have to get these live shows done. She's in the Philippines. I'm here." She waved a hand at Ben. "Ben is helping me."

Theo flicked Ben an unimpressed glance. "And no one else knows? Crew, production team, studio, Ilse's assistant, or anyone else on her team?"

"It's just Ben and me." Jocelyn had to consciously force herself to not hang her head or squirm uncomfortably. She loved Theo to pieces, but the man had stink eye down to an art. Jocelyn shot him her sunniest smile, which usually loosened him up. "And now you."

The smile didn't work.

He lifted a single eyebrow at her, which was Theo for *I'm not buying it*, then turned to face Ben. "I'm surprised you agreed to this. I was under the impression you're not on great terms with Ilse."

Why would Theo think that? As far as she knew, he hadn't talked to Ilse in ages, and certainly never visited the studio.

"When did you find out?" Theo demanded.

Unlike the two of them with their crossed arms, Ben casually leaned against the vanity table, appearing completely relaxed. She had a feeling of purpose. "The day before the first live show," he said, then tipped his head, studying her friend. "I didn't have much choice at that point. It was either cancel all the shows or go on with Jocelyn pretending to be Ilse."

"Uh-huh."

Not good. Theo's "uh-huh" was a signal that he was on the verge of delivering a very long diatribe. He never yelled when he was angry. He just lectured. She had only been on the end of exactly three of his lectures since their childhood, and didn't plan on being on the end of any more.

Honestly, she'd sort of hoped she'd get through these live shows, return home, and feed him some story about her Christmas—not overly idyllic because of course in theory she was spending it with Ilse—then get back to life as normal with Theo none the wiser. Why did he have to go and watch the show and figure everything out? Ignorance was supposed to be bliss.

Actually . . .

Jocelyn slowly dropped her arms, then put her hands on her hips, studying him more closely. "Why *were* you watching *Home & Hearth* anyway?"

Theo was in construction. He had worked his way up to owning his own company. The man was all about tools, and nails, banging, and hard hats, and lots of swearing and sweating. He was not, by any stretch of the imagination, a crafts and recipes kind of guy. His idea of cooking dinner was to make boxed macaroni and cheese, for Pete's sake.

Shock tumbled through her as Theo's cheeks infused with red. Jocelyn was pretty certain she'd never seen him blush. Ever.

"Ilse may have changed," he said slowly. "Grown more distant. But you and she are still the most important people in my life. I keep tabs on her."

Jocelyn stared, even as her insides melted to goo.

For several years Theo had complained about how Ilse had cut them out of her life, and about her choices of boyfriends, and about how she made work her everything. Enough that Jocelyn had eventually asked him to stop. He had, but he'd also stopped talking about Ilse at all, or asking about her.

But he still cared.

And Jocelyn hadn't realized.

"You keep tabs on her?" she repeated.

Theo glanced away. "Probably more than I keep tabs on you." She barely caught his muttering.

Well . . . this has to be the darnedest Christmas I've ever seen.

Jocelyn took the few steps to his side and wrapped her arms around Theo's unmoving form. After stiffening—he'd never been much of a hugger—he slowly wrapped his arms around her, squeezing her back. Knowing not to cling, she let go and stepped away, offering him a smile. "Now that you know everything, how long are you staying?"

Theo blew out a long breath. "There was a problem at the site. Nothing big, but the timing around the holidays means they shut everything down probably until after Christmas just because it'll take that long to get everything sorted. So if I can find a place to sleep, I guess I'm staying until Christmas and helping with . . ." He waved a hand between her and Ben. "This disaster."

Her first thought was that he was referring to her and Ben . . . and their shared kiss. Only because that kiss was still on her mind. She even opened her mouth to ask how Theo knew about it. But stopped herself in time.

"There's not much you can do to help." Ben finally spoke up.

Jocelyn swung to face him, catching a curious expression cross his features a heartbeat before he blanked out all emotions, the way he did.

"Jocelyn and I *always* spend Christmas together," Theo said.

There he went again with the truth wrapped in some weird implications, like he was being deliberately misleading.

Ben didn't even blink. "The studio has bought out the inn and the hotel rooms. You might be able to find something in town, but it's pretty touristy. So I'm guessing not."

Jocelyn frowned at her temporary cohost and partner-in-deception. "You know there's two empty rooms on the third floor." She pointed up.

Ben flicked her a glance. "I don't know how the studio will feel about that."

"If they rented out everything, they already paid for those rooms. If they're paying anyway, might as well have someone use it."

"And who do we say he is? Enough of the crew saw your little act in the foyer to be very aware that you know him well enough to drag him up to your room by the hand. And they also know you just broke up with your boyfriend."

"Jocelyn doesn't have a boyfriend," Theo said.

"Ilse broke up with hers," she and Ben told him in unison.

Theo went very still. "She did?"

Ben was still looking at her. "We're conspicuous enough as it is, given you aren't her and don't have her skills. Let's not bring more attention our way than we have to."

All valid points. Even if a little harshly blunt.

Jocelyn thought for a moment, then a slow smile spread across her lips. Both men shifted uncomfortably at the sight.

"I think it's time Ilse turned diva. After all, she's been so accommodating so far. Maybe she suddenly needs her family with her for the holidays, and her sister couldn't make it, so she invited her longtime childhood friend and sister's roommate."

Ben and Theo looked at each other, then back at her.

"Great," Ben muttered.

At the same time Theo said, "Merry Christmas to me."

I can't sleep. I'm curled up at the end of Jocelyn's bed, chin on my paws, thinking hard. This morning I snuck into the room with Ben when he went up to check on Jocelyn and the man she called Theo. Which means I heard and saw everything.

And now I'm so confused.

Theo clearly cares a lot for Jocelyn. Anyone who would fly all that way at the drop of a hat . . . and he recognized that she wasn't her identical twin sister just from watching her on TV. Does he love her? Do I have the wrong man picked out for her?

I just . . . for the first time I don't know for sure.

Chapter 12

"And we're out," Walter announced, indicating they were on a commercial break. "Three minutes to set up the next segment."

Jocelyn tried her best not to completely deflate. Not because there'd been problems, but in direct reaction to the stress of keeping it together, smile pinned in place, on like a streetlight on a dark night. The pressure was bottling up inside her like a shaken soda can. Ready to pop.

She worked her jaw, stiff from smiling so hard.

"Good job, Ms. Becker!" Kyle flashed her a thumbs-up. He'd been handling her teleprompter from his usual perch on the stairs, his computer in his lap.

"Thanks."

They were halfway through and so far, no disasters. Today's theme was a Toy Drive Party. They'd covered types of toys to bring, things like variety, age appropriateness, generic versus more specific gifts, more practical gifts like coats and blankets, and some of the current most-wanted items. The next short segment should be relatively easy too . . . talking to Lara Wolfe about the custom toys at her shop here at Weber Haus.

But after that . . . after that there would be cooking and wrapping presents.

The food is premade and already-wrapped presents are ready as examples of the final products. Just stir a pot and tape a flap. That's all.

She'd been telling herself that for what felt like a very long time.

Basically, ever since Theo had heard the plan for this show in particular. He'd barked a laugh and said, "Jocelyn wrap a gift? This is going to be good." Another snort. "And by good, I mean a mess."

Ben had looked between them, then focused in on Jocelyn the way he did. "What am I missing?"

"Remember the 'can't craft' bit of my skill-set gaps? It . . . uh . . . applies to wrapping gifts."

Ilse made gifts look like the wrapping job itself was the present. People didn't want to undo them just because they were so pretty. Jocelyn, on the other hand, was lucky if it didn't look like a ball of trash and accidentally got thrown out.

At least her confession had led Ben to the work-arounds that might save her dignity and her secret.

As they got up to move into the sitting room where Lara was already waiting for the interview, Ben ducked his head to whisper in Jocelyn's ear. "Kyle stole my thumbs-up."

She angled her head to see his face, surprised at the humor glinting back at her. Was he trying to keep her relaxed?

Jocelyn played along. "I'll take all the thumbs-ups I can get."

With a grin, he flashed her one.

Catching sight of Theo standing at the end of the hall, Jocelyn teetered over to him on Ilse's sky-high candy-red heels. "Festive" was what Margot had called them. "Death trap" was closer. Theo had been watching her as if she was a bomb on a timer, like he was counting down to detonation and already braced for the explosion.

He'd seen all their rehearsals, which was probably why.

Accepting the bottle of water he held out, she took a grateful swig.

"It's going well," he murmured in a low voice, glancing over her shoulder at the rest of the crew.

"Just wait for the last bit."

"The wrapping?"

She grimaced. He grimaced back, then chuckled. "Maybe you can demonstrate your technique for fast unwrapping." He waggled his brows. "Perfect for the impatient children in your life."

In other words, her efforts tended to sort of fall right off the gift. "Ha. Ha. Ha."

"Ilse?" Ben's voice held a bit of a warning. They only had a few minutes for commercial breaks.

"Coming." She teetered her way to the love seat where she sat beside him and primly crossed her ankles, knees together, back straight. She angled her body toward Lara, who was seated in the wingback chair to their left.

Leaning closer, Ben raised a stack of papers he was holding to shield them from those watching.

"Tony's not listening right now."

She glanced in the direction of the sound guy, who monitored their mics, and sure enough his headphones were off, hanging around his neck.

Ben moved closer, the warmth of his breath brushing over her ear. "Just talk to her like you're talking to a friend. Okay?"

Jocelyn's skin prickled like a snowy wind blew up her skirt, and she clenched her teeth behind the smile she shot the other woman. She knew what that prickle was about, and it wasn't her nerves. That was about his voice in her ear and the memory of kissing Ben in this exact spot. His proximity to her right now didn't help, either. If she turned her head . . .

Ignore it. The kiss was a flibbertigibbet of a moment, brought on by an adorable rom-com and a cozy room at night. Flight of fancy. Romantic whim. Total accident.

Nothing more.

He was just trying to be helpful right now.

"Got it." There. Her voice sounded normal.

Ben's leg brushed hers as he adjusted where he was positioned in relation to her, Lara, and the camera. Pressing closer into her.

Don't move. Don't move a muscle.

She made herself focus on their nervous guest. Lara's leg was jiggling. Jocelyn knew the feeling. "Ready?"

Lara waved a hand, even while her eyes remained wide. "No problem. National TV is nothing compared to figuring out the perfect toy for a shy five-year-old who wants something specific but won't tell Santa what."

Jocelyn chuckled. "I bet."

Walter signaled it was almost time. Jocelyn faced the camera, smile pinned to her lips, Ben doing the same beside her, and waited for the cue. As they'd rehearsed, Ben talked first, getting the transition in, then passing it over to her to introduce Lara.

As expected, the interview went easily. Right up to the part where Jocelyn couldn't figure out a wooden 3D puzzle Lara had brought to share. The parts just didn't want to fit together.

Canting her head, she tried one way, then another, then another combination. Frowning, she pulled it all apart, spreading the pieces out on the table in front of her. Then, tongue caught between her teeth, tried again, starting from a different angle. Then again.

Forgetting about where she was and what she was supposed to be doing.

"Clearly my cohost is absorbed," she vaguely heard Ben say off to her left.

But the puzzle was still beckoning, and she was determined. Focused.

A masculine hand suddenly landed over hers, gently stopping her. "I didn't know you were so into puzzles, Ilse," Ben said in his best teasing cohost voice.

Jocelyn raised her gaze to laughing green eyes, then, at a subtle nod of his head off to the left, swung her gaze forward . . . directly at the red light of the camera. The live camera broadcasting her sudden hyperfocus to the world.

What a time for her ADD to kick in.

She gave an owlish blink. Then another.

Ben squeezed her hand. This time a warning. She was being too quiet. Too much dead air.

Giving a laugh that sounded way too bright and loud in her ears, Jocelyn flung up her hands, knocking Ben's away. "I really want to figure it out. I thought this thing was for seven and under."

Lara laughed. "That one has ten different ways to solve it. The harder puzzles only have one solution."

Oh. Behind the camera she caught the way various crew members were grinning. At her expense. Ilse would be less than thrilled. She wasn't a fan of being laughed at or thought of as anything other than perfect. Jocelyn placed the puzzle pieces on the coffee table. "I'll have to buy this one so I can keep trying." Then aimed a sheepish smile at the camera.

Which got her a thumbs-up from Walter behind the camera.

Lots of thumbs-ups today. Not a complete disaster.

From out of nowhere, a white streak of fluff ran into the

room and jumped right onto the table. Then Angel the professional acting cat proceeded to take one fluffy paw and whack the ever-loving life out of the wood block of the unfinished 3D puzzle. At least the part Jocelyn had managed to put together.

The thing went catapulting, and broke into pieces midair, all flying projectiles aimed at Jocelyn's face, in what felt like the slowest of slow motions and fast forward at the same time.

She barely started to lift her hands to shield herself before Ben launched himself between them, taking a direct hit to the back with a manly grunt before landing in her lap in a heap of limbs. Over his form, Jocelyn met the cat's gaze, and swore for a second the little beast smirked at her.

Shocked silence hit the room, and she glanced up to find everyone staring with jaws dropped. Then Walter gave a sign with his hands, telling her to roll with it.

And do what exactly?

While she was still trying to think of something, Ben suddenly scrambled off her lap and back into his seat, face adorably red.

The only thing she could come up with was to clasp her hands to her breast, damsel-style, and declare, "My hero!"

Ben's eyes went wide, then he burst into laughter. Rolling laughter that was genuine, truly amused, and made her heart flutter like it had sprouted an extra set of wings.

"All in a day's work." He gave an extra frilly bow with lots of hand swirling. Ben also used that as his cue, facing the camera as he came up from his bow. "Thanks again to Lara Wolfe of The Elf Shop here at Weber Haus for joining us. When we come back from this commercial break, we'll look at easy options for toy-wrapping stations to get all the goodies wrapped beautifully and labeled appropriately."

And that was when—if they hadn't already, thanks to two separate Angel attacks—the world would find out Jocelyn was a fraud.

Time to wrap a gift.

As soon as Walter said, "That's a commercial break," and the red light went off on the cameras, Kyle was across the space to kneel in front of Jocelyn. Like he thought he might whisk her off to emergency care, carrying her in his big strong arms.

"Are you okay?"

Which was what Ben was going to ask, but the intern beat him to it.

The bright eyes of concern coming from a youthful and admittedly handsome face were too much, though. The kid's crush was so visible, written into every smooth feature, he was going to scare off Jocelyn . . . or Ilse . . . if he kept that stuff up. Actually, with Ilse he didn't stand a chance. But with Jocelyn . . .

She laughed. The sound wasn't even forced. In fact, if anything, Kyle had managed to break some of her tension, her shoulders dropping a hair. "You should be asking Ben that. He took the hit."

Kyle didn't even glance in Ben's direction. "Are you sure nothing got by him?"

What? Like Kyle's shoulders were broader and could have done better? A vague recollection that Kyle had been a rugby player until recently suddenly popped into Ben's head. And now he was comparing himself to the kid.

What is wrong with me?

"I'm pretty sure something got by him." Theo appeared out of nowhere, standing behind Kyle with his legs set wide apart, arms crossed.

Ben had no doubt there was a double meaning to the man's words, he just had no intention of deciphering it.

"I'm fine," Jocelyn assured both Kyle and Theo. Then glanced at him. "We should move to the wrapping station." Which had been set up in the dining room. Already the rest of the crew were in position.

Theo reached over Kyle's head to hold out a hand, plucking her right out of her seat onto heels that she really shouldn't have let Margot talk her into.

"I'll help her over." Kyle popped up from his crouch, which broke Theo's hold on her but also made her lose her balance.

Ben, already on his feet, wrapped an arm around her waist and physically lifted her out from between the two men to place her on the ground at his side. "Come on, trouble magnet."

"Hey!"

He ignored her protest. Leaving his arm around her, he walked her briskly right out of the room. Under his breath, he muttered, "It's like you need a human shield today, and the universe picked me."

" 'Fasten your seat belts,' " Jocelyn said, just as quietly. " 'It's going to be a bumpy night.' "

"Movie quote?" he asked.

A nod. "*All About Eve* with Bette Davis."

She glanced over her shoulder, probably at the other two men. Ben had no idea if either, or both actually, had followed.

"Is Kyle acting . . . ?" She didn't finish her wondering.

He stopped them in front of the long, waist-height table all set up for the final segment of the show. "Yes."

That earned him a double take. "Wait. He's not that way with my sis—"

Ben pinched her hip, which made Jocelyn yelp, but she'd been about to say *my sister*, and Tony had his headphones on.

She stepped back, forcing Ben to drop his arm. "What was that for?"

"Are we ready?" Walter called out.

Jocelyn swung her gaze from Ben to the director to the camera, then down to the gift wrapping. "Oh Lord," she whispered. " 'You're gonna need a bigger boat.' "

He recognized that one from *Jaws.* Now she was quoting movies in rapid succession, which he could tell must be a stress reaction from her. For good reason, too, given this next segment. She'd shown him a sample of her wrapping last night. After the cat incident—the second cat incident—they really couldn't mess this part up.

"Let me do all the doing," he whispered. Even taping that flap they'd arranged just for her.

Her gaze flashed to his. "But—"

"And five, four, three." Walter mouthed the words "two" and "one" before pointing right at Ben.

They were live again. Ben launched into the transitional intro. As he finished, Jocelyn was supposed to pick up an already wrapped gift and simply fold and tape the final end shut.

But he'd meant what he'd said. She should let him do this part. So he reached out to take it from her. But Jocelyn offered him a teasing grin as she half turned her back on him and took a step away. As if she really wanted to do this herself.

"I'm pretty sure I wrap gifts better than you, Benjamin."

Benjamin. Only his grandmother had ever dared to call him that. Somehow, though, coming from Jocelyn, he sort of liked it.

He held out a hand. "What? You don't trust me? Why don't you give me a chance to prove myself?"

She laughed. "I've seen what you do to wrapping paper. It's worse than—" Her eyes flashed wide a brief second, and he knew she was going to say worse than her. "Worse than my sister," she corrected in time.

"For that, you should let me do the wrapping for the rest of the live shows." Ben grabbed at the gift.

Jocelyn hopped back, waving the partially wrapped gift in the air, and giggled when he missed.

He lunged again.

She hopped again.

Only this time a screech like the Ghost of Christmas Past come to wake the dead, split the air. Ben jerked his gaze down to find she'd stepped on Angel's tail. When had the animal come in here anyway?

The cat went haywire. Retribution in her blue eyes, she turned on Jocelyn, clawing her way up tights-clad legs. Jocelyn yelped. On her stilt-like shoes, she was no match for that cat, and in yet another slow-motion moment that was starting to become their signature move, she toppled over. Ben wasn't quick enough and she hit the back of her head on the hardwood floors with a resounding *thwack* that had to be heard halfway across the world, thanks to the cameras still recording.

Ben scooped up the cat, hissing in pain as it sunk teeth and claws into his arms. Thank goodness he was wearing a Christmas-colored sweater today—long sleeved and nice and thick. "Isaac?" he called for the cat wrangler.

He barely paid attention to the handover, sort of half shoving, half throwing the flailing cat at the man. Then he was on one knee at Jocelyn's side. "Are you okay?"

She blinked at him, slightly dazed, then held out a hand. "Help me up."

What? She wanted to keep going? She could have a concussion.

When he didn't move, she took his hand anyway. "We're still live," she whispered.

Right. Still live. And she'd just been attacked twice in ten minutes by Atilla the Cat, but she was pushing through.

As they got to their feet, Jocelyn turned a smile on the camera, letting go of his hand to rub the back of her head. "Angel and I clearly need to have a heart-to-heart chat," she announced. "I don't know what I did to her, but I will certainly apologize."

Then she held up the slightly smooshed gift she was still clutching. "But I managed to hold on to this!" She thrust it toward Ben. "I'm a bit cross-eyed though. Given the circumstances, your terrible wrapping skills are probably better than what I could come up with right now."

Ben took the gift and stared down at it, then back up at her.

He couldn't have handled that any better himself. What a pro.

I saw everything.

And okay . . . maybe I was responsible for Angel getting out the second time. Her handler saw me and thought I was her, then came after me, leaving the small canvas-sided crate she was in unattended. Apparently, she's figured out how to unzip it.

That devil cat has been sent straight from the fiery pits of hell to torment humans. I've witnessed it with my own eyes now. How could Angel attack Jocelyn—who is an absolute sweetheart? Three separate times? On live TV? What does she have against her anyway?

Jocelyn and Ben did amazing dealing with it. They must be finishing up the show now, because Ben is saying something about, "next time join us" and a "Christmas Movie Marathon Party."

Then the man behind the cameras, who I've figured out is in charge, shouts, "And we're out. Thank God."

Jocelyn teeters off the "set," which basically just means out of the dining room and down the hall. Ben watches her go. He even takes a step in her direction, but his cell phone rings.

She should *not* be alone after all that, so I follow her instead. It would be better for their romance if Ben comforted her, but I guess he can't. Besides, she clearly needs a nice kitty to cuddle with and take all those evil kitty memories away.

Chapter 13

Since they were on location, Jocelyn's dressing room was her bedroom in the house, and she knew for a fact Margot was there right now. She didn't want to face Margot. Which was why she ended up sitting in Sophie's office toward the back of the house, head in her hands. The hotel manager had kindly intercepted her in the hallway, taken one look at her face, and brought her back. Jocelyn didn't have to look up now to see Sophie's sympathetic expression while the other woman very kindly sat with her without saying a word. She could feel it just fine.

Which meant the incident was as bad as she was thinking.

Jocelyn's head was still a little fuzzy from that knock she took to it. How she'd managed to get through that last segment coherently was a miracle. Or maybe she hadn't been all that coherent. Ben had certainly cast her a few worried glances. She honestly couldn't remember much past the horror of the second Angel attack. Hopefully Ben had covered.

"I swear, that cat has it out for me," she muttered.

A small, strangled sound came from Sophie's direction, but all the other woman murmured was, "She really seems to."

Jocelyn lifted her head to find the blonde watching her with open curiosity. "You saw it, right? It's like she's deliberately targeting me. I mean . . . why didn't she go after Ben at least once?"

After a second, Sophie shrugged. "What I can't understand, though, is Angel is on the regular shows that are taped. During all those episodes, she seems to love you. You're the only one she'll let pet her."

Jocelyn blinked. "Do you watch *Home & Hearth*?"

Pink tinged Sophie's cheeks. "I didn't want to be one of those obnoxious fans and fuss over you, but I record every single episode and watch it at night. It's the way I like to wind down. Just happiness and charm for a solid hour."

"That's so nice!"

"Sometimes Emily and Lara join me."

Jocelyn wasn't sure if she should be more nervous now, in case she gave herself away to fans who knew better. But at the same time, it made her heart glow for Ilse. Her sister really had made a show people adored. "I love that."

They exchanged smiles.

"Did you change cat actors?" Sophie asked, still on the question of Angel's behavior.

Jocelyn gave a rueful shake of her head. "Given the way that cat behaves, I would think the entire cast and crew would love to get a new cat for the show, except maybe her handler. But no, same cat."

"Oh." Sophie seemed to deflate a little, as if learning that Angel wasn't the paragon of feline virtue portrayed on the show was a disappointing discovery.

With a warning *purrup* of sound, Snowball suddenly leapt into Jocelyn's lap. Where did the white fluff of a cat come from? The door was closed.

Almost as if she was soothing Jocelyn, Snowball gently pawed at her hands until Jocelyn dropped them to her sides. Then the little cat curled up in a ball on her lap and set to purring. Letting go of some of her tension with a long breath,

Jocelyn ran a hand over the cat's impossibly soft fur. She gave a little sigh.

At least not *all* cats hated the sight of her.

"Well, Snowball clearly doesn't have the same reaction to you." Sophie's voice wavered with laughter.

"No. I usually get along with animals."

"You must edit out all the stuff where Angel gets . . . feisty . . . on the show."

"Feisty" was a mild term for that cat's attitude. Or catitude. Jocelyn managed to keep that one to herself, though she did give a mental chuckle.

Wait.

Was that what they did on the show? Did they edit out Angel bothering Ilse? Her sister had never said anything about it, but Jocelyn slowly straightened in her seat. Then stopped herself. Because no, she was pretty sure this wasn't an Ilse problem. The one time she had asked Ilse about the cat, because it had seemed strange for her sister to even attempt to pet a creature that could get fur on her precious clothes, Ilse had said something along the lines of, "Angel is very well trained, and we understand each other."

That did not sound like a situation where they would have to edit out the cat's behavior.

Which means it's me. I'm the problem.

Or . . . Maybe the cat really did like Ilse and could tell the difference between twins? Animals used their senses in different ways than humans. Jocelyn lifted the collar of her blouse and sniffed.

Maybe I smell off to her?

Someone would have told her if she smelled bad. Right? Ben . . . or Theo now that he was here. Her bestie wouldn't hold back something like that. She relaxed a skosh. "I'll have to talk to Ben about using Angel only for the segments I'm not in while we're doing live shows."

And maybe otherwise keeping her locked in a cage in a

building miles and miles away, because Isaac clearly couldn't keep her locked up.

Sophie's answering smile was interrupted by a brisk knock at the door. Then it cracked open, and Ben popped his head around the corner. "There you are."

She shouldn't be all that surprised. He would want to talk about ways to avert more disasters in the next show. Jocelyn got to her feet. "Time to debrief?"

The twitch to his eyebrows told her Ben caught her use of the word. A term she'd heard Ilse use before. Not a ton of cause for it in Jocelyn's line of work, but it made sense given the circumstances.

Ben glanced at Sophie, but not before Jocelyn caught the way his expression slid into something rigid, grim maybe. "The bigwigs are going to give us a call in about . . ." He checked his watch. "In ten minutes. We're going to take it in the hotel conference room."

Jocelyn's feet rooted to the floor like pine trees in an ancient forest. "Full cast and crew on the call?"

Oh no. Oh no. Oh no.

They were going to call her out in front of everybody. Someone had sussed her out, knew who she was. Ilse was going get fired. Jocelyn would be humiliated. Maybe even Ben would lose his job.

"Just us," Ben said.

Well, at least she could cross out the personal humiliation piece. Mostly. "O-o-okay. Of course. Be right with you."

I'm toast.

She shot Sophie a smile that she knew barely cracked her face. "Thanks for letting me decompress in here for a second."

Sophie's "anytime" floated out the door behind Jocelyn and Ben as she followed him through to the kitchen and outside to walk to the hotel wing. Neither of them spoke all the way there. It wasn't until they were in the conference room with the doors safely closed that Jocelyn finally found the courage. "You didn't know."

Ben was already leaning over the disk of a speakerphone that sat in the middle of the long conference table, but his hand paused over it before he straightened to face her. "What are you talking about?"

"If they ask, tell them you didn't know. About the switch. You were fooled right up to the last minute. I mean you and Ilse aren't close. They'll believe you."

Ben's frown made her want to step back a pace. "I'm not going to lie," he said.

Stubborn man. "Please. For me?"

He took a single step closer, which was when she realized just how closely she had followed him into the room. She had to tip her head back to maintain eye contact, and his warmth reached her even through his sweater and the wool dress she was wearing.

"For you?" he asked, voice going softer. "How would my lying about this be for you?"

Jocelyn cleared her throat but didn't back down. This was important. "I'm about to get Ilse fired. Please don't add your career to the list of damage. You weren't supposed to know. Ever. My guilt would go through the roof."

Never mind the "naughty" list, she'd be on Santa's "banned-for-life" list.

Ben's gaze sharpened, sending silly thoughts through her. Thoughts that had no business in her mind, especially at a time like now. Even so, the air stilled in her lungs, or maybe she held her breath. But she didn't look away.

He made a sound in his throat. "I can't let you—"

"You can. I'm asking you this as a favor."

Ben's lips flattened. "Jocelyn—"

The phone on the table rang and they both jumped. After a long look at her, he leaned over and hit the button to answer it. "You have Ben and Ilse here."

"There are our stars!" a vaguely familiar voice boomed out of the speaker.

Ben and Jocelyn both stiffened, glancing at each other. Stars?

Luckily, they didn't have to say anything because Herbert kept talking. "I think your breakup must be a good thing for you, Ilse."

Ben's scowl at the machine on the table should have singed the man's ears on the other end, it was so fierce. "Want to explain that?" he demanded.

There was a small pause. "Don't take that the wrong way, Ben. When did you get sensitive?"

Before Ben could answer Jocelyn jumped in. "I'm the sensitive one."

Another small pause, then a sigh reached them down the device. "I'm just saying that you've been more relaxed. Looser on screen. It's good."

Jocelyn sank into one of the chairs around the table.

This was not what she'd expected. Didn't they think she was a mess? A total wreck?

"Viewer feedback so far, online especially, is that your little moments with Ben and with the cat and messing up things is more . . . relatable."

Relatable?

Oh dear. This was not good. Not in the long run. She glanced up at Ben, whose eyes were closed as he leaned his fists on the table. Clearly, he thought the same thing.

Jocelyn held in a sigh. Ilse was going to kill her.

"This is a good thing, you two," Herbert said when neither of them talked.

They glanced at each other, then Jocelyn shrugged.

"Is that all you wanted to tell us?" Ben asked.

"That's it. I wanted to tell you we're seeing an increase in online chatter and viewership. Keep it up." Herbert's voice hardened a little on that last bit. He meant it.

"Thanks for the feedback, Herbert," Ben said through visibly gritted teeth. "We'll keep that in mind." Then he hung up on their executive producer, mid-sentence.

"Ilse is going to kill me if she has to keep that up," Jocelyn murmured.

Ben sank into a seat beside her, leaning back. "That's her problem."

Jocelyn stared at him, but he just raised his eyebrows, daring her to deny it. "She brought this on herself, putting you in her place in such a public way. If she tanks her career, it's on her. Not on you."

"I know," Jocelyn agreed slowly. "Of course I know that. But she's my sister. I'd never want to hurt her."

After a long look that she couldn't quite interpret, Ben suddenly sat up, scooting closer to give her a soft, quick kiss on her cheek before straightening again. "You're good people, Jocelyn Becker," he said. Then he stood and walked out of the room, leaving her there alone.

Jocelyn raised a slightly stunned hand to touch the spot he'd kissed, her skin still tingling from the contact. Ben Meyer thought she was good people.

Honestly, with the way he'd helped her so much already, never getting angry at her even though his career was on the line too, she felt the same about him.

Admit it. You have a thing for Ben.

She took probably her hundredth deep breath of the day. Because she couldn't deny it. Ben was . . . Well, he was magnetic. At least to her. But also a kind man. And funny and fun. The way he'd teased her about the wrapping, even if it was for the camera . . . that had felt real. Genuine.

But having a thing for Ben was beyond complicated.

She forced her shoulders back. No more interest in him. No more kisses. He was just helping her out and then she'd probably never see him again after this was all over.

Which was exactly the way it had to be.

*   *   *

Ben sat alone in some random bar located in the downtown strip of shops in Braunfels, the little town close to Weber Haus. The first bar he'd spotted after borrowing a car from Sophie was where he'd ended up. He'd practically sprinted out of the conference room, because after kissing Jocelyn on the cheek, he'd wanted to pull her into his lap and kiss her even more.

The woman wanted to take all the blame and save *his* career by letting him lie about his own involvement. He'd almost kissed her in that moment too. Hence the hightailing it out of there before he did something regrettable.

This was already too complicated as it was. Kissing her was a bad, bad, bad idea. Terrible.

Vaguely he was aware of someone taking the stool next to him.

"This is the only open place serving alcohol in town at this hour," Theo's voice sounded beside him. "And this is the last empty seat at the bar, or I wouldn't be here."

Ben turned his head to find Jocelyn's friend waving down the bartender with a raised finger. "What are you doing here?"

Theo didn't even look over. "I just told you."

"No. You told me why you're sitting next to me in the same bar, not why you're here, in Braunfels, in the first place."

Theo heaved a sigh. "I need a drink after that epic disaster today."

Looked like he wasn't going to answer the question. Ben snorted a laugh. "Me too." He took a sip of the whiskey he'd been nursing since he'd got here.

"What the hell is with that cat?"

"Damned if I know." Ben took another swig. "The thing actually likes Ilse, but Jocelyn . . ." He glanced around him. Maybe a public place full of people wasn't the place to be discussing this.

The door swung open on a burst of cold wind and a laughing, raucous group came in. A group Ben immediately recognized—a good chunk of their crew. Today just wasn't his day. As soon as he came through the door, Kyle spotted Ben and raised a hand in greeting. Then he leaned over and spoke to the others, who all turned and waved before moving to a large table another group was just vacating on the other side of the room.

Kyle, however, made a beeline for him, getting there just as the woman on the stool on Ben's other side got up and left. Kyle slid right onto it. "Hey, boss."

Theo and Ben glanced at each other. The kid just had eager puppy energy written all over him.

Kyle leaned across Ben, shoving his hand at Theo so fast, Ben had to jerk backwards. "I saw you on set earlier but didn't get to say hi. I'm Kyle."

The reluctance with which Theo shook that hand was completely lost on the younger man. He didn't give his name either, which didn't seem to bother Kyle in the slightest. "You're Ilse's friend, right?"

"We live together," Theo said.

"That again?" Ben said, earning a hard glance from the man to his right.

Meanwhile, Kyle's face fell. He almost felt bad for the guy. Almost. "I thought she just broke up with her boyfriend."

"He's not her boyfriend," Ben assured the kid with a sudden urge to grin at the way Theo's eyes narrowed. He took a swig of his beer, settling back.

"That's great!" Kyle bounced back fast. Oh, to be that young again.

Not that Ben was old. Thirty wasn't old. Prime of his life. Right?

Except Kyle, who was in his early twenties at most, somehow felt ages younger. Maybe Jocelyn liked younger guys. Maybe she was into puppy energy.

"I was hoping to get your advice." Kyle directed the question at Ben, then looked at Theo. "But it sounds like you know her well too, so I'd appreciate it if you could help. I mean, us men have to stick together, right?"

"No," Theo said.

"Not really," Ben muttered.

Kyle didn't appear to have heard them. "I think I messed up with Ilse."

They both raised their eyebrows, and Ben immediately relaxed his face, not wanting to be lumped in with Theo. He took another swig of his whiskey.

Neither of them asked Kyle what he did. He glanced between them. "I told her I liked her."

Ben froze with the glass halfway to his mouth. Theo, however, after a long pause, leaned a casual elbow on the bar. "When was this?"

Why did Theo suddenly sound genuinely interested?

Kyle grimaced. "About a week before we came here."

Ben exchanged a glance with Theo. So that was the real Ilse the kid confessed to. Did Jocelyn know?

"Did she slap some sense into you?" Theo wondered almost idly.

Kyle lost the puppy dog, scowling like a rottweiler. "Ilse would *never* do that."

"Clearly you don't know Ilse," Theo muttered under his breath.

Ben was inclined to agree. Not that she'd ever got physically violent with him. But a verbal smackdown wasn't beyond her.

Kyle wasn't done. "The thing is . . . now that she doesn't have a boyfriend, maybe she'd be more open to me. That's why I could use your advice."

Ben sighed. "I think this is something you'll—"

Theo caught his eye, giving him an oddly conspiratorial

shake of the head. Then he turned to Kyle. "You know . . . that breakup left her feeling pretty down on herself. Maybe she could use a guy like you."

What was he doing?

Theo continued. "What Ilse really loves are very big, very public displays of affection. She eats up those social media videos."

That didn't sound like Jocelyn at all. Ilse either, really, though the public part might be up her alley if it was super classy and cost a lot.

"The ones that go viral?" Kyle moved to the edge of his seat. "Any ideas?"

"What about one of those dances?" Theo suggested.

Ben caught on to what Theo was doing. "Or something like one of those promposals."

"Promposal," Kyle whispered to himself, lighting up. He wasn't saying no. Poor sucker.

"Balloons. Flowers. A handmade sign," Theo ticked off on one hand.

Ben nodded along. "With one of those great puns as part of the question on the sign."

"A pun." Kyle looked around like he wanted to write all this down.

"Confetti cannon?" Theo offered next.

Ben had to hold in a snort, managing to nod instead. "Oh, that's good."

"The sign could say, 'I flip for you.' " Kyle jumped in, apparently still on the pun thing.

"Flip?" Ben asked.

Kyle nodded. "I was a gymnast until high school when I gave it up for rugby. I can do a standing backflip. Watch."

Right there, in the middle of the crowded bar, the kid stood up, back to the hallway that led to the bathrooms. Then, like he was just taking a casual hop, proceeded to do a backflip. A gasp ran through the place. Kyle gave the crowd a boyish, lopsided grin, which was when it occurred to Ben that the guy was movie star good-looking. Then he flipped again, and the crowd went wild, applauding, and several girls came over to lead him away to another table and fawn all over him.

Ben and Theo stared after the kid.

"Maybe we should rethink encouraging the public social media promposal thing," Ben said, though more to himself. Apparently, girls liked that kind of display of physical prowess. "At least until Jocelyn and Ilse switch back."

"Jocelyn does get excited about weird stuff," Theo mused.

They both looked at Kyle again.

Ben reached into his back pocket, pulled out some bills and tossed them on the bar. "Feel free to talk him down. I have the next show to prepare for."

Then he bolted from the place, pulling out his cell phone as he made his way to his borrowed ride.

He shot off a text to Jocelyn. **Next show is Christmas Movie Marathon. Want to talk through some ideas?**

The house is so quiet tonight.

Usually there are more guests, especially at this time of year. But with only Ben and Jocelyn, and now Theo, staying in the house with me, it feels emptier. And even more so right this second, because all the humans left to go do human things.

I lie at the kitchen door, chin on my paws, waiting for any of them to come back home. Emily and Lukas are already asleep upstairs. I could probably go up to them, but it's warmer in here at night after all the cooking anyway. I also want to make sure Jocelyn is okay.

At a tiny scuff of a noise, my ears flick. But I dismiss it. This old house is always making noises. Especially at night.

Except, a few minutes later, I hear it again. And it's not the house.

Or I don't think so.

Curiosity is a cat's bane, and I never ignore my own. So I'm heading up the back stairs before I decide I even want to. As I hit the second floor, I catch that glimpse of white fluff in the darkened hallway.

Angel.

Demon cat is loose again.

Sprinting to catch up, I get to the main set of stairs to find her only halfway down. I must make a sound because she glances up, and there's a flash of something shiny in her mouth. Her blue eyes widen, and then she takes off running.

She's fast.

When I get to the bottom of the stairs she's already long gone. Again.

But what did she have in her mouth?

Chapter 14

After an entire day of going over scripts and practicing for their next live show, Jocelyn's brain was pure fuzz. She hardly talked at dinner, although that didn't keep her from noticing the way Kyle was staring at her from across the table. The intern, as nice as he was, had been a bit of a nuisance all day. In a nice way, of course—bringing her water, fluffing the pillow at her back, making sure the room was an acceptable temperature—but also uncomfortable.

Ben eventually took her to a room where they could lock the door.

Speaking of nuisances, what was with Ben and Theo? They seemed to be engaged in some sort of contest. Even at dinner. Making subtle digs at each other all evening. With Ben on one side of her and Theo on the other, she'd felt like the epitome of the rock and hard place idiom. So she'd gone to her room as soon as she'd finished eating, with plans to go to bed early.

Except she was bored.

Lying on her bed, she stared up at the wood ceiling with its beautiful white crown molding. People didn't make houses the way they used to. But it was only seven, and she'd lain here for an hour.

Jocelyn blew out a breath.

She could watch a movie, but after talking about them and watching clips nonstop to get ready for the next show, for once she wasn't in the mood. She could take a long bath and relax. But she always seemed to find the idea of a bubble bath more appealing than the actual act. Usually she got bored and came out feeling lethargic and even sweaty.

So . . .

She sat up. The stores behind the house didn't close tonight until ten. Maybe a little brisk winter air and holiday shopping would do the trick.

By herself. No one watching her every move and expression. Even better.

In less than ten minutes she was bundled up in Ilse's designer jeans, a lovely deep-purple sweater, and leather boots, all covered by the thick jacket Theo had brought her to use. Shabby by comparison, but who cared. She added a hat that probably wouldn't do much to keep her warm but was better than nothing, and made her way to the shops.

She decided to start at the far end and make her way back.

The store at the corner was called Trendz. A boutique, it carried the most adorable home goods, furniture, décor, clothing, and more. She was just picking up a leather handbag that she thought might make a good gift for Ilse when someone brushed against her. Absorbed in checking out the details of the lime-green bag decorated with silver studs, she murmured, "Excuse me," and stepped to the side.

Except the person stepped closer, and then a low voice said near her ear, "That's cute but I don't think it's your style."

On a gasp she jerked her gaze up to find Ben standing beside her, green eyes mildly amused.

A line from the movie *Casablanca* popped into her head and she mentally adjusted it for the setting. *Of all the Christmas shops in all the towns in all the world, he has to walk into mine.*

All day long she'd managed to keep everything professional. No thinking about his amazing jawline, or the way he was so patient with her, or the feel of his arm when he brushed against her, or the sound of his laugh and wanting to hear it more often. She'd focused on getting ready for the episode.

Mostly.

Come to think of it, remembering all those details about him right now meant she'd noticed at the time, despite her best efforts not to.

Out loud, though, she said, "What are you doing here?"

"Shopping."

Not what she expected him to be doing.

She thrust the bag between them. "It's for Ilse. What do you think?"

After a pause, he lowered his gaze to study it. "I don't really know Ilse well enough to guess."

But something in his voice told her he was holding back. "What aren't you saying?"

His lips twisted. "Well . . ."

"You can say it."

He considered her. "You're not allowed to get mad."

"I make no promises. My temper just"—she flung out a hand—"flies on its own."

An answering grin tugged at his lips. "Yeah. You're like Godzilla that way. Total rampage."

Jocelyn nodded, eyes wide like she was very serious. "It's a serious problem."

"Hmmm . . . Well, this"—he took the bag from her hands—"isn't expensive enough for your sister."

He ducked, covering his head with hands dramatically.

When she didn't turn into Godzilla, he peeked out from around his hands. "Is it safe?"

Jocelyn sighed with extra flair. "There's too much truth in that statement for me to go on a rampage."

Chuckling, Ben straightened, putting the bag back on the

display. Then glanced around. "Why don't you shop for you instead?"

Jocelyn gasped like a Victorian maiden, hand to her neck clutching nonexistent pearls. "It's December, sir. What are you thinking?"

Raised eyebrows asked the question for him.

Really? He didn't know? She dropped her hand to explain patiently. "The rule is no shopping for yourself all of December, so that your friends and family can surprise you with gifts and not worry that you already have it."

"Uh-huh. So you do a lot of shopping for you, the other eleven months?"

Jocelyn wrinkled her nose, wondering if she should be honest. Then shrugged. "Not really."

"That's what I thought." He grabbed her by the hand and led her over to a display in the back corner. "I thought of you when I saw this section."

Jocelyn tugged to a halt before they got all the way there, which pulled him up short. Ben looked over his shoulder at her, but she was busy staring. He'd found an entire display dedicated to classic movies. And not movies from the 1980s and 1990s, but the *true* classics, old-school Hollywood from the '30s, '40s, '50s, and '60s.

It was a wonderland.

"Oh wow," she breathed, and was vaguely aware of the way Ben grinned at her response. But she was too busy hurrying over to look at the collection. "How am I going to decide?"

There was a framed movie poster of *It's a Wonderful Life.*

"I like this," Ben said. He picked up a mug that looked both like yellow police tape and a production clapboard that read, "Caution: I may start talking about movies at any time."

She side-eyed him. "I do not."

Ben leaned forward slowly, gaze never leaving hers, and

she was tempted to lean back. But she didn't want him to see the way his nearness or how he was looking at her was affecting her.

What's he doing? Is he going to kiss me? Right here in this store under bright lights and surrounded by shoppers and Christmas music?

He even glanced down at her lips, and she held her breath.

In a low voice, for her ears only, her murmured, "Tell me that when I showed up next to you just now, you didn't think in your head, " 'Of all the gin joints in all the world . . .' "

Jocelyn felt both seen and called out, glancing away from smiling eyes. She debated lying, but there wouldn't be any point. "I may have changed the wording to fit the situation."

Ben's chuckle sent a warm glow through her. "I knew it." Smug. He straightened, and she breathed a little easier. "It's kind of adorable, actually."

Adorable. There went her breathing again. The word spread through her with warmth like butter melting over toast.

He's Ilse's cohost.

"Are you flirting with me, Ben?" The words just popped out.

Ben straightened abruptly, then opened his mouth like he was going to . . . What? Deny it? She was going to be so embarrassed if he said he wasn't flirting. That she'd got it all wrong.

"I don't know if you are or aren't," she rushed to say. "I'm terrible at reading those signals. But if you are . . . we shouldn't." He said nothing, probably because he couldn't get a word in edgewise. The words were pouring out faster and faster now. "I mean Ilse's my sister. And you don't like her. And she doesn't like you. And I could get you fired. And—"

"Oh wow. That's Ilse Becker and Ben Meyer!" A shrill, very excited voice penetrated the low hums of Christmas music and shoppers in the store.

*   *   *

"See, honey!" The overexcited fan was gushing to the poor man being dragged along in her wake through the crowded shop. "I told you this was where they were filming *Home & Hearth*. Weber Haus. Just like they said on TV."

Ben was already starting to get used to being recognized after months on the show now, though it didn't happen a ton. But it happened. Immediately he pinned his most charming TV personality smile to his face as he waited for the fan to reach them, the other shoppers starting to murmur amongst themselves.

Except then he looked down at Jocelyn, who had visibly paled, total reindeer-in-headlights as she stared at their fan like a train wreck coming straight for her.

Why? She was friendly with everyone. He would have thought greeting fans would be the easy part of pretending to be her sister.

He grabbed her hand to tug her closer, leaning over to whisper, "Follow my lead. I'll try to get us out quickly."

Seeming to pull herself out of her stupor, Jocelyn pinned her own very stiff smile to her lips and nodded. But she was hating every second.

He shouldn't have taken her hand though. The fan took one look at it and announced in a voice that carried, "I just knew there was something going on between the two of you. Those looks that passed between you these last few shows . . . I could just die."

He should nip that in the bud before someone filmed it or posted about it and rumors flew. Ilse was trying to get her boyfriend back. If she did, and then returned to the show with a boyfriend in tow . . . Ben really didn't feel like looking as if he'd been thrown over for Baron Cheater Von Trap.

Which meant denying any connection with Jocelyn while she was Ilse. He really should, but the words didn't want to come out.

"We're just friends." Jocelyn suddenly dropped his hand, stepping away from him, but making it look natural as she approached the fan.

The woman glanced over Jocelyn's shoulder at Ben, speculation rife. She opened her mouth, but Ben beat her to it. "Thanks so much for watching *Home & Hearth*."

That was enough to have her gushing. "Oh, I don't miss a show, and the live shows have just been adorable. Have you thought about doing more of them after the holidays? Maybe for other holidays?" She gasped. "How cute would shows for Carnival, or Easter, or Mother's Day, or even Oktoberfest be?"

"That would be fun," Jocelyn agreed in a faint voice. Probably picturing still doing this for Ilse during those holidays.

Which meant now Ben was too. With Jocelyn more live shows would be fun. Ben suspected with Ilse it would be a nightmare. Meanwhile the lady smirked because a well-known TV star had praised her idea, so he left it alone.

"Can I get a picture?" she asked.

Ben ran his gaze over Jocelyn and hid a wince. Not that she wasn't cute, swamped by the oversized jacket with her hair peeping out from under her hat and minimal makeup, but Ilse wouldn't be caught dead in public looking like that. The way she put her hand up to her hair, then winced, lowering it slowly, he knew she was thinking the same thing.

But no getting out of it without upsetting a fan who seemed like the type to blow it up on the internet.

"Sure," Ben said.

The woman handed her phone to her husband, who Ben guessed didn't get to be in the picture, then stood between Jocelyn and Ben as they all smiled. One picture led to more with other folks who were in the store, and it took a solid half hour before he could get Jocelyn out of there.

They had to keep up the charade of smiling famous people as they walked back past the shops. They were just passing the last one when the same woman's voice sounded over the crowd. "If you watch *Home & Hearth*, the stars of the show are here in the shops and taking pictures with anyone who asks!"

Oh, good grief.

Ben grabbed Jocelyn's hand and ran, scooting them around the corner of the building that housed the shops and into the darkened area between it and the main house. He didn't stop there though, running along that side, their boots kicking up snow with a shooshing sound. He didn't stop until they rounded the next turn, putting them on the back side of the shops, barely lit by the glow coming from the hotel wing, though they were hidden from that building by a copse of pine trees.

Breathing hard, they peeked around the corner to see if anyone had followed or seen where they went.

But they were in the clear.

Breathing a little hard, Ben turned to find Jocelyn still bent over and watching, the side of her face to him, and he knew, in that moment, that he wanted to know her better. Ilse and his job and their situation be damned. She was . . . special.

"Yes," he found himself saying. "I was flirting with you."

Jocelyn sort of froze, then slowly turned her head, wide-eyed gaze connecting with his. "What?"

He leaned closer, hand going behind her head to prop against the wall. The way her lips parted on a silent gasp about sent him spinning. "I *want* to flirt with you. I want to get to know you. And . . ."

"And?" she squeaked.

He smiled, and no doubt it was wolfish based on the way she swallowed hard. "And I want to kiss you again."

She stared, then licked her lips. "We shouldn't."

"I know."

He lowered his head. Slowly. Giving her enough time to stop him, to pull away. But she didn't, and he softly brushed his lips across hers before pulling back to be sure she wanted this too.

Jocelyn gave one slow blink, then surged forward, wrapping her hands in his jacket lapels and going up on tiptoe to press her lips to his in a kiss that was *everything*. The only thing it wasn't was hesitant.

Ben smiled against her. They could figure out what came next later. For now, he had every intention of enjoying this part.

I couldn't have missed the man standing at the window, shoulders slightly hunched as he looked outside, even if I tried. Not that I would have. This human clearly needs comfort. His body language is screaming sadness.

What is he looking at anyway?

Trying not to sneak up on him, I pad over and hop up onto the windowsill with no effort. He still jumps a little, then gives me a very odd look.

"Are you the bad cat or the good cat?" Then he snorts, though to himself I can tell. "Or as Jocelyn would say, 'Are you a good witch or a bad witch?' "

Huh? What is this about me being a witch—good, bad, or otherwise?

As if reading the question in my eyes, Theo—I think that's the name of Jocelyn's friend—smiles and pats my back. "It's a quote from *The Wizard of Oz*."

Oh, a movie. I get it.

"I'm tempted to be a bad witch," he murmurs, then looks outside again.

So I look outside too . . . and almost fall off the windowsill ledge.

Jocelyn is out there in the shadowy area behind the barn that is now the shops. She's there with Ben and they are kissing.

Not just a cute little peck or a friendly brush of the lips. They are *really* kissing.

I glance from them to Theo's face and my kitty heart cracks a little. I've never seen a man look so . . .

It's way worse than if Santa gave him coal for Christmas. It's like all his holidays this year got canceled.

"Meow."

I butt at his hand with my head. He glances down and I carefully drop to the floor then wend around his legs, brushing against him.

Theo sighs and scoops me up against his chest, rubbing his cheek against my fur. "Thanks for trying to cheer me up, but I'm afraid the damage is already done."

Poor human. Some just can't avoid broken hearts.

For the second time since meeting him, I wonder if I'm matching the right couple.

Chapter 15

"Everything is going fine, Ilse." Jocelyn kept her voice low. She'd been outside when her sister had called and had tucked herself around the side of the shops. The same place where she'd kissed Ben.

She'd *kissed* Ben.

And it was . . . spectacular. That elusive thing all those holiday rom-coms were made of. Her heart raced again just thinking of it.

All while her sister was on the other end telling Jocelyn that she wasn't coming home quite yet. Ilse, who would not be happy about anything happening on this end of things, with her career *or* her costar.

"Well, that's a relief." Ilse sighed down the line. "They haven't posted the streaming versions yet, so I haven't been able to see the shows."

Streaming?

Which meant Ilse would be able to see the shows before she got back. Shows that were nothing like the versions she had worked on.

Oh help.

"Did you hear me?" Ilse demanded.

"Um . . . sorry. They're calling me. Gotta go, Ilse. Love you." Jocelyn hung up before she put her foot in her mouth and confessed everything. Including the kiss. Ilse was half-way across the world and could do nothing about it. No need to add to her stress.

"I know it's really rude to eavesdrop—" A soft voice sounded from behind her.

Jocelyn swung around to find Sophie, Lara, and Emily, who was pushing her baby in a pram, all standing there with varying expressions of incredulity.

"—But did you say *Ilse* just now to the person you were speaking with?" Sophie glanced at the other two women, then back to Jocelyn. "Aren't *you* Ilse? Do you know another one?"

Oh . . . dear.

The thing was, she really hated lying. On a big sigh, Jocelyn said, "I'm Ilse's twin sister, Jocelyn."

"Jimminy Christmas," one of them, Lara maybe, murmured.

Jocelyn grimaced. "My thoughts exactly. It's been . . . complicated."

"I can imagine." Lara's eyes were as wide as saucers.

But at the way all three of them suddenly broke into wide grins, Jocelyn relaxed a little. "You're not mad?"

"Mad? Why would you worry if *we're* mad?" Sophie asked.

"Well . . . you're all fans of the show. Right?" Sophie had told her about that.

"Fans who are in on the biggest secret in the show's history?" Emily laughed, giving the pram a little jiggle. "You just made our holiday season *way* brighter. Or more interesting at least."

The other two nodded along eagerly.

Jocelyn bit her lip. Actually, she could use someone to vent to a little. Normally that would be Theo, but he was being weird, probably because Ilse was involved. And Ben was . . . well . . . He was great for the show-related stuff, but she definitely couldn't talk to him about the kissing because he was directly involved in that situation.

"Could I treat you all to some coffee or a snack or something? I'll tell you about it and you can give me advice."

All three straightened like they were her toy soldiers and she'd given them marching orders. Then they put their heads together while Jocelyn looked on. "Lukas can watch the baby and I can cover the treats," Emily said. "Any requests?"

"The petit fours," Lara immediately answered.

Right. Because Emily owned and worked in the bakery in the shops. "Umm . . . the chocolate croissants?" Jocelyn added hopefully, and got a thumbs-up from Emily.

"Meet at my place?" Sophie asked.

Sophie had a place? Jocelyn just assumed she lived at Weber Haus, though come to think of it, she wasn't upstairs often. How far away was it?

"Definitely. Perfect for the privacy," Lara said.

Privacy sounded promising.

Lara continued, "I'll help Emily and we'll meet you both there."

Before Jocelyn could voice a single question or offer to help, she was scooped up in Sophie's wake, skirting around the main house and off to the west toward a smaller house tucked into the edge of the tree line, closer to the road.

"I wondered about this little house," she commented, as Sophie unlocked the front door and let them in.

Sophie smiled. "It was the groundskeeper's cottage when the house was original. Now we've renovated it and it's the hotel manager's"—she hooked a thumb at herself—"cottage."

It was basically a smaller version of Weber Haus. One story though, but with similar Victorian details in the wood floors, the crown molding, white siding with black shutters on the outside, and decorated similarly with the green garlands and red and gold bows. "It's adorable."

"Thanks! Daniel and I love it."

"Your husband, right?" Jocelyn had heard his name but not met the man yet.

Sophie nodded. "His company constructed the hotel wing and did all the renovations to convert the barn and carriage house into the shops they are now."

"I see." She smiled. "It must be nice to have close friends as couples who are also your married friends."

The few friends she'd had who'd gotten married had just sort of disappeared from her life, especially after having kids. Not that she blamed them at all. They were in a different place, a different stage. Jocelyn understood. But it made it lonely for her.

"It is." Sophie unwrapped the scarf from around her neck. "Make yourself at home."

By the time they were settled on the comfy sofas in the living area, Emily and Lara arrived with the goodies. In short order, they were all stocked up on hot chocolate and sweet treats, sitting around on the sofas. That's when three sets of eyes turned her way.

"We're ready when you are." Lara gave her an encouraging smile.

Jocelyn paused, then let it all out. *All* of it, right up until the moment Ben kissed her a second time and then Ilse's phone call they'd just overheard.

"So that's everything. And I . . . I just . . ." She bit her lip. Because her heart was pulled in a thousand directions. "What do I do now?"

The three women glanced at each other. "Well . . . do you like Ben?"

Like him? Yes. Want to get to know him better? Yes. Kiss him again? Definitely yes.

Jocelyn nodded.

The three exchanged another indecipherable glance.

"It seems to me your sister put you both in this position,"

Emily said slowly. "Do what you can for her but take care of *you* first and foremost." She glanced at the others. "Don't you think?"

"Definitely." Lara and Sophie chimed in unison.

"*Meow.*" A white cat jumped up onto Jocelyn's lap.

"Snowball!" Sophie exclaimed. "Where did you come from?"

"She must've come in with us," Emily said. "We were carrying lots of things."

"I guess so."

"I don't mind." Jocelyn cuddled the kitty, who set to purring. Then picked her up so that they could go nose to nose. "What do you think, Snowball? Should I give this thing with Ben a chance?"

If he was interested in that too. Maybe he wasn't. Maybe these kisses were something else for him. A blip. An escape. A holiday fling. Who knew?

Before Snowball could answer, Sophie piped up with, "What about Theo?"

That's right. Sophie had had to check him in and get him set up with his room, so the hotel manager knew exactly who he was.

"Oh, Theo is an old friend of mine and Ilse's. He's also my roommate at home."

Sophie moved to the edge of her seat. "And so it's a one-sided love there?"

Jocelyn frowned. "What? No. We're just friends."

Lara pursed her lips. "Are you sure? I thought I caught a vibe from him."

"When did you see him?"

"He was behind the camera, tucked into a back corner, the day you interviewed me." She winked. "That man is hard to miss."

Jocelyn's heart dropped to the soles of her feet, which was a journey given the way she was seated. The thing was . . .

she was fairly certain she wasn't the one Theo was interested in. Not really.

There'd been small clues over the years. He'd been so angered by what he thought of as Ilse leaving him behind when she got rich and famous. But angry in a hurt way. And just look at this situation alone. The man watched *Home & Hearth*, for heaven's sake. And he'd turned red when Jocelyn pressed him on it. That and a thousand other small signs all added up. Didn't they?

"You want him to just be a friend?" Emily asked in a soft voice.

She glanced up to find three sets of sympathetic expressions turned her way.

"*Meow.*" Snowball butted her hand so she'd keep petting.

Jocelyn cleared her throat. "I've never thought of Theo as anything else."

"I think we've all been there in one form or another," Emily said in a dry as dust voice.

Sophie chuckled. "My husband, Daniel, actually had a crush on Emily before he met me. He'd grown up with her and is best friends with her brother, Peter."

Peter was Lara's husband. That much Jocelyn was aware of.

Emily, meanwhile, shrugged like *whatchya gonna do?*

Jocelyn's eyebrows crept upward. "But . . . clearly it all worked out."

All three smiles aimed her way were content. "Lukas and I were meant to be together, and so were Daniel and Sophie," Emily assured her.

So there was hope that whatever Theo was going through wouldn't ruin her longest and closest friendship. Or her roommate situation. That was something at least. "How do I . . ." She paused. "I mean, should I bring it up with Theo?"

"That might embarrass him if he's trying to work it out on his own," Sophie mused around a mouthful of cupcake.

Good point.

Emily snagged a cupcake of her own. "Let him bring it up. If he does, let him down gently."

Gently. Right. Okay. Not that she was convinced she was his crush anyway. Still, she'd been handling Ilse since the womb, and her sister often required the kid-glove treatment. She could do gently.

Just so long as she didn't lose Theo. That would break her heart.

The knock at Ben's door was not expected. Which was why he was in pajama pants and nothing else. He cracked the door open to find Jocelyn standing in the hallway with Theo in tow.

Theo looked less than thrilled.

"Are you ready?" she asked.

He glanced between them. "Um . . ."

"For stringing the popcorn. We were going to do that tonight. Remember?"

He remembered popcorn stringing being a thing for their next party. To go along with the movie theme. But that was supposed to be the night before, and the crew who did all the set decorations were supposed to cover it. "Um . . ."

"Theo said he could help us."

Theo was going to string popcorn? A second glance at the other man revealed an unimpressed expression.

"Feel free to bow out," Theo said. He might as well have dared Ben. "I can help J with this."

J? He called her J? He had a nickname for her. The message couldn't be any clearer. Theo had a long-standing relationship with Jocelyn and Ben did not. But had Jocelyn ever kissed her friend the way she had Ben?

He'd bet this next live show the answer was no. That kiss had been too real. Too . . . perfect.

He returned his gaze to Jocelyn, who shuffled her feet. "I should have texted you a reminder. Sorry."

"No problem," he found himself saying. "I was just changing clothes. Get started and I'll be down in a few minutes."

Immediately Jocelyn perked up, even as behind her Theo did a slow frown.

And Ben closed the door.

Before he'd even made it downstairs the smell of popcorn filled the house, nutty and buttery. He went to the kitchen to find Jocelyn seated at the small table with a skein of thick, red yarn, a needle, and a bowl of already popped corn. Theo was at the microwave, making another batch, which popped cheerfully away with rapid crackles.

As Ben watched, Jocelyn licked the end of the yarn, then, tongue sticking out and one eye scrunched adorably shut, she threaded the needle. "Got it!" she crowed in victory, waving it in the air.

"I told you that you could," Theo said without turning away from the microwave.

"Do we have more than one needle?" Ben asked.

Theo stiffened but didn't turn or speak. Jocelyn, meanwhile, patted the chair beside hers. "Right here."

Then she sort of froze, her cheeks turning red. Something was definitely going on. Trying not to act weird himself, Ben pulled out the wood chair and sat. Jeez, she smelled good. Vanilla mixed well with popcorn.

"Here." She put another needle and already cut string of yarn in front of him. "Do you need any help threading it?"

"I'll figure it out."

"Okay." Then she picked up hers and speared a piece of popcorn, sliding it down to the end of the yarn with a scratching sound.

They worked in silence for a bit. The microwave dinged. Theo poured another bowl, and then took the seat across from them and started stringing.

Silence.

"*Meow.*" Snowball hopped up onto the table between them

and snagged a piece of popcorn from one of the bowls, chewing happily away before they could stop her.

"No, no," Jocelyn scolded, scooping the little cat up and setting her gently on the floor.

Silence again as they worked.

"How much do we need to make?" Theo broke the quiet.

"*Meow.*" Snowball jumped up again and snagged another piece. Ben put her down this time.

"I think three strings this length should be enough to decorate one tree. Don't you?" Jocelyn debated. This had been her idea for a decoration. "It's only going on the one tree."

"Sounds about right," Ben said. Then popped a piece in his mouth only to get his hand smacked.

"No eating," Jocelyn instructed in what he could only deem a schoolmarm voice. "We only have so many bags."

He gave the bowl a forlorn look, stomach suddenly feeling empty despite having eaten dinner not that long ago, then caught the way Jocelyn quickly glanced away from him, hiding a smile.

"What?"

"Nothing."

"What?" He elbowed her.

"Just . . . popcorn is clearly a weakness for you."

She'd figured that out from his looking at the bowl? "Guilty."

They grinned at each other, but the hole of silence on the other side of the table finally made itself felt, so they stopped and went back to work.

"*Meow.*" Snowball was up on the table again.

Ben scooped her. "No," he said firmly, and tapped the end of her nose.

She butted his hand, and he could have sworn gave Jocelyn and Theo a pointed look. Almost like she was warning him about something.

Which was silly. She was a cat.

Snowball needn't have worried anyway. He'd caught the odd vibe between them already.

"So . . ." Theo said after a minute. "You kissed my girl."

Ben froze mid-spear of his popcorn. Jocelyn did not. She missed her popcorn entirely, hitting her thumb, then yelped, hissed, and shook her hand before sticking her thumb in her mouth. "Ouch," she grumbled around it.

Theo looked at her. "Are you going to live?"

Seemed a bit harsh. Except Jocelyn choked on a laugh while she was still sucking on her thumb. "I'm tougher than you are, mister."

A small smile might have cracked Theo's face before he went back to serious. "In your dreams, J."

She rolled her eyes, then pulled her thumb out of her mouth to give her friend a glare that reminded Ben of Snowball two seconds ago. "It's your fault. You can't just drop that like a bomb and expect us all to walk away unscathed."

Theo leaned back, crossing his arms. "What was I supposed to do?"

"I don't know." Jocelyn threw a hand out in frustration. "Lead into it."

The man stared at her, then cleared his throat. "So the other night I happened to glance outside and see two people behind the shops with their tongues down each other's throats. And they looked just like you two."

"I think he was right," Ben said conversationally, because there seemed to be no other way to approach it. "The first way was better."

Theo ignored him, clearly not interested in the help.

Jocelyn, however, was glaring at Theo now. "First of all, our tongues were not down each other's throats."

"Well . . . not *all* the way down, I guess," Ben muttered.

Jocelyn swung her glare in his direction, and he shrugged.

"And second . . ." She swung back to Theo. All the frustration left her face, gentling along with her voice as she said quietly, "It's none of your business who I kiss."

Ouch. In a moment when Ben should probably be triumphant, he actually felt for the guy. After all, Theo was just trying to look out for someone he loved.

"It will be my business," Theo argued, "when you spend six months crying on my shoulder after this doesn't work out."

Fair point. But who said it wouldn't work out?

A small voice in Ben's head immediately started listing the reasons: *Ilse. The studio. My career. The truth about her and her sister. Pick one.*

"When have I ever cried more than a day or two over a breakup?" Jocelyn scoffed.

Not where Ben would have gone with the argument, because Theo was clearly asking where this relationship was headed. The problem was, neither of them could say. They'd barely done more than acknowledge that they shouldn't pursue this thing between them, but they were going to anyway.

"It felt like months to me," Theo grumbled. Then pinned Ben with a hard gaze. "If you hurt her . . ."

He had no intention of defending himself this early on. "It wouldn't be on purpose."

Theo was not impressed. "Ilse will kill you with her bare hands when she finds out. Probably smile over your body as she shovels the dirt on top of it, too."

He wasn't wrong.

Jocelyn set her needle and yarn down with a *tink* of sound. "She is not *that* bad."

Theo huffed a laugh as he pushed back from the table. "You never have seen her clearly, J."

"Neither have you," Jocelyn pointed out.

Theo stilled but didn't say anything.

There was history there that Ben wasn't about to touch.

Jocelyn took a deep breath. "I think you've been a little bit in love with her since we were eighteen," she said quietly. Gently. "But I'm not her."

"I *know* that, J."

"Do you?"

Suddenly, Snowball ran between Theo and Jocelyn with a *"meow"* that sounded suspiciously like, *Stop fighting, you guys.*

Theo seemed to take that as his cue. "I do. And I'm doing something about it." He moved to the shadowed corner by the back door, where he hefted a stuffed backpack, which Ben hadn't noticed before, to one shoulder.

Jocelyn also pushed to her feet. "Wait. Where are you going?"

"The Philippines."

"What?!" She was around the table and standing in front of her friend, staring at him with mouth agape before Ben could even stand up.

"Yeah," Theo said. "To talk some sense into your sister." He grimaced. "Or argue it into her. Hopefully."

Jocelyn shook her head, then shook it again before walking right into Theo and wrapping her arms around his waist, her head buried in his chest. "Don't be too harsh with her. She's heartbroken."

"Her heart's got nothing to do with it. Her pride's broken." He kissed the top of her head, then looked across her to Ben and raised his eyebrows.

"I'll take care of her," Ben promised. And meant it. Even if whatever this was between them didn't work out, Jocelyn deserved to be looked after, protected.

After a second, Theo nodded. Once.

Then he squeezed Jocelyn hard before setting her back from him, and opened the door to head outside. On the small set of steps outside, he paused and looked back at Ben. "Good luck with Kyle."

Then he was gone, the door closing quietly behind him.

Jocelyn stared at it with a worried little frown. Then finally seemed to pull herself from her thoughts and glanced his way. "What about Kyle?"

I'm staring at the closed door that Theo left through. Theo, who I thought was heartbroken over Jocelyn, but there's a tone in his voice when he talks about Ilse. Is Jocelyn right, and Theo's heart is with the sister? Or is he grabbing on to the excuse she provided so she doesn't worry about him?

Either way, he left. He left so Ben could step in. Any fool can see that's true.

Wow. I did not see that coming.

Chapter 16

Margot tweaked the last curl into place around Jocelyn's face. "There," she said. "Perfect. Even if I do say so myself."

Jocelyn turned her head back and forth, admiring the other woman's work. "I don't know how you do it."

Because Margot was standing behind her in the mirror, Jocelyn caught the funny look that passed over her features. "You taught me everything I know."

Right. Because Ilse, in addition to singing and crafting and baking, also knew fashion and makeup and hair. Something she had been into ever since Jocelyn could remember. In high school, Ilse had been horrified by Jocelyn's own utter lack of interest, especially the things she would wear; or worse, the fact that she would go to school with absolutely no makeup on. Ilse could no doubt put Jocelyn's current look together even better than Margot had.

Backtracking wouldn't salvage the comment. Jocelyn decided to lean into it. "I think you've surpassed even me."

Nope. That didn't work. She only got another funny look. *Maybe you should shut up.*

The line from *Saving Private Ryan* popped into her head and Jocelyn buttoned her lips closed, then stood up, brushing nonexistent wrinkles out of the silvery material. The outfit looked more like pajamas than anything. She had to admit, they were very golden-age-of-Hollywood-esque with the long flowing pants and sleeves, made sexier by cutouts at the waist that nipped in. And the sparkling material definitely screamed silver screen. Margot had even styled her hair à la Marilyn Monroe.

Perfect for a movie-watching themed party.

"Now for the finishing touches." Margot hefted a box that reminded Jocelyn of a massive fishing tackle holder onto the bed, removed a hefty-looking padlock, and flipped it open. In short order Jocelyn was dripping in rubies. At her neck, ears, wrists. "To go with the ruby slippers," Margot pointed out proudly. "Plus, it stands out against the silver."

It was a little much, but she liked the reference.

Ilse's assistant moved over to the small bedside table. "Umm . . . Ilse . . . where did you put the ring?"

Jocelyn was still debating the rubies situation, angling her body this way and that in the mirror. The bracelet Margo put on her was that heavy. And the necklace felt like a collar. This must be how cats and dogs felt when their owners tied things around their necks. It even tinkled a little like a bell when she moved. Tony, the sound guy, was going to love that.

"Ilse?" Margot's voice had tightened. "The ring?"

Ring? Oh right. The diamond. "It's on the bedside table."

"It's not here."

Jocelyn dropped her hand to her side and slowly turned to look for herself. Sure enough, no massive rock glinted at her from the lace doily that covered the antique wood of the table. She frowned. "Maybe the cat knocked it off?"

Snowball was always in here.

She and Margot look at each other a beat before instantly dropping to their hands and knees, searching frantically under the bed and everywhere else on the floor. But it wasn't there either. It wasn't anywhere in the room.

Ilse was going to lose it if Jocelyn lost her precious ring.

"It's got to be here," Jocelyn muttered, lifting a pillow on the armchair that was tucked into the corner of the room.

Margot meanwhile was anxiously riffling through drawers and pulling apart the already previously made bed. Anxiety filled the room until Jocelyn was practically suffocating on it as they ran around like elves who had lost Santa's favorite toy hammer.

"Okay, think." Margot's words jerked them both to a halt. "When is the last time you remember seeing it or wearing it?"

Jocelyn racked her brain. "I don't know," she wailed.

Margot goggled. "What do you mean, you don't know? You were once able to tell me the exact block and storefront in New York City where you thought you'd heard the *tink* of a small emerald falling off your dress, and it turned out you were right. You don't remember where you put a ten-carat diamond ring that never leaves your finger?"

Ten carats. Jocelyn's lungs tightened like they'd been put in a vacuum with all the air sucked out.

Ten. Carats.

Ilse had never told her that. Ten? And probably flawless and all the other things jewelers said made a good diamond. What on earth had her sister paid for that thing?

Margot was still waiting for her answer.

"Um . . . I've been really stressed."

Plus, she didn't like wearing it. It was heavy and she knocked her hand into so many things every single day. In fact, she may have left it on the bedside table for the last few days on purpose. The last time she remembered actually wearing it was the last day of filming.

"The cleaning staff must have taken it." The way Margot's face pinched suddenly made her look ugly.

It took everything in Jocelyn not to snap. "You do not know that, and there is no evidence to suggest it."

"Except the missing diamond ring that you're sure you put

on your bedside table and left there for anyone to pick up. Who else would have been in here other than me?"

And Ben, but he wouldn't take it either.

Jocelyn held up both hands like she was warding off an evil spell. "We are not accusing anyone. I'm going to go talk to Sophie. Maybe it fell off my hand while I was walking." Which meant it could be anywhere on the grounds, including in the shops. If someone had returned a ten-carat diamond ring to lost and found, she was pretty sure word would have spread. She was trying very, very hard not to panic.

"You were just complaining a few months ago about how it was a little too tight." Margot was still arguing.

"It's colder here," Jocelyn pointed out as calmly as she could. Why was Margot so hung up on blaming some poor maid who came in once every few days to straighten things up?

She picked up her phone.

In short order, Sophie was up in the room listening with enviable professional calm as Jocelyn and Margot got her up to speed with the situation. Of course, she assured them both that no one would have come into the room and taken it, including their cleaning service. Margot shared a picture of the ring that she had taken for insurance purposes. That same picture was sent to Sophie's phone and then out to all of the staff, not only in the inn and hotel, but the shops too.

Ten minutes later, the Weber house and grounds probably looked like an ant hill that had been kicked over, with everyone scrambling around to look for the darn ring. Jocelyn herself was on her hands and knees in Sophie's office, looking under the chair where she'd sat after the last episode when she'd come in here. She hadn't been in the room since, and she was pretty sure she remembered putting the ring on her bedside table after that, that night even. But it was worth a look.

The door opened with a bang. Then closed with another bang. Startled, Jocelyn tried to jerk up to sitting, but smacked her head on the bottom of the chair's armrest that stuck out. "Ouch." She rubbed at the spot as she more carefully sat up to find Ben glaring at her, hands on his hips. Not happy.

"We are filming today, Jocelyn."

He said it in that dangerously quiet way he did when he was truly angry. If he'd ever talked to Ilse this way, no wonder her sister's back had gone up like a cat arching in a fight. She did not need this right now.

"I'm aware of that, Benjamin," she replied in a voice that she tried to make as coldly soft as his. It wasn't nearly as intimidating, darn it.

"You lost that massive, expensive, ugly as sin thing Ilse wears?"

Despite the fact that she was still on her knees, Jocelyn mimicked his body language, putting her hands on her hips and glaring at him. "Maybe."

"Doesn't she have some kind of safe to put it in?"

"According to Margot, she never takes it off her finger."

"So why did you?"

"Have you ever tried to sleep with a diamond ring the size of a meteorite digging into your cheek? It's not exactly soft and comfy." She glanced away, more guilt sinking through her at making the entire household search for this thing. "And it's really heavy," she grumbled.

She honestly didn't know how her sister wore the thing. It was constantly falling to one side or the other, catching on materials, knocking into things. She'd already had to confess to Sophie about leaving a one-inch scratch in the wood of her door from when she'd tried to turn the knob with the ring on. "I already feel bad enough without you piling on."

Although if Theo were here, he would be laying into her even harder. The man had serious issues with taking care of anything that was worth a lot of money. And a lot, in his mind, was anything over about fifty bucks. Came from growing up with nothing.

The stuffing went out of Ben, and he held up both hands. "Okay. I guess it could happen to anyone . . ."

She heaved a sigh of relief.

"Or at least anyone named Jocelyn Becker."

She shot him a glare. "Oh, ha ha. Let's just concentrate on finding it."

He glanced at his watch. "If we don't find it in the next fifteen minutes, we'll have to leave Margot and the staff to it, very quietly, because we have to film."

A stealth piece of popcorn smacked Ben in the middle of the forehead before dropping into his lap.

He deserved it.

After all, he'd started it. In the middle of filming a live show, no less.

But mostly because Jocelyn had been visibly worrying about the stupid ring while they were filming, and he'd been trying to knock her out of it.

Rather than pick one movie to screen parts of for their Holiday Movie Watching party, they'd decided to do a clip from twenty different films, giving people ideas of what could be popular for different age ranges, party themes, and so forth, as well as what had a lot of party potential in terms of aspects like food and decorations and music.

During the first clip they'd shown, from the new modern classic *Elf*, he'd launched a popcorn missile at Jocelyn and scored a hit.

Juvenile? Yes.

Probably a poor decision? Not a doubt.

Worth it just for the sound of her surprised gasp followed by an expression Snowball would make when she was irritated? Absolutely.

The popcorn had been flying ever since, and they were getting close to the end of the show. They were showing another clip now, which he could see rolling on the nearby monitor.

That meant the folks at home weren't seeing his and Jocelyn's faces.

"You two better get that off your clothes and out of the shot in the next ten seconds," Walter warned from his hiding spot behind the camera. "Thank goodness we went with kettle corn, or you'd both be butter-stained messes."

Ben and Jocelyn both sat up straighter in their Christmas-themed director's chairs that the crew had provided for them to sit in today. Nice touch.

Ben brushed at his lap. So did Jocelyn.

The last lines of the clip from *A Charlie Brown Christmas* played. Walter pointed. And Ben smiled directly into the camera. "Any kid who grew up before streaming watched that special on TV every holiday season. Me included. In fact, I always try to find the saddest tree on the lot when I shop for Christmas trees. What about you, Ilse?"

"Me too, definitely. And . . ." He didn't look over immediately at the pause. "Only . . ."

Was she fumbling her spot in the script?

He turned his head to find her looking directly at him, lower lip caught between her teeth and eyes twinkling.

Twinkling. Not panicking.

"Only what? You can't tell me it doesn't fit in your giant living room. You could probably give a home to all the pathetic-looking trees on the lot."

Jocelyn rolled her eyes. "Only I hope everyone at home will forgive me but . . ." She actually got to her feet, which Walter was going to hate, given the way the cameras were positioned. "My cohost just couldn't help sneaking some of the kettle corn during that last clip." She leaned over him, the scent of her shampoo suddenly elusively around him, and plucked a massive piece of popcorn out of the collar of his button-down shirt. Something that no doubt had been perfectly visible to the viewers at home.

Ben swallowed a groan. He could see the memes coming.

Better to lean into it then. So he peeped around Jocelyn to address the camera. "I'll have you know that I wasn't *sneaking* popcorn. Ilse was *throwing* it at me."

And now the entire viewing public would think he'd been flirting with Ilse Becker. He had not thought that through very well.

"Just for that . . ." Jocelyn stuck the popcorn right back where she found it in the collar of his shirt. Then returned to her seat, now facing the camera. "I would also like to state, for the record, that he started it."

She switched on a smile that was becoming more and more professional looking, and more like Ilse's with each show. "And to answer your earlier question properly, Benjamin, I have proof that I like to pick the smallest, saddest, least likely to be bought tree on the lot. See?"

Walter gave a thumbs-up and, on the monitor, they could see that viewers would be getting images from Ilse's own house. Ben had gone there for a holiday party earlier in the year. He'd been brand-new to the show. That was the last time he'd gone to her house. Now, on the screen, it didn't look remotely the same. No doubt some poor intern had been tasked with the colossal feat of taking down the obnoxious plethora of modern décor that littered Ilse's home, and putting up simpler, cheerier, more traditional items that would match the Charlie Brown special and the poor, pathetic Christmas tree they'd found who knew where.

The thing even tipped over on the top under the weight of the star, just like in the cartoon.

Right in time with the shot returning to them on set, Ben gave Jocelyn a suspicious look. "Did they photoshop that in? Come on, be honest. That's not *really* your house."

She wrinkled her nose at him. "Really my house. Really not photoshopped." Technically that was true . . . ish . . . given that this was Jocelyn and not really Ilse. "And for doubting me . . ."

He saw, too late, that she'd snuck her hand down to the bowl on the table at her side. A handful of popcorn smacked him in the face like bugs hitting the windshield of a moving vehicle. Shock had Ben staring at Jocelyn for a long beat, possibly even longer than he would've, because her hands immediately flew up to cover her mouth, her eyes widening behind them like she'd surprised even herself.

"Don't think there won't be retribution, young lady," he warned.

Slowly she lowered her hands to reveal twitching lips that would just not contain her smile. Jocelyn opened her mouth like she was going to say something, but couldn't get it out around a breathy chuckle. An adorable chuckle that he should not find sexy . . . but did. On live TV. What was he thinking?

She had to try three times before she finally said, "There's popcorn in your hair."

Then, with all the casual confidence of someone who had been doing this for years, not just three shows, she faced the camera with a blinding smile. "After this commercial break, we'll be looking at the movie *A Christmas Story*. I hope you'll stick around to join us."

It wasn't actually time to break for a commercial, but Walter had no choice after that, and immediately the monitor switched to show a placeholder while local stations aired the commercials.

Jocelyn was out of her seat and by Ben's side in a rush, plucking the popcorn out of his hair. "Sweet baby in a manger, I did not mean for that to happen. I don't know what came over me."

"Makeup," Walter called out.

What Ben really wanted to do was laugh. Like happiness was welling within him, coming out in a release of sound. The entire segment had been ridiculous, and childish, and his heart hadn't felt this warm or content in a long time.

What he wanted to do was kiss her.

Again.

"I think we'd better separate you two." Margot appeared out of nowhere, grabbed Jocelyn by the wrist and tugged her away to make sure that there were no illicit pieces of food lingering on her. Meanwhile Ben's makeup artist, a local woman who'd been hired just for these shows, did the same.

Something about Margot's expression snapped him back into exactly where they were and exactly who he was with. Jocelyn. *Not* Ilse, like everyone around him thought. And his career ambitions rested on these shows going well, let alone staving off the disaster that was Twin-Gate.

Clearing his throat, he sat up straighter in his chair. No more popcorn throwing. No more going off script. Definitely no more flirting on screen.

Not that he was giving her up. He'd just keep the flirting private. For now.

In short order they were both back in their chairs, the set cleared, and ready to face the next segment. Ben kicked it off, as usual, and Jocelyn followed his lead in a more seriously appropriate way. Had she come to the same realization?

Except now they felt stiff together.

All that natural chemistry was buried under fear, if he was honest. And subterfuge. There was that too.

Just get this done.

They stuck to the script exactly, with no more mishaps, right up to the last few minutes of the segment. Probably because Ben had relaxed a bit again, and so had Jocelyn.

She was mid-rave about how funny she'd thought the movie was as a kid, when a very loud screech tumbled down the stairs from somewhere on the upper floors of the house. "I found it! I found the ring!"

He and Jocelyn looked at each other.

Ilse's ring?

Should they address it? There was no way the mics hadn't picked that up.

Walter made a rolling motion with his finger, a signal to just keep going with what they had been discussing, and Jocelyn said, "You know what I learned about this movie when I was researching it once? 'The Old Man' was originally written with Jack Nicholson in mind. He was even interested—"

Ben reached across the space between their chairs, hand on her arm. Their filming bat-signal.

He caught the second she realized her mistake, because she jumped a little under his hand.

"I should explain that my sister helped me get ready for this show," she rushed to fill in. She turned to Ben. "Did I ever tell you she's a film historian?"

Nice save.

"Anyway," she continued. "Jack Nicholson was apparently too expensive for the budget, but I can't picture it with anyone but Darren McGavin."

From there they showed a snippet of the movie and then went into the food and music selections to go with it, which included Chinese takeout, sugar cookies that were cut and iced to look like glasses with one eye of cracked glass, fudge with a tag that quoted the movie, and Ovaltine chocolate martinis.

"And if you can find a gem like this online"—Jocelyn did a terrific model-hand-wave at an actual leg lamp—"it will top off your décor beautifully. I'd like to thank Kyle, our crew member who hunted this one down for us."

Ben glanced in Kyle's direction at his spot on the stairs just in time to see the kid's head pop up like a gopher out of a hole, then grin while his ears turned bright vermillion. Kyle really did have it bad, and now he'd only have it worse.

Maybe I should warn Jocelyn about that particular crush. Except he'd probably come off sounding jealous.

They wrapped up the show, signed off, the light on the camera went out, and everyone in the entire house felt like they took a big breath of relief and let it out slowly.

"Well . . . that was an adventure," Walter commented loudly.

Margot hurried up to Jocelyn, proffering the gaudy diamond ring before her like a herald bearing gifts for the queen.

"Thank heavens." Jocelyn snatched it from her assistant's fingers, putting in on her own and staring at it like she'd never take it off again.

"Where'd you find it?" she asked.

"Snowball's bed in Miss Tilly's room."

That brought Jocelyn's head up as she blinked at the location. "What? How did it get there?"

"The owner's son or nephew or whatever—"

"Lukas Weber?" Jocelyn clarified.

Margot shrugged. "He said that sneaky cat is a bit like a magpie; she likes to take and hoard shiny things."

After a pause Jocelyn gave a short laugh. "Well, I'm just glad it wasn't any of the alternatives considered."

She was looking at the ring again, so she missed the way Margot's lips flattened, her ears, like Kyle's minutes before, turning red. Only this looked more like anger than embarrassment. Which got Ben to wondering who Margot had thought the culprit might be.

Kyle stuck his head in the room. "We're all eating the goodies now, and the Ovaltine martinis are going fast."

Was he even old enough to drink them?

"I saved you one, Ms. Becker," Kyle added.

And Jocelyn, clearly oblivious to the kid's adoration, smiled and followed him out of the room. Though she did glance surreptitiously back at Ben.

He waved her on. Better to not make any of their previous flirting worse by staying in any kind of close proximity. Except Kyle put his hand at the small of Jocelyn's back when they went through the dining room.

On second thought . . . too much distance was being ridiculous.

Ben followed.

I sit at the top of the stairs, tucked into shadows so no one notices, and watch as all the humans enjoy their food.

Me. They blamed . . . *me*.

How did Angel know to put that ring in my bed? Come to think of it, how did she know I like shiny things in the first place? And worse, how did she get into Miss Tilly's room at all?

I picture the devil cat destroying things in that room, and it puts a pit in my stomach. Not only did she get me in trouble, but was that a warning? Was she threatening my humans?

Someone needs to show the humans that that cat can't be trusted.

The question is, how am I going to do that?

Chapter 17

Jocelyn was escaping in a corner of Emily's bakery, nursing a now cold cup of hot chocolate. Just one day to not think about the show before they started the intense prepping for the next one. Was that too much to ask?

Plus, Ben was being weird.

Like he'd changed personalities back to the uber-professional TV producer mid-show the other day and hadn't switched back. So . . . yeah. She needed an escape for a hot second. She glanced at the window at swirling snowflakes dropping in picturesque perfection. Make that a cold second.

At least no one had recognized her as Ilse. It helped that she was sitting with her back to the room and a thick hat hid her hair. She was even wearing her very real glasses, although she'd always thought anyone who couldn't recognize someone with and without glasses was silly. But she wanted to give her eyes a break from the contact lenses too.

A hand suddenly landed on the table in front of her, the other on the back of her chair, and Ben leaned over to murmur in her ear. "We have a problem."

Was it a bad sign that, even a week ago, that would have sent her heart rate skyrocketing and nerves dancing a jig in her stomach? But right now, her response was a heavy sigh. "What now?"

He pulled out the chair catty-corner to hers and scooted it around the leg of the table to sit close so they could keep the discussion between them. "The execs want to see Ilse cook on the next episode."

Cook?

Now the heart rate and nerves took off, and she glanced around. "But I can't cook."

"I know. But Ilse usually does, and viewers have been commenting."

Great.

"How bad is it?" he asked.

"I burn toast." That might have come out as a very hushed wail.

Despite the seriousness in his eyes, Ben's mouth twitched. "Ilse doesn't do everything on air, it would take too much time. Maybe a specific step?"

"It had better be simple." Jocelyn frowned, thinking. "Remind me, what foods are we doing for the next show?"

"The Ice-Skating Party?" Ben rubbed a hand over his jaw. "We tried to keep it to stuff you can eat while wearing gloves. So chili in bowls . . ." He looked at her. "Can you brown meat?"

"I could maybe do that. Is it enough? Doesn't Ilse usually bake?"

"You're right. She does." Then he rolled his eyes. "We're doing sugar cookies decorated like ice-skates and snow-flakes."

"Definitely too complicated unless you just show me cutting out the pieces. Even then, I tend to mess up the dough. Stretch it out and stuff."

"Okay. Something easier that's baking and can be held in gloved hands . . ."

Pure instinct had Jocelyn glancing around again, to make sure they weren't being overheard. Her gaze lighted on Emily, who was behind the glassed-in counter, slipping a tray of freshly made stollen into the display.

"Emily," she murmured.

"Huh? Is that some kind of cookie?"

She shook her head, then nodded over his shoulder, so Ben turned to look too. "Emily Weber. She can come up with something and show me how to do it."

"Why would she do that?"

"Because she knows who I really am, and I think she's the type who would be happy to help . . ."

She trailed off as Ben swung a slowly incredulous—turning into thunderous—frown her way. "She knows? How—"

Oh geez. Might as well get it all out there. "Um . . . she and Sophie and Lara all know."

Ben's jaw worked for a full twenty seconds. "I am trying to hold on to angry words very hard right now."

"I can see that."

"Did they guess?"

"They overheard me talking to Ilse."

"You were somewhere not soundproof doing that?"

If he wasn't careful, he was going to blow a blood vessel at this rate. A very concerning one was pulsing at his temple. "I pick up when she calls because if I don't, I might not get her back on the phone."

He ran a weary hand over his face, taking a deep breath. "Right. It's done. Anyone else know, that I should be aware of?"

She shook her head.

He nodded, then glanced back toward Emily. "Worth a try, I guess."

This was a terrible idea. Emily had agreed, quite happily, to help Jocelyn practice baking. In fact, she'd been the one to suggest doing soft pretzels, which went well with the parameters for the party theme. She claimed she could show Jocelyn several easy steps and they'd practice together until Jocelyn got it down.

But—and this was the disaster part—she'd insisted Jocelyn should do all her learning and practice in the kitchen where she'd be taping the show. That way she wouldn't be thrown off by any differences in tools or space that might crop up.

Which made sense from a logical standpoint, but from a logistical, not-letting-anyone-else-witness-the-practice standpoint . . . disaster waiting to happen.

Especially since there were four different access points into the kitchen—the back door, the back stairs, the door into the hallway, and the door into the dining room. They'd decided to wait for evening at least, after the crew had been fed and left the house. If anyone did come in, the plan was for Emily to duck.

That was the best they'd come up with. Now here they were.

"Are you sure about this?" Ben asked for the umpteenth time.

Emily and Jocelyn shared a glance and both shrugged. They were probably as sure as he was, which was not at all. "Why don't we just tell people that Ilse and I got to talking all things baking, and she is showing me a technique I was interested in."

Jocelyn sighed. "Because my sister doesn't share recipe tips with anyone except her audience. She's notorious for it after someone stole one of her recipes before an airing. It's a whole thing."

Emily bit her lip. "I knew that, actually." With a sigh she thumped a large bowl covered in cheesecloth on the counter. "We'd better get started, then."

As would happen on the show because of timing issues, the dough itself was already finished and had time to rise. Emily dug right in explaining the basics of making the dough and even insisting on walking Jocelyn through a new batch just so she could talk about it with ease. All of which went fine. Only two small scares, but Sophie, their plausible lookout in her office, the window of which faced the walkway from the hotel wing, gave them plenty of warning, and neither person had come into the house anyway.

Next, Emily showed Jocelyn how to section out the dough, followed by stretching it into the shape of a pretzel. Not as fine. Jocelyn's pieces kept breaking in the middle or were too thick or stuck to her fingers.

They hadn't even got to the actual twisting yet.

Ben's fingers itched to step in and help her with it. Not that he could bake, but he was pretty sure he could do that much better.

"I can see what you're thinking, Benjamin," Jocelyn said without lifting her head. "I dare you to try it."

He knew danger when he heard it. He stayed where he was, standing between the back door and the stairs.

"Can I help you with something?" Sophie's suddenly raised voice sounded from the foyer.

What was she doing in the foyer? No one should be coming in through the front door.

She was still talking. "I was told to keep people out of the kitchen—"

The door from the hall swung open abruptly. On a stifled gasp, Emily dropped to her stomach on the floor, blocked from the intruder's view by the large butcher-block island in the center of the room.

Margot.

She stopped at the sight of Ben and Jocelyn, then paused as she got a better look at Jocelyn, her gaze doing a once-over at least three times. Ben took a closer look at Jocelyn himself, then realized why.

She'd only been sectioning and pulling dough, but the woman was already covered in flour, including a cliched streak across one cheek. Which was kind of adorable, but not when she was supposed to be Ilse. Her sister was notoriously fussy and clean in the kitchen. A perfectionist in every way.

Jocelyn's cocked head was just the right touch of impatient that Ilse would give, because she didn't like others in her kitchen. "Do you need me for something?" she asked.

Margot hesitated only a fraction. "I was going to run through wardrobe options for the next show."

With an impatient little nod, Jocelyn said, "I'm busy now, but tomorrow we can."

"Okay," Margot said slowly. But didn't leave.

Jocelyn went back to the pretzels. "I'll see you at dinner. Thanks, Margot."

Ilse wouldn't have included the thanks, but he suspected Jocelyn couldn't help herself.

After a sidelong glance in Ben's direction, clearly wondering why he was allowed to stay, Margot left. They all held their breath for a long moment until Sophie stuck her head in. "All clear. Sorry I couldn't give you more warning. I heard the bell and ran out there as fast as I could."

"It was fine," Ben assured her.

Jocelyn made a face.

Emily groaned as she pushed to her feet, brushing off her hands and then going to the sink to wash them. "Remind me to have the cleaning crew mop in here daily. The floor is filthy."

"We'd better clean you up too." Ben also moved to the sink to wet a cloth, then beckoned Jocelyn over.

Just in case someone else came in.

He wiped away flour on her hands all the way up to her elbows. "Face," he requested. She lifted her head, tilting toward him like a flower to sunlight, gaze on him as he wiped her clean.

He swallowed, because up close, she was . . . beautiful. Clean, clear skin. Stubborn chin. Sculpted brows that Margot had no doubt taken tweezers to recently. But his favorite part might be the smattering of freckles. Ilse was missing those.

"All right?" she asked when he dropped the cloth to his side.

Not all right. He wanted to kiss her something terrible. Only he couldn't. Not here and now. But what really wasn't all right was they were in the middle of stuff for the show. Where had the business side of him, the smart side, gone?

Instead of kissing her, he flicked the tip of her nose. "You'll do."

The door from the hall suddenly opened, banging into Sophie, who was still standing there. Immediately Ben shoved Jocelyn out the door to the dining room, then braced for the sound of a crash because he'd accidentally pushed harder than he meant to and his last sight of her was pinwheeling arms.

No crash came, thankfully.

Kyle, meanwhile, managed to force his way past Sophie, looking around eagerly. "Is Ilse here?"

"No." Ben pointed at the back door. "I think she's at the shops."

Zero guilt followed the kid out into the night. Then Ben carefully pushed the dining room door open to find Jocelyn sitting half in, half out of a dining room chair, one hand clamped over her mouth no doubt to hold in a screech.

"You okay?"

She nodded, eyes wide over her fingers. Then slowly lowered her hands. "Maybe a little bruised, but I'll live. Where did he come from?"

"Who knows." He held out a hand to help her up.

After a quick break to check that no one else was in the house, everyone returned to their stations. Emily was still trying to show Jocelyn different dough-twisting techniques. Only the stuff kept getting tangled or the end result was a mangled, indistinguishable blob.

Jocelyn held a new attempt up like a drooping mustache, and said in a nasally voice, " 'I intend to live forever . . . or die trying.' "

Emily wrinkled her nose. "Huh?"

"Groucho Marx," Ben offered.

"Exactly." Jocelyn beamed at him through the dough that was slowly sinking between her fingers.

A movement outside caught his attention. Ben jumped in front of the back door, blocking the small window in it with his shoulders. "He's back."

"Who's back?" Jocelyn asked.

"Kyle."

A knock rattled the door, but Ben refused to move. "We're working on something," he called out.

"I just need—"

"Come back later."

It was pretty impressive the way even Kyle's footsteps sounded disappointed.

Ben sighed. "This is not working. Too many interruptions."

"I've almost got it," Jocelyn said. "Another five minutes. I refuse to let Ilse down."

As if the cosmos heard her, Walter walked in from the hall with zero warning from Sophie. Why did they all keep coming in through the front door? Was there a faster way around that way?

Immediately Emily faced Jocelyn, saying, "I'm sorry, but I need this space to start getting breakfast prepped for tomorrow."

Jocelyn, right on cue, scowled. "Can't you do scrambled eggs or something? Our group won't mind, and I've got to get this right."

Walter looked around at the disasters that were the pretzel blobs, then looked at Ben, who shrugged. Then he looked at Jocelyn. "What's this about?"

She crossed her arms, getting streaks of flour on the pushed-up sleeves. "I want to make handmade soft pretzels for the Ice-Skating Party, but I've never made them before."

Walter frowned. "You usually don't bake with anyone watching."

Jocelyn clicked her tongue. "Exactly." Her voice was tight between her teeth. "That's why I waited for everyone to be gone, but people keep coming in and out of here."

She really was impressive at imitating her sister when she wanted to be.

Walter puffed up a little. "Let's clear them out then."

"Like I want to be here for this. I was going upstairs anyway," Ben said. He headed that way while a protesting Emily was sent out the back door to her own bakery. Listening from halfway up the stairs, Ben could tell when Walter left "Ilse" to it. He waited a few minutes then popped his head into the kitchen. "Now what?"

But Jocelyn was already on the phone. "I think we're going to have to video chat," she said to whoever picked up. Must be Emily.

As the two women started talking, Ben figured it was safe to return, plopping himself on a stool at the end of the counter and watching.

Jocelyn gave him a disconcerted glance. "You're not supposed to be here."

"I'm your cohost."

"Who Ilse dislikes and distrusts."

"Ouch." He waved a hand. "It'll be fine."

She didn't object more, so he stayed.

He stayed as she finally got the twisting down to a consistent level. Not as good as Emily's, but they could do a little camera art to a preset tray. Then they had to wait twenty minutes while the dough was allowed to rise some more. Not too little, because apparently then the pretzels would explode. Not too much, or the yeast would be out of juice for the baking part, which apparently helped them stay soft. When Emily was satisfied, then they had to brine the pretzels—dipping them into a solution of boiled water, baking soda, and salt.

Every pretzel Jocelyn tried to "dip" came out a soggy, melting mess. Until Emily, on the tiny phone screen, threw up her hands. "I'd better come show you in person."

Minutes later, they were all three standing over the boiling pot, the next pretzel victim on Jocelyn's slotted spoon.

"Okay," Emily said. "Now—"

"Are you still in here, Ilse?" Walter's voice called out from the other side of the hall door. Again.

Ben, Emily, and Jocelyn all looked at each other in horror. Then, faster than Angel could attack wrapping paper, Ben grabbed Jocelyn by the hand and swung her out the dining room door only to yank up short at the sound of other crew members coming in the front door of the house.

With nowhere else to go, he backed her into a corner, blocking her with his body, close in. Close enough that the scents of dough and brine covering her hit him. Why the evidence of her disaster of baking made his mouth water, he had no idea. Meanwhile, he could hear Walter going into the kitchen. "I was looking for Ilse."

"She finished with what she was doing, and I'm getting breakfast started," Emily lied through her teeth.

"She left you to clean up her mess?" Walter asked, irritation rife in his voice now.

"I offered."

Walter harumphed like he doubted that truth.

Not a bad cover, actually.

"Fine. Fine," Walter said. "I'll talk to her later."

Ben let loose a small sigh of relief. Except in the next second the dining room door swung in toward him. Luckily, where they were tucked meant the door blocked them from view as Walter walked past. At least for the few seconds it stayed open.

Jocelyn squeezed her eyes shut like a child hiding under a bed from a monster. Ben braced but didn't move.

But Walter didn't stop or say anything.

As soon as his footsteps left the dining room, Jocelyn opened her eyes. And just for a split second, all he could think was that he wanted to kiss her.

Common sense, and the sound of people in the house prevailed, and Ben tugged her back into the kitchen, where Emily was standing in the middle of everything, arms at her sides, eyes wide. They all stared at each other before smothering their laughter.

"Let's not do that again," Jocelyn pleaded. "I'll just do the twisting onscreen. That should be enough."

Ben wasn't so certain, but it's the best they could do.

"I'll clean up in here just to be safe," Emily offered.

Jocelyn brushed at some flour on the counter and shook her head. "I can't let you do that."

"Better than getting caught again."

Ben waved Jocelyn away. "Let me help. Ilse would never bother to clean a mess like this. First of all, she bakes much cleaner, and second of all, she has people for that."

Truth, but he regretted saying it when she winced. After all, Ilse was her sister. He gave her a gentle shove toward the stairs. "Go get yourself cleaned up."

"All right," she said reluctantly.

Then she was gone.

He still wanted to kiss her.

I've been waiting in Jocelyn's room for her. I had been in here alone for the longest time, until the door opened, but when I lifted my head, it wasn't Jocelyn but that Margot woman who is always around her and asking her questions.

She came in with an armload of clothes, so I laid my head back down, figuring she was here to do that thing they do with picking the exact right outfit for a specific occasion.

Except after sorting through the clothes, Margot didn't leave.

She didn't sit next to me either. Instead, she pulled out the chair at the vanity, sat down, and took out her phone, scrolling through video after video. The entire time she's been ignoring me, watching videos, and every so often shooting the door an annoyed glance.

There's something about her energy that is just . . . off.

This doesn't feel like she's waiting to discuss clothes with Jocelyn. But I can't put my finger on what it does feel like. Just . . .

I watch her closely.

I hear Jocelyn's footsteps before the rattle of the key in the door sounds. Margot gets to her feet as Jocelyn comes in. "Oh!" Jocelyn says, and they both pause, looking at each other.

Then Jocelyn glances around. "I thought we were going to talk tomorrow. How long have you been here?"

"You're not Ilse."

I hop to my feet because . . . whoa. But also because that something I couldn't figure out earlier is really bothering me now. There's a tone in Margot's voice. A *not* nice tone.

Jocelyn pulls her shoulders back, expression a cool mask. "What on earth are you talking about?"

"Don't bother denying it. I stood outside the kitchen long enough to hear what I needed. Ilse could do pretzel twists blindfolded and only using her teeth."

"Eww," Jocelyn sniffs.

"Everyone knows she has a twin sister. But no doubt they haven't figured out you switched places because . . ." She gives a laugh that's like walking on broken glass. "What adult in their right mind would pull something like that at all, let alone on live TV."

Margot crosses her arms like she's daring Jocelyn to keep playing dumb.

After a long beat, Jocelyn's shoulders slump a little. "Actually, it's quite a relief that you know. I've been dying to tell you, but I didn't want to get you in trouble. I could really use help—"

"I'm not here to help you. Or Ilse."

Jocelyn's frown looks like my frown feels on my face. Very confused.

"What?" Jocelyn asks slowly.

Margot's smile makes my fur ruffle. "I'm here to help *me*."

Chapter 18

"Ilse had better be in there—"

Jocelyn's eyes popped open at the sound of Walter's voice. It wasn't coming from right outside her door exactly, but nearby. She was still groggy from sleep, but she was pretty sure he was coming down the hall. Or was that just a nightmare?

Ben's voice sounded a second later. "Of course she's in there. You just saw her yesterday in the kitchen. How could she have been in the Philippines by last night?"

Philippines? Oh no!

"I don't care," Walter declared. "I need to see her face."

Bang. Bang. Bang.

Any grogginess that wanted to linger dissipated in an instant as Jocelyn bolted straight up in bed, clutching the covers to her breast like a Victorian maiden. "Yes?"

How would Ilse approach a situation like this?

The answer was pretty obvious. Essentially what it came down to was, her sister would be more than a little irritated at being woken up so early for no good reason. Hopefully no good reason. Because that reference to the Philippines and Walter's need to see her face already gave her a pretty good idea what was going on outside her bedroom.

God bless Ben for giving her as much of a warning as he could. What did her sister do now?

Walter—she was assuming it was Walter doing the banging—knocked on her door again. "Ilse, open up. We need to talk."

She channeled every ounce of her sister's ability to go coldly imperious. "Then you can wait a damned minute, Walter. I was dead asleep when you thought waking me up so rudely was convenient for you. I am not exactly decent."

Jocelyn held the covers away from her and looked down. The black satin and lace nightgown—negligee more like—that Margot had set out for her last night was racy. And Ben was out there. Jocelyn wouldn't have slept in it, because it wasn't exactly winter-friendly. But Margot had also taken all other sleepwear with her. As what? A juvenile attempt to manipulate? She was already blackmailing Ilse.

At least she'd left the matching wrap.

Jocelyn got out of bed, put it on, ran a quick brush through her hair, then went to the door and opened it a crack to find Walter blocking most of her view.

Ben popped his head around the man's shoulders, face a study of concern. "See. Definitely Ilse. She's not in the Philippines, and we can go tell the bigwigs exactly that."

Jocelyn didn't even have to fake her scowl. "Why in heaven's name would I be in the Philippines?"

Walter gave her the hardest look she'd ever seen from the director for a long enough beat that Jocelyn's own scowl wanted to slip. She tugged it back in place with effort. Then he looked down, jerking his phone up to turn the thing on and scroll and then shove it in her face. "This is why."

Jocelyn didn't even need to read the headlines. The picture said it all.

There was her sister, standing in what appeared to be a hotel foyer, and looking very un-Ilse-like. She was in a baby-blue satin and lace negligee not unlike the one Jocelyn was wearing, only without the wrap. At least the softer lighting was kind, and Jocelyn couldn't make out any bits she wasn't supposed to.

But there was more.

Ilse's hair had clearly been in a ponytail, but something had gone wrong, and it was perched sideways on her head like a bad 1980s hairdo with tendrils of hair pulled out and sticking out in all directions. Even more conspicuous . . . she had not a scrap of makeup on. In public. And she was clearly yelling at the top of her lungs as her embarrassed Baron Ex-Boyfriend stood there . . . holding another woman's hand.

Oh, Ilse. Jocelyn's heart cracked for her sister.

"Why don't you and I go to the conference room and give Ilse a chance to get dressed and join us there before we call Herbert." Ben reached between them to take Walter's phone out of Jocelyn's numb hands. "Take all the time you need," he said to her.

No doubt in response to that, Ilse would have snapped something like, "Why? So you can settle this with the execs without me?"

According to Ilse, Ben had been trying to get her off the show since the second he'd arrived, and this would be his big opportunity. Except Jocelyn didn't believe that. The bigger opportunity would have been outing their twin switch.

Ben was on their side. She could trust him. So she just nodded.

He dragged Walter off down the hall. A grumbling Walter who was saying something about, "I don't know why you're being so calm about this . . ."

Jocelyn closed the door and after a long moment staring at the wood grain, it hit her that she shouldn't dawdle. Dressing at the speed of Santa's sleigh on Christmas Eve, she was riffling through the clothes hung up in the armoire when she suddenly paused with her hand on a bright red blouse. Because yesterday's interaction with Margot hit her with a new meaning.

First of all, Jocelyn hadn't told Ben about that yet. She'd been hoping to shield him from at least one ugliness in this mess. But would Margot speak up now that Ilse had outed herself?

Jocelyn shook her head. No. Margot wanted something from Ilse, so she wouldn't use this catastrophe to blow her own opportunity.

Twenty minutes later, dressed and shaking slightly, Jocelyn let herself into the conference room in the hotel wing to find Ben, Walter . . . and Margot . . . all waiting for her. Trying not to stare at the other woman, she closed the door. But a knock immediately sounded, making her jump.

"The entire crew have seen that article, so I asked them to join us for this," Walter explained.

She was beyond certain Ilse would not have liked that. "You should have discussed that with me first."

Somebody tried to open the door and hit her in the backside. Jocelyn spun around, opened it a crack and said, "Just a moment." Then shut the door.

Crossing her arms, she faced the three in the room. Ben was positioned slightly behind the other two, and the way his face was pinched was a bad sign. She deliberately turned her gaze from him. If she couldn't pull this off, it was best if the others had no idea he had been involved in any of it. This was her sister's nightmare. Ben didn't need to be dragged down too.

"There is an easy enough solution." She brazened it out.

"Easy?" Walter's eyes narrowed. "What?"

She shrugged. "A quick statement and possibly a live interview on the steps of Weber Haus to show that I'm still here."

Walter leaned his hands on the table. "You think a statement and a brief appearance are going to fix this? People will just say you returned to film the show."

So what? she wanted to say. Ilse wouldn't have been breaking her contract if she'd done that. The problem was . . .

Jocelyn tipped her head, arranging her expression in her best pursed-lipped, unimpressed Ilse impersonation. "Clearly you don't know how to do math."

While Walter garbled over that insult and Ben winced visibly, she kept going, giving a dramatic, put-upon sigh. "Since there's an easy explanation, and the crew are already here, I guess they can listen in."

Before Walter or anyone else could say anything, she ushered a wary group of people into the room. People who were aware Ilse had a twin sister. Jocelyn was really hoping Margot was right and that full-grown adults would never think that she and Ilse would do something like this. Although Ben had figured it out.

She pinned a determined smile to her lips and waved them inside.

Kyle stopped in front of her with an expression that was so dejected puppy she almost smiled at him. "So did you get back together with your boyfriend?" he asked.

Based on that picture, Jocelyn felt fairly safe giving a bald denial. "No."

Kyle perked up so fast it was almost comical. Poor kid. He had it bad for Ilse.

"Not when she's been openly flirting with Ben this entire trip." Margot slid the dig into the silence.

The rest of the crew shifted uncomfortably on their feet.

"We are going to keep this professional," Ben said in a voice that brooked no argument. Then gave Margot a pointed look. "And if any of you can't do that, feel free to fly on home. Start looking for a new job while you're at it."

Margot shot a look at Jocelyn, and it didn't take a genius to figure out Ilse's blackmailing PA had just realized that Jocelyn hadn't told Ben about her. When Ben turned his attention away from her, Margot shot her a triumphant smirk.

Ilse was going to have to deal with her, because Jocelyn just couldn't.

She waved at Walter to connect the call to Herbert.

Two seconds later an irate Herbert was yelling about stars thinking they could do whatever they wanted and disappearing in the middle of live shows. When there was finally a break in the diatribe, Jocelyn leaned closer to the disk on the table. "If you would just stop talking for a minute, you'd find out that I am right here, Herbert, and not in the Philippines."

Dead silence followed that statement.

Then . . . "Did you catch the red-eye back?"

Jocelyn scoffed, while wincing inside at the rudeness of the sound she'd made. "Apparently you're as bad at math as Walter."

Walter garbled again. Herbert barked her name . . . or technically Ilse's name. And Ben ran a hand over his face. Okay, so angering both the director and the executive producer was probably a bad idea. But Ilse absolutely would have. In fact, she'd probably have been more aggressive about it.

"There isn't enough time to fly from there to here overnight," she pointed out.

Another pause of silence. "Then how do you explain that article?" Herbert demanded.

"That picture is from three years ago. I thought we'd buried it, but I guess it leaked again." Would it be too obvious if she stuck crossed fingers behind her back at the blatant lie?

"Why would anyone post an old picture when that would be easy enough to prove?" Herbert was still suspicious.

Good point. Jocelyn scraped her brain for an answer.

"Clearly Ilse's ex is trying to get back at her for breaking things off," Ben said.

A wave of gratefulness hit her, and she jumped right onto that idea. "Exactly. When that picture first happened, he was the one who paid off the photographer. I guess he kept a copy."

Silence. Then, "I'll get the PR team on it now."

"No need," Jocelyn said. "I have my team already on it." Or she would right after this meeting.

"They can join forces."

Great. It wasn't going to take them long to prove that the picture was brand-new. She needed Ilse back here. Now.

Ben hung back as the meeting broke up, not wanting to be obvious that he was following Jocelyn. He waited until the room cleared, then slowly made his way back to the main house. He assumed she'd gone back to her room to escape the speculative glances and more questions. And Kyle.

Going up the front stairs, the murmur of two women's voices floated to him, though he couldn't make out the words. He rounded the corner, but no one was there. It wasn't until he raised his hand to knock at Jocelyn's door that he realized they were in Jocelyn's room, the door cracked slightly.

Margot and Jocelyn's voices were easily recognizable.

He opened his mouth to let them know he was standing there, then closed it sharply when Margot's next words hit him.

"I told you, get me on the show."

What?

"A regular spot," Margot insisted. "Do that, and I won't be the one to spill your secret to the world."

"I have to talk to Ilse," Jocelyn said. "It's up to her. Not me."

Which meant Margot had figured out what was going on

and which sister was doing these shows. A stirring of hot anger swirled in him.

What was she doing? Blackmailing Jocelyn?

"No, no, no." Margot sounded like he'd never heard the assistant before. Hard. Cold. And oozing with poison. "Ilse won't have a choice if you announce that I'll be a new regular before she comes back."

"I thought you were her friend."

Margot's scoff took the heat of his anger up a few more degrees. "No one is friendly in this business. Not really. It's all about leverage and who you know."

Wow.

Unfortunately she wasn't entirely wrong, but to use that to justify her actions was a jerk move. Ben went to open the door and set her straight by firing her. Mid-step, Jocelyn's voice stopped him. "Don't tell Ben you know, and I'll do it."

He jerked like he'd been hit with an electric current.

Don't tell Ben.

Why?

Why didn't she want him to know? Margot was a threat to both of them.

"So . . . Ben knows?" Margot asked.

"No, he doesn't," Jocelyn rushed to say.

What was she doing? He crossed his arms, head down as he listened.

Another scoff from Margot. "He does. Holy shit. Mr. Career-Television-Man is actually in on the scam. This is brilliant—"

"Wait!" Jocelyn's call had him backing up a step, bracing for Margot to emerge suddenly.

"What?" Margot was closer to the door by the sound of it but didn't come out. "He has more power than you do."

"You tell Ben and I make sure Ilse knows what you're doing right now."

"Put your phone down," Margot finally said. Then hummed a speculative sound. "You must really have a thing for him."

Ben's heart flipped over in his chest, and he strained his ears for the answer.

"He found out after we got here. He wasn't in on it from the beginning. He doesn't deserve to be hurt by this."

"Uh-huh. You think he'd give your sister the same consideration if the roles were reversed?"

Silence greeted that. A silence that stung. Did she think he wouldn't? Actually, if he was honest, it would be a close thing. Ilse wasn't his favorite person.

"Fine," Margot snapped. "This is between us and us alone. I want on the next show."

Ben straightened.

"It's tomorrow," Jocelyn protested. "Ben will want a good reason for switching the script and plans so late."

"I don't care. Figure it out."

He didn't have to hear her footsteps to know she was leaving. Ben rushed down the hall, hopping into the cover of the stairwell leading up to the next level as Margot emerged. If she'd turned her head right instead of left, she would have seen him. Heart pounding, he let out a silent breath of relief as she headed the opposite direction.

Then he stood there, wondering what the heck he should do now.

Jocelyn didn't want him to know about Margot. Clearly, she was doing her best to keep him protected from the worst of the possible fallout from this thing. No one did that for him. Not even Mike, and Mike was his agent whose entire job was to insulate Ben and make sure he was working without interruption.

He gave his head a shake, his earlier anger burning through his veins.

Striding directly to her door, he didn't even knock, walking right in.

Jocelyn, sitting on the edge of her bed and petting Snowball, who lay beside her on the quilt, jumped to her feet with a yelp. "You scared me—"

Ben walked right to her and yanked her into his arms, wrapping them around her in a tight hug. She stiffened at first, but he just held her as he waited for his anger to burn out. Gradually her arms came around his waist and she snuggled into him like a cat.

"What's going on?"

"You tell me," he murmured into her hair, still holding tight.

Silence. "You heard?"

"Enough," he confirmed.

He felt her breathe in and breathe out. "She wants a permanent slot on the show."

"Yeah. I caught that."

"You should stay out of it."

"No way."

"Ben—"

"I said no."

Jocelyn wiggled in his arms until he loosened his grip, and she stepped back to look him in the eyes. "It will be worse for you if—"

"And what about you?"

She shrugged. "My career isn't affected if this goes sideways. At the end of all this, I go back to my basement office and my vlogs that only four people watch. Ilse will have to fix the mess she made. But you were an innocent bystander all along. I don't want that to get worse than it already is."

Ben couldn't help the smile that welled up from within, burning away the rest of his anger. "You're kind of adorable when you're in mama bear mode."

Jocelyn huffed a half a chuckle. "Mama bear? Really?"

He nodded. "Protecting her cubs."

"You are definitely not a cub."

Ben posed. "Glad you noticed." Which made her laugh out loud, the sound going right through him and into him. "I'm going to kiss you now."

She sobered, though her eyes continued to sparkle, even as they widened. Then a whispered, "Okay."

I watch Jocelyn and Ben kissing until I get too embarrassed and cover my eyes with my paw. These two are doing my matchmaking for me. Easiest couple of humans I've worked with in years.

Chapter 19

Jocelyn sat on one of the benches that were scattered around the edges of the frozen pond on the Weber Haus property. Kids zoomed by on skates, people laughed all around her, and she was trying to keep her smile pinned in place.

Bent over, she was lacing up the ice-skates somebody on the crew had bought to match her outfit, which, thank goodness, involved jeans, a sweater, and a thick coat, along with a scarf and a hat and gloves. All in Christmas colors, so the skates were white with little ruffled fur cuffs at the ankles, so she made sure to tuck the edges of her skinny jeans inside.

"Let me help you with that." Before she knew it, Ben was on one knee in front of her, taking over tying her laces. Which was what he was supposed to do. All part of the script so that they could point out that Ilse had never been ice-skating before.

Ilse would probably hate this moment when she saw the show. She'd say something about not needing a man to tie her laces. Jocelyn got it. But her classic-Hollywood-movie-loving heart considered the gesture romantic more than misogynistic. Maybe it was the way he'd approached her? Or the tone of voice?

Or maybe she just liked having him at her feet, giving her strong Cinderella vibes.

The way butterflies had come to breathtaking life in her tummy, and how she wanted to reach out and brush back the floppy lock of hair that had fallen over his eyes, honestly, she really didn't care right now.

Except she was supposed to be on TV acting like Ilse.

True to Ilse's character, Jocelyn said her line. "I do actually know how to tie a shoe, Benjamin."

She looked directly up into the camera trained on her face and winked.

"There's a trick to tying laces for things like ice-skates." He glanced up at her with a grin that was so boyish, her heart flipped a little. "I played hockey for a bit. It's all about making sure your ankles have enough support."

He tugged a little harder and Jocelyn couldn't help her wince. "Just so long as you leave me enough room for blood circulation."

Behind the camera, Walter flashed a grin. They really were loving something about the way she and Ben interacted. Though she suspected what they loved more were the positive comments on social media, not to mention the speculation about their chemistry. Positive was fine. The problem was the romantic angle. Her sister definitely wouldn't appreciate coming home to learn she had to fake a romantic interest in the cohost she didn't get along with.

And I wouldn't want her to. Not with Ben.

Which meant she needed to stop staring, stop responding, and stop whatever flirty tone kept creeping into her voice.

Treat him like Theo. Like a brother.

Finally finished, Ben looked up, then over his shoulder at the camera. He delivered some line about ice-skating not just having to be for kids. How part of the finding of the magic of Christmas every year was to actively remind yourself what it felt like when you were a child.

Great line. And Jocelyn would totally be into it, if she wasn't about to risk life and limb on a gliding deathtrap.

It wasn't that she hadn't ever skated, like they were imply-
ing on the show. It was that she really sucked at it. Coordi-
nation and she had never really gotten along.

Ben got to his feet and held out a hand to help her to her
feet. "Ready?"

Not in the least.

As soon as she was up, he let go of her hand, and moved
down the small, snowy embankment to the ice of the frozen
pond on the Weber Haus property. He stepped onto it, took
two gliding steps, then flipped around and immediately
started skating backwards, doing things with his feet that she
had to admit were just downright sexy.

How was she supposed to watch that and think "brother"?

Except . . . now that she thought about it, he was going to
make her awkwardness look way worse by comparison. He
needed to tone it down.

Jocelyn wanted to toss her head back and wail. Life really
wasn't fair sometimes. Couldn't the powers that be have dis-
tributed abilities so that each and every person only got one
thing they were really good at? But no. Some people got all
the things. Ben was smart, and charming, and kind, and now
apparently athletically inclined. Add that to the good looks
and the shiver-inducing voice, and anyone who liked men
didn't stand a chance against him. Jocelyn included. Worse,
she also knew what it was like to kiss him. So she was a
goner.

Brother? Yeah, right.

As far as she was concerned, Ben's only true detraction
was that he was in the public eye. She could do without that
part. That and how Ilse didn't like him.

After skating one quick loop around the pond, masterfully
avoiding collisions with everyone else out there, he did a
hard stop in front of her, spraying ice with the blades of his
skates. By the way his eyes sparkled, she knew he was gen-

uinely having fun. Meanwhile she was still standing at the edge gathering her courage.

"You really like this," she said.

Not on script. Anything to delay her own skating.

Ben didn't miss a beat. "I already feel like a kid again."

Then he beckoned her onto the ice with a little wave. No time like the present. In front of gazillions of watching fans of the show. Well, maybe not gazillions, but numbers that were impossible for her to wrap her head around all the same.

Don't think about them.

With one foot still on the snowbank at the edge of the pond for stability, she put the other foot on the ice, and it immediately went a direction she wasn't expecting, which made her fling out her arms and bobble. "Whoa!"

The only reason she didn't go over was because Ben grabbed her hands and steadied her. "You want to keep your center of balance upright and over your skates," he told her.

She tried not to snort her doubt. "That'll be the next thing I focus on after I manage to keep my feet under me at all."

He chuckled. A warm sound that surprisingly reached inside her despite the moment. But then he mumbled something very softly, under his breath, just for her. "You are too cute."

She wanted to make a face at him, a warning, because the cameras were still on, and Tony was listening. But of course she couldn't, so she pretended she hadn't heard.

Taking his hand, she managed to get her second foot onto the ice. Clutching at Ben, she struggled as her feet slipped and slid in polar opposite directions until she finally got them both under control and managed to stand upright. Breathing hard.

She was probably a mess already.

"Got it?" Ben asked.

"I really hope so."

"Okay, I'm going to pull you so you can get a feel for it. Just keep your eyes on me." But he didn't count down or anything. He just started going backwards, tugging on her to follow.

Not remotely ready, instinct had her pulling against him, which meant she leaned back. Both of Jocelyn's feet shot straight out in front of her. And because she was stiff as a board trying to stay upright, her entire body laid out backwards.

It happened so fast, all she got was a flash of Ben's shocked face, the feel of her hands yanking against his, and then somehow, they both landed on the snow with Ben beneath her, chest to chest and nose to nose.

She stared into concerned green eyes.

How had he managed to flip them that way at all? It seemed to go against the laws of physics.

"Did I hurt you?" she asked.

His grin was pure mischief. Sincere. And somehow the cameras and the audience melted away and this was just the two of them having fun. Jocelyn grinned right back, a giggle bursting from her, followed by another and another.

" 'Don't try to get on my good side,' " he drawled, Southern-gentleman style. " 'I no longer have one.' "

She laughed. "*Steel Magnolias?*"

"That's the film."

Then they both blinked as they remembered where they were and who she was.

Ben lifted up on his elbows so fast, he forced her to use his chest as a prop so that she could lean back and not get smacked in the face . . . or give in to the sudden urge to kiss him. He looked over his shoulder and grinned again, but this one was more professional, no emotion behind his eyes. Not really.

"After this commercial break," he said, "we'll have Ilse up on her feet and doing spins."

A few seconds later Walter indicated the commercials were running, and several of the crew hurried over to help Jocelyn and Ben to their feet.

"Aren't you a dancer, Miss Becker?" Kyle bounded up to her with all his puppy-dog energy. Then before she could answer, he kept going. "I would have thought that would help make ice-skating easy."

It probably would have, if she'd been Ilse. Her sister had been on the high school dance team, on scholarship since they couldn't afford the fees or costumes, but she'd loved it. That had probably been where her love of performing started.

"I wasn't doing pirouettes on a floor that moves, or makes me move," Jocelyn pointed out dryly.

"That's a great line," Walter boomed. "I want you to say exactly that in the next shot."

She glanced over at Ben, who still had snow in his hair, and without thinking, she reached up to brush it away, only to stop after two swipes as she realized what she was doing. In front of everyone.

I am never pretending to be someone I'm not ever again.

"Let's get you on the ice and moving before the next segment," Ben said. "The next part of the script needs you upright." He winked. "Me too."

Jocelyn had no choice. So with Ben's help, this time she managed to keep her feet when he started her moving around the ice. Unfortunately, what that meant was that rather than skating backwards and trying to get her to do it on her own, Ben had to skate at her side with one arm manacled around her waist, practically holding her feet off the slick surface. But they could stay upright and keep moving, and that was all that mattered.

"And where the heck is the darn cat?" Walter called to one of the crew.

Wait, what?

"The cat?" Jocelyn looked at Ben, then slipped, only to have him bodily haul her back up.

"Orders from on high," he muttered under his breath. "Came in this morning. Viewers think Angel attacking you is hilarious."

And they wanted to see that on ice? "You know . . . there is a mean streak to humanity in general that, up until now, I just haven't wanted to acknowledge."

"How anybody ends up on Santa's 'nice' list at Christmas is beyond me."

Why, oh why, does the pond have to be down a hill a bit? Don't they know that this hill gathers drifts of snow that are too deep for little cats? I leap over what appears to be a pile, only to *ploof* into a pit that's well over my head. The third ploof so far, and I'm not to the pond yet. I'm close, but not close enough.

I wouldn't be out here at all, only I have to warn Jocelyn and Ben.

Unable to see where I'm headed, I aim in the direction I was already going—toward the pond—and, with a wiggle of my tush, jump. This time the ground where I land is more solid and I'm able to run almost the rest of the way. I can even see Jocelyn and Ben standing side by side on the ice, talking into the camera and gesturing behind them.

I'm so focused on them, that I don't notice the way the land dips until I tumble into another drift of snow with another *ploof*. As an added insult, a glob of snow falls on top of my head.

Maybe I should turn back.

Gathering my determination, I wiggle and leap again.

"The cat!"

I *ploof* back into a continuation of the drift I'm already in. But I pause instead of jumping right away. Because I'm pretty sure one of those humans spotted me. I listen carefully, ears twitching. And I can hear them talking about a cat. But they're talking about Angel and how they should get her because the next segment would be good to have her.

I'm not sure how they think that's going to happen. Because the reason I'm out here is to try to tell Jocelyn and Ben that that Margot woman took Angel away in a car. She was muttering to herself about how she'd better be on the next episode, and that this was just a taste of the havoc she could visit on Jocelyn if she continued to dismiss her.

I don't think she's very nice.

I wiggle and jump and *ploof* again.

A cry goes up. "There she is!"

Then, before I know it, human hands reach into my snowy hole and scoop me out. I'm held against a chest—I can't say cuddled because this person is wearing a vest with rough, stiff pockets and it's a far cry from cuddling. They lug me the rest of the way to the pond and say, "Here."

I'm held unceremoniously toward Ben and Jocelyn, my legs dangling in the air. I'd squirm, but Jocelyn backs up with her hands in the air like she doesn't want to even touch me.

So instead I meow. Because ouch. I thought we were friends.

Ben reaches for me, but as he does, Jocelyn frowns, stepping closer suddenly to inspect me.

"Got her?" the Walter guy behind the camera asks.

"Um, Ben . . ." Jocelyn tries to get his attention. But he's pulling me in close and positioning them both in front of a table off to the side of the pond set up with the food already made.

"I'll keep her from attacking you," Ben murmurs to her.

"That's not—"

Walter starts a count down. "And five, four, three . . ."

"That's not Angel. That's Snowball." Jocelyn whispers the words at Ben in a rush.

Ben stiffens, squeezing me a little tighter, before they both suddenly smile brilliantly. "Look who joined us today, folks. Angel the cat!"

Ben lifted the cat he was holding, turning her so that they were nose to nose. Damn. Jocelyn was right. This was *not* Angel.

Somehow, they'd ended up with Snowball.

Because of course. That they hadn't blown up these live shows in a spectacular way up till now was still a Christmas miracle. But there was still time.

Somebody had to be playing a joke on them, right? Then again, at least this particular cat wouldn't attack Jocelyn and cause all sorts of chaos. The question was . . . would anybody else notice? Viewers could get really weird about things like that. They didn't like to be lied to or tricked, and using a cat body double and an Ilse body double at the same time was pushing it.

So . . . next question. *What should I do now?*

Point it out or lean into it?

He made the decision in a blink, because they didn't have time to debate. Time to catfish the nation. Again.

He spoke directly to Snowball. "You and Ilse have made up and become friends again, right, *Angel?*"

The cat scrunched up her face at the name. Like she understood and really didn't want to be associated with the TV kitty.

He didn't blame her.

"You two are friends now?" he insisted.

As if on cue, like the best trained cat would, Snowball meowed, then she pawed gently at his face. No claws.

Good kitty.

Ben smiled at her, then tucked her in close to his chest and redirected that smile at the camera. "Ilse and Angel sat down and had a long talk the other night. Didn't you, Ilse?"

He didn't dare look at Jocelyn. Hopefully she played along.

She paused just long enough that he was about to turn his head, then said, "Sometimes it just takes opening the lines of communication."

Another hurdle cleared.

He had to give it to Jocelyn, four shows in and she was already a pro at the ad-libbing. Possibly better than her sister, at least at that. Ilse didn't really like to go off script.

Ben ran a hand over Snowball's soft fur. "Why don't I hold her while you tell the folks at home about the incredible goodies we've concocted for our Ice-Skating Party today?"

"I'm pretty sure I did all the concocting, Ben." Jocelyn looked directly into the camera with a big smile.

Then she rolled right into the cued script. "Clearly we couldn't bring a kitchen out here to do most of the prep."

"Clearly," Ben interjected on a laugh. Also on script.

She wrinkled her nose at him like they'd rehearsed. "And there's not enough time on a live show between breaks for us to run back and forth from the pond to the house."

"I actually thought that would be pretty funny to watch," Ben admitted to the camera. "But I got outvoted."

Jocelyn's shoulder bumped him. "So we prerecorded how to bake these treats. For an Ice-Skating Party we recommend foods that can be easily carried to where you're skating, held while eating, possibly even when you're wearing gloves or mittens, and are very easy to clean up. So take a watch as we walk you through the baking!"

At Walter's signal, Ben and Jocelyn relaxed, knowing viewers were seeing Ilse/Jocelyn in the Weber Haus kitchen making the pretzels and then talking about making the other items. So far, so good with the cat. Maybe after this segment they could send her home.

Instead of staying behind the camera where he usually did, Walter moved right up to Ben and shoved his face in Snowball's, who blinked back at him with her big blue eyes. Innocence personified.

Ben held his breath, waiting for Walter to discover this was the wrong cat. The thing was, they'd already been live on TV. If the cat disappeared now, it would look odd. Worse, if anyone found out they used a different cat, it seemed like that would just point a big flashing neon arrow at the fact that they were using a different host too.

Besides, Snowball was sitting quietly in his arms, perfectly content to be petted. Why rock the sleigh?

As Walter studied the cat intently, Ben met Jocelyn's gaze for a quick second. Clearly, she'd come to the same conclusions. "You're not attacking anybody today," Walter said to the cat.

Ben blew out a silent breath and was pretty sure Jocelyn did too. Actually, he got the impression that Snowball did too.

"Maybe she had a thorn in her paw or something before," Jocelyn murmured.

Which was a stretch.

Walter straightened, but he didn't take his gaze off the cat, tipping his head and still studying her. "Does she look different to you?"

He raised his gaze to Ben, who put on his best acting face, giving a confused frown. "Different? What do you mean?"

"Yeah . . ." Walter nodded more to himself. "Smaller maybe? A brighter white?"

Ben angled his body just slightly, trying to hide that Snowball really was slightly smaller than Angel. "It's probably the natural lighting and setting."

"I did see Isaac giving her a bath yesterday," Jocelyn offered.

Walter crossed his arms, still looking at the cat. "Maybe that's it."

Only he still didn't move away.

Ben glanced at Jocelyn again, and even opened his mouth,

vaguely trying to come up with some distracting comment, but Tony called out, "Ready to go live in thirty seconds."

Walter shuffled his way back behind the camera. For someone who worked in TV, Ben had never met somebody more determined to never be in front of one. Although a lot of the crew could be that way, preferring behind-the-scenes work.

Actually, Ben preferred that as well, but he could do both.

At the end of the thirty seconds, they were cued back to live. Jocelyn picked up the tray of pretzels on the makeshift table the crew had set up for them to stand behind and held it up so that the camera could zoom in. "Doesn't a warm Bavarian pretzel, all soft and gooey on the inside and crisp on the outside, sound like the perfect ice-skating food? You can even bring different dips like mustards or cream cheese icing or cinnamon." She read right along with their script that Kyle was queuing up. Then she paused. Longer than she should have been pausing. They'd practiced this and were in the relatively easy part.

Ben glanced at Jocelyn, who flicked him a glance that looked almost nervous, before returning her gaze to the prompter at the side of the camera.

Had something changed?

He glanced in the same direction and also stilled. Someone had definitely changed the script. Not in a way he would have ever agreed to. He was going to kill them.

Jocelyn cleared her throat, then picked up a pretzel and tore it apart so she could pop a small piece into her mouth, which she chewed and then appeared to have to force down. Then she tore off another piece and held it out to Ben. "You've got to try this."

Ben looked at her, looked at it, looked at Snowball, then back to her. "I'm kind of holding a cat."

"Well, then I'll help you." She was so hating this.

Rather than hold it out so that he could nibble it from her

fingertips, like the altered cue card indicated, she said, "Open wide . . ." in a singsongy voice.

He did, only to have the bite unceremoniously shoved into his mouth. She jerked her hand away like he might bite her. Then Jocelyn grinned, eyes twinkling and confidence returned. Because while she'd stuck strictly to the script, they were both well aware that that was not what whoever changed it had wanted to happen.

They'd wanted chemistry and romance.

"It's really tasty," Ben said to the camera around the piece he was still chewing.

"Let's talk about these other goodies," Jocelyn said.

She then proceeded to walk the folks at home through the other items like churros, pigs in blankets, and a hot chocolate station including personalized mixers to change the flavor or give it an added little kick for those who wanted a boozy party. Unlike the other parties they'd hosted so far for these live shows, for this one they had decided *not* to include a themed cocktail. Mostly because it had occurred to somebody in Legal that ice-skates could technically be lethal weapons in the wrong hands.

"I can take her now." Jocelyn held her hands out for Snowball, making little grabby fists. Just as Ben let go of the cat and Jocelyn snuggled her, Emily Weber, who was on the ice, suddenly said very loudly, "Lukas, look. Snowball is on TV."

Oh . . . hell.

He didn't even dare look at Jocelyn.

Most of the people on the ice while they were shooting were locals who frequented Weber Haus or were friends of the owners. That had been deliberate, so that the crew could be sure everyone behaved while filming and looked happy as they skated around. But that also meant *all* of them knew Snowball. Which meant every person on the ice stopped and turned to look . . . and point.

"No, no," Jocelyn called back. Making Ben wince, because he knew Tony, working the sound mixing, was going to lose it if she kept that up. Which she did. Jocelyn held the cat up like a trophy. "This is Angel. She's our show's cat."

Then she looked at the camera. "For the folks at home, Weber Haus boasts an adorable resident kitty who looks a lot like Angel. But she's not a trained cat like this one."

What was she doing? The trick to magic was that the audience wasn't aware of the illusion mechanism. Why was she pointing out that another cat even existed?

"Are you sure?" Emily called across, frowning her confusion. Lukas, at his wife's side—Lara was somewhere at the side of the pond holding their baby—was also frowning. Because of course they knew their own cat.

"Would an untrained cat be this calm and easygoing out here in all this chaos?" Jocelyn asked.

That was a poor excuse, and he could see even Jocelyn knew it based on the tiny wince she gave. Hopefully too small for the camera to catch.

"I even taught her a new trick when we were making up and becoming friends again," she said.

Getting any cat to do a trick was tough. But getting one to do anything on cue while on camera, and while ice-skaters were staring and people were all around . . . even Angel would have trouble focusing in this environment.

But Jocelyn set Snowball down on a nearby stool. Then broke off another smaller piece of pretzel. "Nose," she said.

Snowball stared at her and did nothing.

Jocelyn clicked her tongue. "Come on. We did this the other night." She held up the treat. "Nose."

Snowball cocked her head as if to say, "I don't understand human."

Then she hopped down from the stool and trotted across the packed snow straight to Emily, who was waiting now at the edge of the pond.

Jocelyn stared after the cat with her mouth open.

Ben couldn't help it. He burst out laughing, which made her swing around to glare at him with her hands all akimbo.

"At least she didn't attack you this time," he teased.

Shaking his head, he turned to face the camera. Time to put a stop to whatever this was and get the show back on track. "After this word from our sponsors, we'll get into fun parting gifts. Be right back."

Chapter 20

Ben walked Jocelyn down to the dining room for breakfast the next morning. Apparently, he wanted to see her choke, because he waited until she had forked a large pile of scrambled eggs into her mouth before he busted out with: "I heard from Herbert. They want our final show to be the Christmas Caroling Party."

Jocelyn sucked in hard, then immediately started a round of violent coughing as her lungs tried to dispel the chunks of eggs she'd just tried to inhale.

Ben pounded her on the back, while Kyle jumped to his feet. After a second he shoved a glass of water into her hand. When she could finally breathe without devolving into more fits of coughing, she turned to Ben, trying not to look gobsmacked. She thought she'd avoided the singing. "What?"

He flashed a smile while, under the table, he gave her hand a consoling pat. "I know. But at least we're all ready for it."

But that required singing. "I told you about the nodules."

He nodded. "Herbert understands, so they're arranging a guest star to come sing so that viewers aren't too disappointed."

Okay. There was that at least. Because Snowball could probably sing carols better than Jocelyn ever could.

"I could sing for you," Margot piped up from the other end of the table.

Jocelyn didn't even want to look in her direction.

Yesterday, she hadn't been aware until they'd finished filming the ice-skating show that poor Isaac had been desperately searching for Angel the entire time. But it wasn't until Margot suddenly appeared holding the feline devil in her arms and claiming she'd found her outside that Jocelyn started to get suspicious.

A sinking feeling that turned into cement in her stomach when Margot had looked directly at her and said, "I hope something like that doesn't happen again. Or worse."

A not-so-subtle threat.

No doubt in Jocelyn's mind.

The trouble was what to do about it. Tell Ben? She didn't want to bring him deeper into the rabbit hole. Tell Ilse? Her sister would have to do something about it eventually.

Or I can just put Margot on the next show.

It was the last of the live shows. The last before the winter break too.

That would give Ilse time to get home, learn about everything going on, and come up with some way to address it. Right?

Oblivious, Ben leaned around Jocelyn to tell Margot, "Herbert wants a big name for this one, since it's the finale."

Margot sent Jocelyn a pointed stare.

Heat flared in Jocelyn's face, traveling down her chest and through her body. She had no choice. It was this or get outed. With only one more show to go, she could see the light at the end of the tunnel.

Or was that a train barreling down the tracks right at her? Difficult to tell.

"Margot could sing with the special guest, maybe," she said slowly. "A duet?"

Across the way Margot perked up, but Ben did not. "It will depend on the contract they negotiated and if they're willing to share the spotlight."

Right. Contracts. Spotlights. Egos.

Not Jocelyn's world, but knowing Ilse and witnessing her sister's experiences, she got it.

"It doesn't hurt to ask."

Ben didn't frown exactly. More like his expression set, and she could practically see the questions spinning. He was going to ask her why she was pushing this. She could see it coming. Better to ignore and avoid? Or maybe divert by addressing head-on.

She went with option number two. "We can discuss it while we're going over the script."

He leaned back, considering her. "Fair enough."

"Do you want to get started after breakfast?"

Ben checked his phone for the time. "I asked Lukas about the carolers who dress up in Victorian holiday costumes to sing around the shops when the Christmas Market is going here. I'm meeting the woman who organizes them today to see if they'd be willing to sing on the show with us."

"That's a good idea."

"Why don't you come with me?"

Anything to get away from Margot. "All right."

"Can I come?" Kyle asked.

Jocelyn tried not to stiffen. She hadn't missed the cue card tech's goo-goo eyes or constant attempts to be around her. Or around Ilse, who he believed she was. The poor guy had it bad for her sister, but he was so far from her type. Ilse didn't need golden retriever energy. She needed rottweiler energy. Someone who could go toe-to-toe with her.

"Not this time," Ben said.

Guilt and relief mixed together was a funny sensation. Like a release and a tightening at the same time.

*   *   *

As soon as breakfast was over, after grabbing Ilse's purse and a jacket, hat, and gloves from her room, she and Ben took the rental and headed into town.

"Want to tell me what that was about with Margot?" he asked before they'd even pulled out of the long drive onto the road.

Jocelyn huffed a laugh. "Not one to sit on your laurels, are you?"

He flicked her a glance before returning his gaze to the road. "I can't tell if you're stalling or teasing."

"A little of both." She sighed.

Another flick of a glance. Then, "I knew something was up."

Which for some reason made her smile. Maybe because she found it sweet that he cared enough to notice.

"Theo says that I'm an open book only to people who care enough to read the instructions first."

Ben lifted a single eyebrow. "Are you saying I fall in that group?"

Oh no! Maybe she'd been assuming too much. They hadn't exactly defined their relationship beyond the whole "It's worth the risk to figure it out" thing.

"Um . . ."

He chuckled. "I hope I do."

Jocelyn's relief came out in the form of batting at his arm. "You're a secret tease, Ben. You know that?"

His lips tipped up in a wide grin.

"Does anyone else on the show know about this side to you?"

Ben pulled up to a four-way stop, which gave him time to give her a longer look. "Why do you ask that?"

Jocelyn shrugged. "I don't know. I get the impression that you're a bit of an island. The man in charge always is."

He eased into the intersection. "Technically I share being in charge with Ilse and Walter."

"But that's not what you really want." She had no idea why she was so sure about that. She just was.

Ben tapped a thumb against the steering wheel. "I didn't tell you this because I didn't want you to be under more pressure . . ."

That didn't sound good. "What?"

That thumb tapped double time. "If the live shows do well enough, they're going to give me my own show. Not to host necessarily, unless I want to. But I get to come up with a concept and produce on my own. I'll be the showrunner . . ."

He sort of trailed off, and it wasn't lost on her that he wasn't glancing her way anymore but staring straight ahead.

"That's fantastic!" The initial shock wore off quickly and all the possibilities struck her at once. "You'd be amazing at that. Look at the way you've calmly handled last-minute changes and worked through all the logistics for these live shows. Including having to work around a person who has never hosted live TV before. The crew respect you. They listen to you. And your ideas have all been great. Just think what you could do . . ."

Oh Lord, she was gushing. Like he had a second ago, she trailed off.

"You really believe that," he said slowly. Not a question.

There was enough of something odd in his voice that she gave him a closer look. "What? Did you expect me to be doubtful of your abilities or something?"

He shrugged. "It's taken me years to convince the studio. But actually, I expected you to get a little upset."

"Why?"

"Because I didn't share that with you earlier. Given that my deal hangs on the success of the live shows, it does kind of involve you. It impacts Ilse as well, and I know how much you love your sister."

Or she wouldn't even be here. He didn't have to say it. "I mean . . . knowing about the deal helps me understand why you jumped in to make things work with me a little better."

Her excitement dimmed like a Rudolph's nose covered by dirt as it finally sank in that all Ben's help hadn't been because he cared about her, but because of the opportunity he was chasing. Not that that changed anything, really, but she'd kind of hoped . . .

Silly things. She'd hoped silly things. Of course when she'd been a total stranger, his motivation wasn't going to be her.

"I did it for me to start with," he admitted. Then reached across the console between them to wrap his hand around hers and squeeze. "But I've worked extra hard lately because I got to know you."

Was she that obvious? Or was he a mind reader?

He gave her hand one more squeeze and let go.

The thing was, Jocelyn got the sense that he knew her. Well enough to figure out what she was thinking. Which was yet another silly idea. They had only known each other for a few weeks now. And yes, there was the chemistry and the kissing and the agreement to see where this went, but somehow, she felt like she'd known Ben as long as she'd known Theo. She was that comfortable with him. Which was saying a lot.

There was no rhyme or reason to it. No logic. It just was.

"Regardless, I'm really excited for you. Your new show is going to happen."

"You think so?" His lips quirked.

"Of course. The execs seem pretty happy with the live shows so far." She thought about that a second, then tacked on a dry, "By some miracle."

"I hope so. I've worked hard for it."

She had no doubt about that. Ben reminded her of Ilse that

way. Or at least Ilse when she wasn't in the throes of being dumped by European royalty.

"Even if it doesn't happen now, although I think it will, I know it will happen eventually. You're too good at what you do for it not to."

Ben stayed quiet for a long beat then in a quiet voice said, "Thank you. That means a lot."

Again, a tone in his voice struck her as off. Did no one else tell him things like that? "You do have a support team, don't you?"

"Support team?" The side of his mouth crooked up.

"Yeah. The people who support you chasing your dream and are there to cheer you on." She lifted a fist in solidarity. "Go Team Ben."

He didn't look over, but she was pretty sure he was secretly laughing at her fist pump.

"I do have Mike."

"Who's that?"

"My agent."

His agent? Nope, that didn't work. His agent was essentially paid to be a cheerleader, because Ben's success equated to Mike's own success. "That doesn't count. I'm talking about people who get no benefit if you do well."

"Mike and I are friends."

"Still . . ." She crossed her arms.

"I do have friends."

That was vague enough to make her eye him narrowly.

"How close?"

"Does it matter?"

Did it matter? She shifted in her seat to turn to face him as much as she could, even if she was addressing the side of his face. "It's like this. . . . Yes, Ilse has her agent, and her PR team, and Margot." Although the PA's level of support was debatable these days. "And they're there for all the minutiae of Ilse's career. They're also there to help her do everything she can to take the right steps to succeed. Very important people in her life. That's her career team."

"I hear a 'but' coming."

Smarty pants. "However . . ."

Ben's lips quirked at her choice of alternate transition word, and Jocelyn couldn't help a quick chuckle.

"However, if she needs to vent, including about people on her career team, or she wants to just brainstorm something she thinks that the people in that career team are going need convincing to get on board with, or anything that has nothing to do with her work, or she just needs a hug—Ilse is so not the type the support team people would even attempt to hug, and I get the impression you're the same way." She paused to take a breath. "That's when she has her support team. Me. And Theo. And she had her boyfriend for a while there. A support team. The people in your life who are there just to love you through the ups and downs of the ride."

Ben didn't say anything, his silence telling, and Jocelyn's heart cracked a little bit for him. Was he really that much of an island? Even the Island of Misfit Toys involved a group of friends.

"What about your family?" she asked.

He gave a shrug she suspected was supposed to be casual. "My parents love me very much. I had everything I could ever want growing up. But they were very busy with their own businesses. My dad is in finance, and my mom runs a boutique shop that is very high-end and caters to the uber-wealthy."

She vaguely remembered him mentioning something about household staff. So were his parents too busy to bother with their kid? Or not impressed with his choices? "And what do they think about your career goals?"

"I don't really share my specific goals with them," he admitted slowly. "But they're very happy for me to have connections in the entertainment industry."

Wow. He said that like it was no big deal. And maybe he was so used to it that to him it wasn't. But that was a big deal.

Jocelyn had lost parents who loved her very much and told her that every day and made her the center of their world. Even as young as six years old, she remembered that much. After they died, her only family had been Ilse and later Theo. She used to wish that she'd find an adult or a couple who might adopt all three of them and support and love them through their lives. And that had been hard.

But she could see the small way Ben was closing in on himself as he talked about his parents, the smile completely gone from his face. Maybe indifference from the people who were supposed to care about you might be just as bad.

"Okay. What about a found family?" she asked.

"What is that?"

"There are people in your life who are not blood related, but who you become really close with. They are the ones who become your family, who you spend holidays with, who you share the daily minutiae of your life with, and who love and support you no matter what. Unconditionally. Theo is our found family."

Ben thought about that a second, thumb tapping at the steering wheel again. If he had to think that hard, then she guessed he didn't have a found family either.

"Maybe I'm just too independent," he finally said. "I don't need that."

Her heart set to aching even more. Everybody needed somebody.

She really wanted to offer to be his somebody, but doubts

peppered her like a hailstorm. It was too soon to be making that kind of offer. They were still feeling things out. "Well . . ." Maybe she could give him the best she could offer in the moment. "I happen to be a very good cheerleader."

His thumb stopped tapping. Then his hands wrapped around the steering wheel, gripping it more tightly. Was he thrown off by her friendly offer? Offended maybe? Scared off?

"I thought Ilse was the cheerleader in the family," he finally commented.

She could not get a read on his reaction at all. "An actual cheerleader? No. She was on the dance team. But I wasn't a cheerleader, either. I'm just talking about the metaphorical kind."

He said nothing.

Awkward silence filled up the car.

Which was when they reached the main part of town, and Ben suddenly pulled off, parking along the street. In a rush of movement, he put the car in park, unbuckled his seat belt, and turned toward her. Then he reached out and took her face in his hands, gently tugging her across the divide between them as he leaned her direction and gave her a long, sweet, lingering kiss.

After the initial shock, Jocelyn relaxed into him, even smiling a little as she kissed him back. The man really could kiss. Her heart set to fluttering, sending warmth through her.

He released her slowly, but only leaning back enough so that they could look each other in the eyes. "Where did you come from, Jocelyn Becker?"

She could see a thousand words he couldn't say in the sparkle in his eyes, in the tenderness of his smile, in the way he softly brushed the pads of his thumbs over her cheekbones. She couldn't voice them aloud either, because it was still too soon, but those thoughts were there just the same.

Unsaid words that buoyed her heart with hope. She felt so light, she thought if he let her go, she might just float away. Maybe that's how Santa got up those chimneys. It wasn't magic, but hope. Hope for the world.

Jocelyn wanted to hold on to that feeling and never let it go.

Chapter 21

Jocelyn believed in him and wanted to be his cheerleader.

The thought hadn't left him in the days since. They were filming the Caroling Party today. The last of their live shows. Then . . . what?

They'd go back to their lives? Continue to see how this played out after they returned to real life? Between his career, her sister's opinion of him, and not wanting to let anyone else on the show know about the twin swap, that was going to be tricky.

But he didn't want to let her go. He was . . . comfortable . . . with her. Like he could relax with her.

That was rare, and he knew it.

Ben stared at the ceiling of his bedroom as the morning light turned the white plaster brighter and brighter. He should get up and get dressed before heading downstairs. Margot would be going to the airport today to pick up their guest star. Fresh off one of the many voice competitions on TV, Quentin Jorgen was a bit of a hot topic right now. They'd been lucky to book him with so little notice and especially at this time of year.

Jocelyn wanted to do one more walk-through, just the two of them, to be sure they had their timing right. They should get started to finish in time to greet their guest and walk him through the show. But all Ben could picture was Jocelyn and her sincere, eager expression as she offered to be one of his support team.

The only and founding member, if he was honest.

And maybe that's why he was falling so hard and fast for her. He'd seen what she would do, how she cared, for Ilse, and he wanted that for himself. He wasn't sure if that made him selfish or incredibly smart. He'd never met anyone quite like her.

What he needed to do was talk to her about it.

He'd thought maybe after the shows were over, he could do that. But he wanted her to know now that he wanted her. To be with her, whatever that looked like as long as they were together.

He wasn't going to walk away from this opportunity.

On that thought, he flung back the covers and showered and dressed in record time. Halfway through, he shot Jocelyn a text, which she answered in seconds, agreeing to meet him up on the third floor in their secret room. Since Theo had left, they'd been using it as a clandestine rehearsal space.

When he walked into the room half an hour later, Jocelyn was already there, sitting on the bed and bent over a ream of printed paper, which he assumed had to be the most recent version of the show script. She looked up and smiled when he came in, and Ben just couldn't resist.

He strode across the room to lean over her, placing a swift kiss on her lips. A kiss that was supposed to be a peck but turned into something lingering. More than a little while later, he lifted his head and smiled down into her eyes.

"Good morning," he said.

Her eyes crinkled with her own smile even as delicate color surged into her cheeks. "Morning. What was that for?"

He shrugged. "Just because."

"Hmmm." She squished up her nose, reminding him of Snowball suddenly. "I like your reason."

Then she surprised him, leaning forward suddenly to initiate her own kiss. This one just a teasing peck.

Ben laughed, then dropped onto the bed to sit across from her.

She looked down at the script. "I was thinking about the segment with the food. I think, since I won't be singing, I can make my way back to the house in time to film it live, rather than using the prerecorded segment."

Caroling, like ice-skating, was going to be shot away from the house, this time among the Weber Haus shops.

"Mm-hmm," he agreed noncommittally, too absorbed in skating his gaze over her features and trying to figure out how to start the conversation he really wanted to have.

Jocelyn glanced up, cocking her head. "It's not like you not to have an opinion about the show."

No time like now. "I wanted to talk to you about when we—"

On the bed beside her, Jocelyn's phone went off. She glanced down at the screen, stiffened, then frowned, picking it up slowly. After a second where she seemed to debate with herself, she swiped to answer. "Ilse?"

Ilse? Ben glanced at his watch.

He could hear Jocelyn's sister speaking on the other end of the line but couldn't make out the words. Which meant all he had to go on was Jocelyn's expression. Which started out mildly curious, but quickly descended into a frown, her brows practically meeting in the middle over her eyes.

"What?" Jocelyn bounced to her feet.

Ben jumped up a beat later. "What's going on?"

She waved him off. Then sighed. "Yes, that's Ben. We were about to rehearse the show . . ."

Jocelyn listened more while Ben's frustration started climbing.

"I don't think that's a good idea—" Jocelyn cut off. Then

blew out through her nose, then jumped in again. "Because we're filming in a few hours, Ilse, and—"

Frustration notched up a level to worry. What was Ilse saying?

"I'm sorry, but—" Jocelyn sucked in a sharp breath. "You're *where?*"

"Where is she?" he asked.

She didn't answer. Instead, she surged around him to go to the window, jerking back the white lacy curtains to look outside. Right behind her, Ben looked over her shoulder. Sure enough, a black SUV was turning onto the drive leading up to the house right that moment.

That better not be what he thought. "Ilse's not in that car, is she?"

"Ilse, this is a terrible idea . . ." Jocelyn put a hand to her forehead. "Fine. I'll send Ben out."

She hung up and, head tipped forward, didn't look at him. "Jocelyn—"

"Ilse's arriving downstairs right now. Can you bring her up here?"

He'd figured out that much. "Why is she here now? Doesn't she realize—"

"Let's hash it out with her. Maybe she has a good reason." Jocelyn still wasn't looking at him.

What he wanted to do was pull her into his arms and hug her until she stopped looking so lost. Until she'd look him in the eyes again. Did Ilse not realize what her behavior was doing to her sister? Her sister who'd worked so hard and worried so hard to take Ilse's place for these shows.

What he did was nod. "I'll be right back."

He made his way down to the first level and out the front door to the circular drive where guests were dropped off. He pulled up at the sight of a second car pulling down the drive. One that suspiciously looked like one of the crew's rentals.

Sure enough, Margot was in the driver's seat. Bringing their guest-star singer to the set.

What were the odds on this timing?

Ilse was just stepping onto the snowy drive. She spotted him, her face pinching in visible anger, and snapped, "You and I have a *lot* to discuss."

Ben ignored her and ran down the stairs to the driver who'd brought her, whipping out his wallet at the same time. He handed the man a bill and said, "Pretend you're a ride-share driver. Leave, and come back with her luggage in twenty minutes. Pull around the back of the house and I'll meet you at the back door to unload it."

The man looked at the bills in his hand, back up at Ben, then nodded. "You got it, boss."

"Hey!" Ilse protested as the driver got back in the car and revved the engine. "My—"

Ben scooted to her side, stopping her with a hand on her arm. "The car behind you is Margot with Quentin Jorgen in tow. He's our guest-star singer today since you have nodules."

"I do not—"

He'd had enough already. "Either play along or I tell everyone who's really been filming these live shows."

He wouldn't. He'd never hurt Jocelyn that way, not to mention his own career opportunity. He didn't give Ilse enough time to reason that out, though, deliberately raising his voice as Ilse's car pulled away and the people in the car parked behind opened their doors. "Did you get the costume?"

Ilse frowned. "I—"

Ben lifted his gaze and froze, everything around him going dead quiet as blood rushed to his head. If it had been snowing at that moment, even the snowflakes in the air would have come to a stop.

He swore under his breath, and, her back still turned to the other car, Ilse stiffened. "I don't appreciate—"

Ignoring her, Ben lifted a hand. "Herbert. What brings you all the way to our remote location?"

Ilse sucked in a sharp breath and spun on one heel to face not only Herbert and Quentin but three other execs getting out of the car. At least she had the wherewithal to stop acting the way she had been. "Yes," she called, switching to sweetly pleasant in the bat of false eyelashes. "This is a lovely surprise."

Herbert's sharp-eyed gaze darted between them. "Why was Ilse being dropped off at this time in the morning?"

Ilse opened her mouth, but Ben beat her to it. "We had a problem with one of the caroling costumes at the last minute, and she was dropping it off at a local seamstress who said she could fix it before we go live this evening."

Beside him, his cohost made a small hum of agreement, nodding her head.

"And Margot was busy picking us up," Herbert murmured, more to himself. "But why wasn't somebody else on the crew taking care of that?"

Good question. And the fact that it was Ilse doing the errand made it even more suspicious.

Ilse plunked her hands on her hips, pulling a dainty frown that everybody standing in front of Weber Haus recognized as the signal that her temper was brewing. Ben could almost feel the men before him take a mental step back.

"You think I can't be helpful?" she demanded.

For the first time since meeting her, Ben questioned whether or not she was putting on an act. He knew she was, to a certain extent, because of the situation. But was she really irritated in this moment, or was she using her famous diva reputation to deflect the conversation?

He honestly couldn't tell. But Jocelyn had him questioning

the truth in a way he never had before. A small part of him even wanted to smile. Like he was in on the joke.

"Of course you can be helpful." Herbert rushed to assure his star. Then he glanced around as if he was searching for any other topic in the world. Something that might head off a full-blown tantrum from her. "Do you two have time to give us a tour of the property?"

"Of course," Ilse said, just as Ben said, "Not really."

They glanced at each other, and Ben cleared his throat. "We were about to rehearse the script," Ben pointed out in his best reasonable-producer voice.

He could tell the second Ilse remembered she was angry with him and Jocelyn. She tipped her head in a move that put him in mind of the movie *The Exorcist*. "But these folks have flown all this way, Ben," she said through a gritted-toothed smile.

Through equally gritted teeth, he replied, "We have a lot to talk through."

"We'll get Walter to walk us around," Herbert assured them both, flapping a hand.

Again, Ben found himself questioning Ilse's true feelings. Had she done that just to get the exec to let them off the hook, rather than creating excuses? At least this group were used to seeing Ben and Ilse's version of "polite" arguing. This was normal.

They all bundled inside together, and Ben deliberately hung back, whipping out his phone to text Jocelyn: **Herbert and team showed up out of the blue. They saw Ilse. Do NOT show your face anywhere.**

Not that he expected her to come downstairs looking for them, even though they were taking a while. His girl had more common sense than that. Unlike her sister, who never should have shown her face here, and definitely not without a warning.

It took another twenty minutes to get the bigwigs all set up with Walter, who looked beyond thrilled to have them there.

As soon as they were out of earshot, Ben took off toward the stairs in the foyer. "Come on."

By the time they got to the next set of stairs leading up to the third story, after checking that Jocelyn's room was empty, Ilse was complaining. "Where on earth are you taking me? Are you going to stuff me in the attic until the last show is done, like Mr. Rochester's wife or something?"

"We're going to where we rehearse, of course." He picked his words carefully. Not that anybody else was staying up here. But he didn't want to take the chance of being overheard.

The second he opened the door to the bedroom, he braced, expecting Ilse to light right into both of them. Instead, Jocelyn shot up from where she was sitting on the bed, hurried across the room, and threw her arms around her sister's neck, squeezing Ilse tight.

As Ben shut the door behind them quietly, he couldn't miss the way Ilse stiffened hard in a knee-jerk reaction, almost like she was going to reject her twin's hug. But, after a brief hesitation, her arms went around Jocelyn, and she sort of melted into her sister. Not a full defrosting. More like a deep snowbank slowly dwindling on a suddenly warm and bright day.

"Are you okay?" Jocelyn mumbled.

Ilse's shoulders moved up and down in a long, albeit silent, inhale and exhale. Then she let go of Jocelyn and straightened, expression turning chillier by the second. Ben almost shivered.

If he hadn't seen it with his own eyes, he never would have believed that all that tantrum throwing, and hard businesswoman, and heartless-human-being stuff Ilse did, had always been posturing. A wall built so thick and high around her that only Jocelyn could get through.

How had somebody with those walls managed to create a show like *Home & Hearth*?

Or was the real Ilse the person she showed to the watching public?

"What in the name of all things holiday disaster have you done to my show?" Ilse was looking at Jocelyn as she said that, but then turned a wrathful gaze on Ben.

Jocelyn mouthed, "I'm sorry," at him from behind her sister.

Ben stared. Now, having them side by side together, he honestly wondered how the hell he'd missed the switch those first days here.

They were *nothing* alike.

"Answer me, Ben," Ilse snapped.

It was so tempting to revert back to the relationship he'd had with her right up until the day he'd figured out Jocelyn was standing in. And he wanted to jump right in with something along the lines of, "Have you seen the stats? They're way up."

But he didn't.

Instead he looked at Jocelyn, pleading with her to understand that he wasn't throwing her under the Ilse bus. "You'll take it all better from your sister, I think."

Ilse shook her head. "I should have known you were a coward."

"That's not fair." Jocelyn jumped right in. "We'd have been found out for sure if it wasn't for Ben."

"I doubt that. He's been angling to get me out since—"

Jocelyn took Ilse by the hands. "Sweetie. Why don't you sit down so we can talk through this? There's a lot you don't know."

Ilse didn't budge. "I don't want to sit down." Tugging out of Jocelyn's grip, she crossed her arms and set her foot to tapping against the hardwood floor.

Jocelyn gave Ben a look that basically was her version of, "I give up."

But she sat on the bed all the same. "Well . . . it all started the day Herbert called me into his office."

The foot tapping stopped, and Ilse straightened. "When was this?"

"The same day you left for the Philippines."

Ben jumped in. "It was to tell her . . . or you rather . . . that we were going to change the format of the live shows, and that you needed to collaborate with me."

Ilse's expression transformed into something so chilling, even Jack Frost would envy her, and at the same time Jocelyn cringed. That had been the exact wrong thing to say.

"I *knew* it." Ilse stabbed him in the chest with a single finger. Which really hurt because of the perfectly manicured, long, and very pointy-tipped nail. "I *knew* you were after my show."

"He's not."

"I'm not." He and Jocelyn spoke at the same time.

Ilse glanced between them, then scowled. "Oh my God. He's really got you fooled, hasn't he? That soft heart of yours—"

Jocelyn shook her head. "Ilse—"

Enough was enough. "I'm not taking your show. They want to give me my own show."

She sneered. "And canceling mine so they can replace it—"

"One that won't compete in the slightest, I assure you."

She narrowed her eyes. "I don't believe you."

"Ilse, that's enough," he snapped.

Ilse breathed in hard through her nose, then out through her mouth. "We need to get Jocelyn out of the house."

He and Jocelyn both startled at that, Jocelyn coming to her feet. "Why?"

"I'm here now. I'll do the show today. Let's focus on getting me up to speed. We can talk about all this"—she waved a hand between them—"when it's over."

They both stared at her, stupefied.

"At the last minute? Are you actively trying to ruin your career?" Ben demanded.

"I'm trying to save it," she insisted. "With the execs here in person . . . my timing is lucky, I guess. It should be me."

Actually. She was right. This was her show. She was here. She was a professional. "You're right."

"Ilse, I don't think—" Jocelyn cut herself off to jerk her gaze to Ben. "What?"

"She's right. It's her show. Her call."

Ilse narrowed her eyes. "Exactly."

"But I'm ready—"

Ben shook his head. "She's done this so much, she'll pick it up fast."

Jocelyn's face fell.

He wasn't expecting it, and the impact felt like a kick to the gut.

He wanted to say more. To hug her because she suddenly looked like she needed one. But Ilse wouldn't like that and would want explanations. They needed to focus on finishing this last show. Talking could come later.

"All right," Jocelyn finally agreed, the words drawn out like she still wasn't certain she'd heard them both correctly. "But I'm not leaving. There are too many people. I'll stay in here until tomorrow after all the crew leave."

Ilse was nodding. "I think that's best."

Ben disagreed. "You can't—"

Jocelyn turned to him. "Just send Sophie up. She can feed me. I have my phone, but I need my charger. Other than that, I'll be fine."

"Who's Sophie?" Ilse asked.

Jocelyn waved her off. "The hotel manager. She's aware of who I really am."

"Geez, Jocelyn. Who doesn't know at this point?"

Ben rounded on her. "Given the way you dumped your entire career in your sister's lap, I suggest you be a little more grateful."

Ilse jutted her chin out stubbornly. "I'll—"

"Margot knows," Jocelyn shot between them.

"She . . . what?" Ilse asked, blinking. "When did that happen?"

Jocelyn winced. "Not too long ago. But she wants a permanent spot on the show. I've been putting her off, but she's been doing some underhanded things." She shot an indecipherable glance in Ben's direction. "I'm pretty sure she took Angel, trying to mess up our Ice-Skating Party."

He'd known about Margot, but not the underhanded things. Several moments—glances between the women, comments Margot had made—finally fell into place. "You should have told me that part."

"I didn't want to worry you."

"Worry him?" Ilse scoffed. "Nothing worries Ben except not getting his own way."

"That's enough, Ilse," Jocelyn snapped.

And Ben had the pleasure of seeing his cohost stunned silent. Except it had taken Jocelyn using a tone he was pretty damn sure never came out of her mouth to do it. So "pleasure" was a loose term in this moment.

"I—"

"You two better get going." Jocelyn didn't let Ilse finish. "Find somewhere else to rehearse so no one looks for you up here. Okay?"

Then, before he could object, Jocelyn hustled both of them right out the door, closing it in their faces.

Ilse stared at it for a second, still in a way he'd never seen her before.

Ben sighed. "You owe her. Big-time."

And I thought the last few Christmases had been adventures . . .

I had followed Ben and Ilse upstairs when I saw them downstairs and could instantly tell she wasn't Jocelyn. From the hallway, I'd heard everything. I still can't wrap my head around how Jocelyn's sister showed back up, and Jocelyn is hiding, and Ben and Ilse are going to do the show together instead.

Evening is turning everything outside to shades of purple and I know they're about to start filming, so all the cast and crew, except Jocelyn, are gathered outside in the area of the shops.

"Has anyone seen Angel?" Isaac asks.

"Good grief, man," Walter snaps. "Can't you keep tabs on your own cat?"

I glance around. Margot isn't here either.

I take off running for the hotel wing, but a quick search shows neither of them there. So I head to the house, making my way up floor by floor. I'm not quite up the stairs to the third floor when I hear a sound.

My ears prick and flick as I catch a hint of what sounds like a pathetic squeak. A familiar sound, but I can't place it. It could be an animal. But it could also be. . . . Is Jocelyn crying? I hurry to the bedroom where I know she's been hiding all day. I'm about to paw at it to get her to let me in.

Until I catch the sound of Margot's voice.

I know I've been looking for her and Angel, but I really wasn't expecting them to be here. What's she doing up here?

My kitty instincts are prickling.

Another murmur of her voice and it hits me that she's not up here. She's even higher . . . in the attic. Then I definitely catch a kitty growl, which sends up the fur on my back. That is a scared growl, not a vicious growl. Kitties know the difference when we hear it. A survival mechanism, I'm sure.

I crouch low to the ground and slowly creep closer to the attic door.

"I know you don't like me after I stole you away last time," Margot is saying. To Angel, I guess. "But you don't like Jocelyn, so work with me on this. I'm going to keep you up here and release you at the opportune time—"

She's going to unleash the hell cat? But does she know Ilse and Jocelyn switched back? Either way, she's trying to ruin things for them.

What a . . .

I don't like to use bad human language, but right now I'm tempted.

Not on my watch, she's not going to hurt either of them.

It's a good thing the attic door has that new keypad lock. It's so when people stay in the third-floor rooms, they don't go up to the attic. I may not be able to unlock those suckers, but I *can* lock them. All I have to do is push the lock button.

It takes five tries for me to jump just right, but I hit the keypad, and the thing beeps, a red light flashing, and then makes the most satisfying sound ever—the bolt of the lock sliding into place.

"What was that?" I hear Margot ask.

Then the sound of feet running down the steep wooden stairs from the attic to the door at this level.

"Oh no!" She's on the other side of the door.

That's followed by the sound of the doorknob rattling, then beeps as she tries to enter a code that works. But she doesn't have the number password and won't be able to unlock it from the inside. After a second there's a loud thump. "Help—"

She cuts herself off and I smirk to myself. Because how would she ever explain why she's locked in the attic with Angel?

Good luck getting out of that!

This is when it would be handy to have hands, so I could brush them together like humans do. One problem handled. Done and dusted.

Chapter 22

Jocelyn really wished the room she was hiding in had a window that faced the back rather than the front of the house. All the filming tonight was happening at the shops, and those were on the other side of the house. Which meant she couldn't see a thing.

Night had fallen, and a fresh blanket of snow sparkled in the bright white glow of the Christmas lights that decorated the outside of the house. Cars had stopped arriving a while ago, the production crew limiting the number of shoppers allowed in during filming.

Checking her watch, she made a squeak, because the show was about to start.

Hurrying over, she flopped onto the bed, but immediately had to steady the plate of untouched food on the bedside table after she knocked it a bit. Food crisis averted, she unlocked her phone, which was already set to the TV-station app she'd downloaded years ago so Jocelyn could watch Ilse's program, which usually came on during the working day, while she was at her job.

The top of the hour came, and then it went, and no matter how many times she refreshed, the show didn't start.

Was there a problem? Had they been found out? What was going on?

She was on her feet, pacing and refreshing over and over, until, suddenly, the introduction rolled with the intro music and all. And then . . . there they were. Ilse and Ben. Filling up her screen.

Her heart contracted at the sight of him.

He wanted to do the show with Ilse.

That shouldn't hurt. Logically she knew it shouldn't. But it had. It still did. Even though she'd had all day to talk herself into all the reasons he was right. It was Ilse's show. The execs were there as witnesses. It wasn't that Ben actually wanted to be with Ilse or anything, or that he didn't want to be with Jocelyn.

But it hadn't been until the moment he'd agreed that Ilse should do it that Jocelyn had realized that . . . somewhere along the line . . . she'd started to enjoy it.

She'd liked the entire process of coming up with the ideas, and jointly working with the crew to bring it to life, of practicing the script, and even being on TV. She'd actually been looking forward to this final episode.

She had not seen that twist coming.

But even heavier was the realization that the reason she liked it was because she'd done all of that with Ben. Every second with him had been . . . fun. An adventure. And she'd started to feel as though even the time shared on camera with millions watching, was just the two of them.

But it wasn't.

This was his job. His and Ilse's. And now that her sister was back, Jocelyn had no part in it. She would go back to her basement hovel of an office and her life. Except she loved her job. She should be thrilled that this was over. All those worries, and they'd pulled it off. They'd actually pulled it off.

She ran a finger over Ben's image on the screen, then snorted in irritation when she inadvertently paused the streaming. Starting it back up, she settled in to watch.

"Good grief, she's so much better at this than I am," she muttered not five minutes in.

And of course that would be true. Ilse had been doing this for years after having come up through the TV industry. That she would be smoother, more flowy, and more charming was a given.

No wonder Ben had eagerly jumped on Ilse's return.

Forty minutes in, Jocelyn had stopped holding her breath. No one had called them out on the switch, and the show . . .

Jocelyn sat up straighter, actually bringing the phone closer to her face. All dressed up in Victorian-era garb, her sister had decided to sing with Quentin, who'd agreed to a duet. They were standing on the gazebo at the center of the shops, no instrumental music, just their voices. But that wasn't what caught Jocelyn's attention.

Was it her imagination or was Ilse actually more herself right now?

More like the sister she knew who could laugh easily and enjoy the things she was showing the viewers. Who got joy out of singing. She was almost glowing.

Why?

Bang!

Jocelyn was off the bed in a flash, heart pounding against the inside of her ribs. "What was that?"

Another bang, and she flew to the door, but didn't open it, instead, pressing her ear to it to listen. No one was supposed to be up here except her. Was someone breaking into the house while the filming had emptied it out?

Crack. Slam. Thump.

Jocelyn threw a hand over her mouth to hold in a scream, her body freezing so hard her muscles hurt.

Someone had just broken something. It sounded like a door had been busted open.

She glanced at the lock on the door she was standing in

front of. If they were busting in doors, was it worth locking this one? She bit her lip. Would they hear her lock it?

Better than letting them just walk right in.

She hurriedly clicked the lock, wincing at the *tink* of sound. *What next?*

Turning toward the window, she was considering climbing out that way—trying to convince herself a three-story drop to snow-covered ground wasn't that bad—when a new sound reached her from the hallway. The sound of a woman's voice. A familiar voice.

Margot.

Jocelyn pressed her ear to the door, listening hard.

First came the sound of tromping, angry footsteps, along with muttered words she couldn't quite catch, until Margot passed directly by the door. Then she heard just fine.

"If they think they can shut me up, they've got another think coming."

What on earth?

Carefully, not wanting to alert Margot that she was there, Jocelyn unlocked the door and, cringing, cranked the handle slowly over before inching it open a crack to see Margot disappearing into the stairwell that led to the next floor down. Right on her heels was a white fluff of a cat.

Not Snowball though. Angel.

Jocelyn stepped into the hallway and looked to her left, only to gasp, then slap her hand over her mouth again, because that had been too loud. But it looked as if Margot had taken an axe—"Here's Johnny" in *The Shining*–style—to one of the bedroom doors. Or . . . on second thought, looking beyond the wreckage and seeing more stairs leading up, apparently to the attic door.

"What was she doing in the attic?" Jocelyn whispered to herself. Then sucked in a breath. "What am I doing standing here?"

She bolted for the stairs. Because no matter what Margot was doing, she was clearly about to do something worse. Probably to Ilse.

Jocelyn saw no sign of the woman on the second floor and shot down the back stairs, coming out in the kitchen to bowl right into a solid, man-sized wall in her way.

"I'm so sorry. I—"

She looked right up into Theo's deep brown eyes. "You're here!"

He didn't bother answering that. "What's wrong?"

It came spilling out as fast as she could summarize—Ilse in the middle of filming and an angry Margot busting down attic doors and heading off to do bad things.

Theo grabbed her hand. "Come on."

But Jocelyn pulled up against him. "I can't be seen."

"Right," he muttered. Then—having clearly just arrived— put the backpack slung over his shoulder on the ground and proceeded to fish out and dress her in an oversized sweatshirt and a baseball cap, telling her to tuck her hair up under.

He eyed her narrowly. "That'll have to do."

Together they ran out the door in the direction of the shops.

I'm watching the end of the filming from a spot up in a tree that gives me a great view. So far so good.

Until I see a streak of white fluff hurry past underneath me. Angel! Followed by Margot of all people.

Oh no! They got out of the attic!

I leap to the ground and run after them both, passing Margot as I try to catch up to Angel, who is headed directly at the gazebo and the filming crew.

Ben stood on the gazebo in the middle of the Weber Haus shops, looking out over the crowd enjoying the caroling show. After Ilse and Quentin's duet, they'd gathered Ben and the carolers, who were regulars in the shops at Christmas, to sing a song.

Almost home free.

They'd done everything. All they had to do was finish this song and say goodbye until the new year when *Home & Hearth* would be back in the studio at their regular time.

No one had blinked an eye at the "different" Ilse. And actually, maybe the professional in her had come out to play, because beyond a few dirty looks as she'd learned each change and the format for the show, she'd gone along. Too late to change it.

Ben glanced over to where Walter was positioned with the camera, and beyond him to the line of execs standing, arms crossed, faces if not wreathed in smiles, at least bearing pleasant expressions.

Did we really pull this off?

Because as soon as filming wrapped, the crew would break it all down and pack up. They'd already had dinner before the show, so it would be off to bed, and then head out to the airport in the morning with Ilse in tow. Ben would make sure Jocelyn, who would have to stay hidden and stay behind, would have a way to get home before he had to leave too.

They finished the song and Ilse turned to him with a smile he almost mistook for sincere. "You actually have a nice voice, Ben."

"Well, thank you—"

A streak of white bolted up onto the stage. With a gasp and a smile, and without missing a beat, Ilse stooped over and cried, "Angel. There you are! It wouldn't be a show without you."

The word "no!" was on the tip of his tongue and he even took a step toward her to stop her from reaching for the cat, who was probably going to go ballistic on her at any second. Except another streak of white let out a kitty challenge of doom and ran up on stage.

Snowball.

She plowed right into Angel. In a frenzy of snarls, claws, teeth, and yowls, the two cats went at it. The gazebo erupted in chaos for a moment as every human either tried to get out of the way or tried to step in to separate the two animals.

Ilse finally managed to scoop Angel up in her arms. Angel, who immediately snuggled into her.

What was with that cat?

Ben managed, around his shock, to pick up Snowball.

"There are two Angels?" A bemused Quentin seemed to be the only one able to come up with words. "I've been watching this show for years and had no idea."

"No," Ben said. "This one is the cat who lives here at Weber Haus. Her name is Snowball."

"Oh." Quentin glanced between the two cats. "Is she the one who kept attacking Ilse then?"

End this. They needed to end this now.

Ilse must've had the same thought because she said, "Unfortunately, we are all out of time. Then she turned to their guest. "Thank you so much again for joining us tonight, Quentin. It made it so special for us here at *Home & Hearth*."

"My pleasure," the younger man murmured, still looking slightly stunned. "I'd be happy to come back for a visit anytime."

Ilse glanced at Ben, who was just standing there, cuddling Snowball, and trying to think. Right. It was his turn.

Ben looked at the camera. "Thank you so much for joining us this month for all our holiday-themed parties. We hope you had as much fun as we did. Now go celebrate the season with your loved ones. We will too—"

"Stop the show!" a female voice shouted. But from far enough off that he couldn't pinpoint where she was. Everyone around the shops, who'd been quiet for the wrap-up, looked around with expressions of confusion and concern.

Walter circled a finger for Ben to finish his line.

"We'll see you in the new year, back in the studio and—"

"She's a fake," the voice yelled. One he recognized now. Margot. "That's not the real Ilse."

Ben rushed through the rest. "Have a very happy holiday!"

He waved. Ilse waved. Everyone on the stage took their cue and also waved, even though he could feel the confusion radiating from them.

"And we're out," Walter called.

It took everything he had to keep from collapsing in relief. They'd managed to keep the looming disaster off the air at the very least.

But it was still looming.

Handing Snowball to Lukas, who'd run to the stage when the cats were fighting, Ben took Ilse by the hand.

"Wait." She tugged against him, only to turn and give Angel over to Isaac.

Then, together, they headed down the stairs. Two steps down, he happened to look across the crowd and clocked Theo purposefully plowing through the crowds in the same direction. When had he got back?

Ben faltered on the next step as he caught sight of Jocelyn—at least he thought it was her in a frumpy sweatshirt and baseball cap—hanging back at the edge of the shops.

"What are you waiting for?" Ilse demanded.

Jocelyn, meanwhile, pointed off to her right and mouthed, "Margot."

So that had been Margot shouting those things. Hell. This was about to go down and probably get ugly on the way.

"That woman is a fraud." Margot appeared at Herbert's side before Ben could get there, pointing right at Ilse.

Ben and Ilse rushed over, Ilse scowling, and for the first time in his life Ben was happy to let his cohost throw her weight around, diva style. "What the hell are you talking about, Margot?" she snapped. Then she turned to Herbert. "She's been demanding that I put her on the show and got ugly when I refused. So I fired her. She's talking nonsense."

"You can't fire me," Margot—who hadn't cottoned on to who she was talking to—scoffed. "Your sister would never let you. She relies on me."

"Not that much, I don't." Ilse's chin went up. "I value loyalty above all things."

Margot slowly closed her mouth, eyes narrowed as she searched the face in front of her. "You're Ilse," she said. Accused.

"Of course this is Ilse," Ben snapped.

"What is going on?" Herbert was looking between all three of them and starting to get a little red in the face.

Margot snorted, then shook her head, gaze trained on Ilse. "You're going to fire me? After everything I've done for you?"

"I paid you well," Ilse pointed out. "And apparently you only did those things for you."

"That's how this industry works." Margot crossed her arms, then turned to Herbert. "Since I'm fired anyway . . ."

Ben stepped forward. "Herbert, let's let Ilse deal with this, and the rest of us can head inside."

The exec actually turned with him, but Margot rushed into speech before they got more than a step away. "You need to know that until tonight, the person doing the live shows wasn't Ilse but her twin sister, Jocelyn."

Herbert jerked to a stop in his tracks, then spun back to Margot. "Explain," he barked.

"She's just trying to make trouble," Ilse insisted.

"I have proof," Margot crowed. Then pulled out her phone, flicked at the screen for a second before holding it up for Herbert to see.

Ben too.

He winced at the sight of Jocelyn in the kitchen working

on the pretzels. The video was taken through a crack in the door, and she was the only one in the shot.

"I've almost got it," Jocelyn said, obviously talking to Emily, who was off camera, or possibly this was when they'd been doing the pretzels by phone.

Ben tried to remember what she said next. Did they at any point say anything about Ilse as if she wasn't there? "Another five minutes. I refuse to let Ilse down."

Everyone in hearing distance around them gasped.

Ben grimaced. And there it was.

Walter entered by the kitchen through the other door, coming into frame, which is where Margot stopped the video. "There's a little more, but that's enough for proof. She wouldn't talk about herself in the third person that way. Not unless . . ."

"That was the sister," Herbert muttered. Then went silent as a self-satisfied smirk spread across Margot's face.

Herbert's face then started turning purple.

Not good. Very not good.

Ben glanced at Ilse, who seemed frozen, tied to the train tracks by her own actions and decisions as the freight train barreled down on her.

"You're fired," Herbert said in a dangerously soft voice.

"Serves you right," Margot crooned.

Herbert shot the PA a narrow-eyed glared so hard she stopped talking. "You too. You obviously recorded that as blackmail to get on the show."

Ben had never thought of the exec as stupid, but the man was sharper than he let on.

"But I—"

"Get out of here before I decide to bring Legal into this."

Margot's lips pressed together so hard that they almost disappeared, the skin around the edges turning white. "You can't do this. I'm exposing her fraud—" She stabbed a finger in Ilse's direction. "You can't—"

"Get her out of here." Herbert issued the order to no one in particular, but two of the crew stepped forward and led a loudly protesting Margot away.

Which was when Herbert swung around to stare at Ilse. "The Philippines. That *was* you, and not years ago. While you were supposed to be *here*. Fulfilling your contract."

There was nothing Ilse could say. She closed her eyes and took a long breath. "I'm sorry—"

"It's too late." Herbert cut her off abruptly. Then cut his gaze to Ben. "Did you know about this?"

"No. He didn't," a voice rang out.

The crowd around them parted to reveal Jocelyn standing there.

Ben's heart squeezed so hard he almost put his hand over it. Jocelyn was here and she was stepping in. He already knew why, but he couldn't let her throw herself at Herbert's mercy. Not for him. He'd made his choices.

She was amazing. Truly. Because he knew her, and Jocelyn wasn't a confrontational person. But for her sister, and now for him, she was standing up to a man with a lot of power in an industry she worked in tangentially. She was too smart not to realize that.

Ben shook his head at her, but after a tiny shrug that he knew was an apology just for him, she pulled the cap off her head and marched straight for Herbert. "The only person who found out was Margot," she insisted. Then, as if she'd remembered the video, hurriedly tacked on, "And Emily, one of the owners of Weber Haus, who was helping me with baking. Ben had no idea."

Herbert stared at her, then without turning his head said, "Is that true, Ben?"

"I—"

"Everyone knows Ben and Ilse don't really get along." Jocelyn cut him off. "Do you think he'd actually go along with something like this?"

Based on Herbert's pursed-lipped, narrow-eyed scrutiny, he was still thinking that through. "He might if his own future was on the line."

The deal they'd made. Yup. The exec was definitely sharp.

Jocelyn shook her head. "My sister was heartbroken and maybe even had a mental break."

He wanted to wrap Jocelyn up in his arms and hold her tight. She was blaming her own sister—rightfully so, but still—just to save his career.

Beside him Ilse hissed like she'd been slapped across the face. "Jocelyn—"

"Ilse knew you'd be unreasonable, and the timing was terrible. But she had to do this, for her own sake. This was me and Ilse and no one else."

Herbert stared at her a little longer, but Jocelyn didn't even blink.

Then he said, "Ilse and Margot are fired. We'll dig into this more to see if anyone else will be as well."

On that he spun on his heel and marched off; the other execs towed along in his wake.

After an uncomfortably long silence following their departure, Ilse spun on Jocelyn. "How dare you take Ben's side."

The way Jocelyn blanched, he knew that hurt. He knew she'd risked that hurt for him. The thing was, he needed to do something about the fallout. Now. While Herbert hadn't had time to really think it through. At the same time, a compelling sort of desperation swept through him to take her in his arms and shield her from her sister's wrath.

"That's enough, Ilse," Theo boomed.

Ilse snapped her mouth shut, turning in the sisters' friend's direction as he stalked through the crowd. "Stay out of this, Theo."

Theo didn't stop moving. "I've stayed out of it long enough."

Ben had his answer. Theo would handle the sisters.

He cast one last glance at Jocelyn, hoping she'd look his way so she could see the regret in his eyes. But she had her head bent forward now, staring at her feet.

He couldn't wait though. He took off after Herbert and the other bigwigs.

Chapter 23

Jocelyn had never felt so drained in her entire life. She let herself into her room—hers and not the room where she'd been hiding. Ilse was probably up there now, along with Theo. Sophie had kindly offered to find them both rooms to stay in.

Honestly, Jocelyn was too much in shock to care.

Maybe because Ilse, after giving her the most hurt look her sister had ever given her, said, "I can't even talk to you right now," before walking away.

Theo had taken one glance at Jocelyn's face—she couldn't even begin to hide her own hurt—then stalked off after her sister.

She plopped into the chair that faced the windows and sighed. The heaviness in her heart and in her gut were to be expected. This had gone terribly. Ilse was fired, and they weren't speaking now, and Ben was—

Movement outside caught her eye and she got to her feet to get a better view, only to find Herbert and the other execs piling into a car. Another figure emerged from the house, and she jerked forward so fast to be sure she was seeing correctly, that she cracked her forehead into the window.

"Ouch," she muttered, rubbing at the spot, but still staring.

It wasn't until he turned to look back at the house that she knew for sure. That was Ben.

Herbert said something, and Ben responded, then got into the back seat. He was leaving.

The heaviness in her heart turned into a stone that threatened to crush her. He was leaving. Without talking to her. Without saying goodbye.

It was over.

All those kisses, those stolen moments, the way she'd felt with him. She'd believed it was real. She was sure it was real.

I guess just not real enough.

She watched, despair adding to the weight inside her, as the cars drove off into the night. She watched until she couldn't see their taillights down the road any longer.

Then she went to her bed and curled up in a ball. With a small *purrup* of sound, Snowball jumped up with her. She wasn't even sure where the cat had been since her fight with Angel. She just knew she was grateful to have the sweet little thing to snuggle into as silent tears trickled down her cheeks.

Which was where she found herself the next morning. She'd cried herself to sleep, and Snowball had stayed with her the entire night. The first rays of sunlight woke her, and the crushing weight returned with the vivid memories of what had happened.

She'd thought maybe . . .

No. It didn't matter what she'd thought. It was all over now. Ilse would have to figure herself out, and Jocelyn would return to her job and a life without Ben. Funny how fast he'd become a fixture in her days . . . and even some of her nights.

Jocelyn sighed, then forced herself out of the bed, disturbing Snowball, who lazily got to her feet and gave a long, satisfying kitty stretch and yawn before sitting down to watch Jocelyn with her head tipped as if to say, "what next?"

Exactly.

What came next was getting home. The crew would be

leaving this morning, and Ilse would take Jocelyn's place on that flight. Or rather, the real Ilse would go, since the ticket was in her name. Meanwhile, Jocelyn would book a flight for this evening if there was one, just to give plenty of buffer time between them.

A long, hot shower later, dressed and ready to go in the most casual set of Ilse's clothes she could find—jeans and a boutique-style, long-sleeved T-shirt, all sparkles and soft material in pink—she at least felt more human and less wrung-out dish rag.

She put her hands on her hips, looking around. "Margot has already been booted, so she's not here to pack for Ilse."

And Ilse was probably still too upset to do any packing. Besides, Jocelyn was still stuck in her room. Hopefully someone remembered to bring her up some breakfast.

"Better than having nothing to do like yesterday," she mumbled to herself.

Plopping one of Ilse's suitcases on the bed, careful not to startle Snowball, who was watching intently, she started packing. She was halfway through the clothes in the wardrobe when it struck her that many more of Ilse's clothes were still in Margot's room.

She shot a quick text to her sister: **I'll pack all the things in my room. Please send one of the crew to handle the stuff in Margot's room.**

No response. She wasn't expecting one. Ilse in upset mode tended to need space and time. She'd just have to trust it was getting done.

Five minutes later a knock sounded at her door and Jocelyn jumped. Then looked at Snowball, who stared back at her with wide blue eyes.

"Should I open it?" Jocelyn mouthed at the cat.

What if it was one of the crew needing to talk to Ilse?

What if they'd already seen her sister dressed one way, only to find Jocelyn dressed another—

They already know.

Jimminy Christmas, she'd forgotten that part. Or . . . not forgotten exactly, because she remembered the firing and then Ben leaving and whatnot. . . . She was just still in "keep the secret" mode after weeks.

It didn't matter who was at the door. And she could go get her own darn breakfast.

In fact, it might even be Ilse, ready to rehash everything and talk it out. Or, more likely, share her grievances. Forget that. Jocelyn had more than bent over backwards for her sister. She'd listen to her sister only if Ilse was ready to apologize.

Which was why Jocelyn strode to the door, shoulders back and purposeful, and jerked it open.

Whatever she'd been going to say stuck in her throat coming out as a strangled squeak.

Because the person knocking wasn't Ilse . . . it was Ben.

She squeaked again, shock stealing her words. Ben's expression gave away nothing as he looked back at her. When she didn't move or speak, his eyebrows crept up. "Hi."

Hi? That's what he had to say to her?

"I saw you leave last night." It was top of mind, so it might have come out a little accusatory.

"I did." He paused, glancing over her shoulder then back to her face. "Can I come in? We need to talk."

They did?

She wanted him to be here for her, to have come back for her, but she was afraid to believe that was why. Her heart was fluttering so hard, she wanted to shout *yes!* and throw her arms around him. But he was in serious mode. Was this about the show? Or Ilse's job? Or his job maybe?

"Um . . . sure." She stood back, ushering him in.

After she closed the door behind him, she took a second to breathe in and out, steady herself for whatever was coming next. She turned to face him.

"I quit." He said it quick and hard.

And it so wasn't what she was expecting that she squeaked again. "You what?!?" Then scowled. "After I saved your backside last night, you quit anyway? What the heck, Ben?"

She'd made things a thousand times worse with her sister. For *him*.

He held up both hands. "Hear me out. Quitting was a shock tactic to force Herbert to listen to me. Really listen to me, because he knows exactly how serious I am about my career. It's the lever he pulls to get me to do stuff I don't want to."

"Like *Home & Hearth*?"

He nodded. "Exactly."

He'd quit . . . and then he'd come back here to tell her? What was she missing? "What happened?"

"It worked. I shocked him into listening, and then I told them every single thing that was wrong with the show came down to them letting Ilse try to be perfect on camera all the time. Everything she does has to be just so, or she redoes it a thousand times. And God forbid a hair be out of place. But our ratings have gone way up with the live shows, and I think I know why."

"Why?" She couldn't even begin to guess, because the live shows were her, and she'd messed up so much.

"You were *real*. The fact that you would have goof-ups or get caught doing something odd or flub your lines made you relatable. But even last night's early numbers are looking good because she didn't have time to perfect everything. She was still spontaneous. She still flubbed."

"I didn't hear any flubs," Jocelyn muttered.

"I had the cues in front of me. She flubbed. And she was easier with our guest than I've ever seen her. It came across to the viewers, I think."

Jocelyn thought about that. It made sense. Ilse would hate people not thinking she was perfection personified, but it was easy to see how more relaxed and more spontaneous would be more relatable.

" 'Well . . .' " she said. " 'Nobody's perfect.' "

Ben tilted back on his heels. "You just quoted a movie at me, didn't you?"

He caught that? She allowed herself a small smile. "*Some Like It Hot.*"

"Right."

Better to keep things on track. She'd let her heart run away with hopes and dreams around this man once already. Steeling herself, she dropped the smile. "So why are you back here?"

Jocelyn was being so distant with him.

He didn't know what he'd expected when she'd opened the door. But it hadn't been this walled off, expressionless person who was watching him with a wariness he'd never seen from her before. She suddenly reminded him much more of Ilse than she ever had.

The movie quote and tiny smile gave him hope, but what if he'd messed up? Clearly, he'd messed up. Letting her lie for him, then leaving without talking to her. He'd been trying to fix everything for everyone, but what if he'd lost her in the process?

"I—"

The knock at the door sounded irritated. Then, without waiting for permission, Ilse opened it and sailed right in, saying snippily, "A text about packing my clothes is how you want to handle this?"

She cut herself off mid-tirade to stare at Ben. "What are you doing here? I thought you left." Then, before he could answer, she snapped her gaze to Jocelyn. "What's he doing in your room? It's bad enough that you took his side—"

"That's enough, Ilse." Theo spoke the commanding words from the doorway, which he was filling up with his tall frame.

Ilse spun on him. "Don't you talk to me that way."

Theo's face went from neutral to thundercloud in half a second. "I am your oldest friend, and I love you, but you would test the patience of a saint."

"Then feel free to not try for sainthood." Ilse pointed. "There's the door."

But even Ben caught the whisper of fear that crossed her features.

"Maybe you need a good lecture, that's what common sense tells me," Theo said.

"And you're the one to give it?" Ilse scoffed.

Theo just shook his head as he prowled forward. Ilse, impressively, held her ground, chin tipping up in a stubborn challenge. "No," he said. "I'm going to try a different method."

"I don't need—"

Theo reached her and jerked her into his arms. "I think you just need someone to take care of you and love you."

Ilse's eyes went wide, and she opened her mouth to speak, but Theo stopped her with a kiss. A long kiss. Jocelyn and Ben both stared on in utter astonishment as Ilse's stiffly held body gradually eased until she melted into Theo.

Jocelyn glanced over at Ben, eyes wide, and then shrugged, as if to say, "Didn't see that coming."

Theo raised his head, looking down into Ilse's eyes, and Ilse stared right back at him. They clearly needed to have a talk, but Ben needed to talk to Jocelyn more. So he said, "I brought Herbert and all the execs back with me to talk to Ilse about the show."

Blinking as if having to pull themselves out of their own world, Ilse and Theo slowly turned their heads. "You did?" Ilse asked, almost dreamy. Then snapped out of it and frowned. "What about the show?"

"Just listen to him," Jocelyn said.

Which made Ilse's scowl deepen. "You're taking his side again."

"Just listen to him for a second," Theo growled.

And to Ben's relief, Ilse closed her mouth. Then, after a second, said, "Fine. I'm listening."

Ben quickly repeated what he'd told Jocelyn, at the end of which Ilse remained quiet. Was she thinking? Angry?

"Sounds like you got your job back," Theo murmured. "You might want to go find them and at least talk about it."

Thank goodness for Theo.

Words Ben never thought he'd think. He nodded. "They're looking for her right now."

After a splash of hesitation, Ilse bolted out of the room. The first time he'd ever seen her eager about anything. The show really did mean a lot to her. Theo shook his head again, then followed at a slower pace, leaving Ben and Jocelyn alone.

Ben shut the door behind them, then turned to face her.

This time, the expression in her eyes fed his hope. Maybe he hadn't messed up. "You did all that for my sister?" she asked.

Ben shook his head. "For you."

"Me?"

With a grin, he crossed the room to tug her into his arms, looking down at her. She didn't pull away, which gave him even more hope. "There's more."

"What else could there be?"

"That Movie Party episode received the best ratings of any show in studio history. It's part of the reason they decided to come in person."

"Okay . . ." she said slowly.

"To see our chemistry."

"Our . . ." She blinked. "Oh." Then she wrinkled her brow, adorable, confused. "But if they're giving Ilse back her job, you don't have chemistry with her. Or . . . I hope you don't."

Ben chuckled. "I don't."

"Good," she muttered.

Happiness filled him up on a long inhalation. "If Ilse agrees, they suggested something else."

"What?"

"They want me to run *Home & Hearth* as the producer, not the cohost—since I could see what it needs."

Jocelyn grimaced. "Good luck with my sister."

"I'm kind of hoping that saving her job will make her like me more. Plus, as not a cohost out to steal the show from her, I'm more of an ally than an enemy." At least he hoped Ilse would see it that way.

"True." She cocked her head. "What does that have to do with our chemistry?"

"They want to start a new regular, weekly segment on the show . . ." Here was the big part. "One where you and I watch and discuss movies together."

"I . . ." She was still frowning. Why was she frowning? He thought they'd had fun on that episode. "Me as Ilse?"

Ah. "No. As Ilse's twin sister, Jocelyn, who is a movie expert."

She stared at him. When she kept staring, he gave her a little squeeze. "Jocelyn, 'Congress doesn't take this long'—"

She chuckled, then named the movie he was quoting. "*The American President.*"

But didn't say anything after that, still staring at him.

"Are you . . . interested at all?"

"I don't—" She squished her nose. Clearly debating something in her head. How could he help? "Why did you do all this?"

She didn't have to clarify. He knew what she was asking. Last night had broken her trust in their attraction, or at least his attraction for her. He'd run off, seemingly to save his own backside, dropping her like a hot potato, only to come back to save Ilse's job.

He wanted to be crystal clear. No misunderstandings. No assumptions. "Somewhere in all of this mess . . . I fell in love with you."

She gasped.

Did she really not know? "Everything I did, even risking my own career by quitting, I did because of you. Because I couldn't stand to see you hurting."

"You did?"

He nodded. "I'm also right about the show and Ilse, and it all worked out. But I was prepared to walk away. Start all over."

"For me?" she whispered. Like she still wasn't quite believing this.

Ben nodded.

"But . . ."

What was going through her head?

"But I can't craft, or sing . . ."

"Or cook," he reminded her.

Which made her frown, and he grinned. "And none of that matters, because I fell in love with you. *You*. Not who you were pretending to everyone else to be. Because with me, I don't think you were ever pretending. Even in the beginning."

"I wasn't," she whispers. "I . . . couldn't."

That's all he needed to hear.

Ben lowered his head and kissed her. Long and satisfying. Heart to heart. Happiness blooming and growing until he could hardly contain it. He lifted his head, sucking in a sharp breath at the same happiness in Jocelyn's eyes reflecting right back at him.

"I fell in love with you too," she rushed to tell him. Then turned bright red.

All that happiness burst inside him, and Ben threw his head back on a laugh. Then dropped his forehead to hers. "What a Christmas."

Epilogue

A very pregnant Sophie is holding me, Daniel at her side. Miss Tilly and Mr. Muir, Lara and Peter, Emily and Lukas, who is holding their baby, are all with us. We all stand off to the side of the "set," which is the gazebo in the shops again. It's a year later and the *Home & Hearth* crew are back at Weber Haus for another round of live holiday shows, kicking off the first one today.

Ilse, who I didn't get to know well last year, is one of my favorite new people. She is clearly a cat person if even Angel snuggled with her, and she pets and snuggles me every chance she gets. Thank heavens they didn't bring the devil cat back though. Which is why we are all standing here.

Ilse is opening the first show now.

"And I'd like to share a very happy announcement to get us started." She holds out a hand to someone off screen. A nervous-looking Theo moves from where he's standing beside Lara and me and goes up the gazebo steps to take Ilse's hand. "Theo and I got married last week in a small, intimate ceremony."

Ilse holds up her left hand, showing off her rings. She no longer wears the big diamond that caused such a ruckus last year.

I am so happy that she and Theo worked out. She's glowing. So is he, actually, even around the visible nerves at being on live TV. I'm just glad I wasn't wrong about the right person for Jocelyn after all.

"And yes," Ilse says, "of course, my sister was there. Speaking of which . . . she and Ben are here with us and will be sharing a Christmas movie on each and every one of our live shows."

Ben and Jocelyn hop up on the gazebo stage with Ilse and Theo and wave.

Ilse grins right into the camera. "And while happiness is in the air . . ." She and Theo step back, giving Ben and Jocelyn center stage.

Immediately Ben goes down on one knee, whipping out a ring. I am so thrilled that I can't even stand it. I don't even hear what he says as I leap from Lara's arms and sprint up to where they are, meowing happily and winding around both of them.

Another couple so very happily matched. I just have to be part of this moment with them. Although, for some odd reason, both Ben and Jocelyn burst out laughing.

Ben said it last year, and I think it's even more true this year. *What a Christmas!*

CHRISTMAS PARTY IDEAS

These are the five parties that Jocelyn, Ben, and Ilse focused their live *Home & Hearth* shows around. Even though not a lot made it into the story, I actually did a ton of research for each individual party, and thought I'd share the ideas in case you'd love to try one (or all, if you're ambitious) of them!

STOCKING STUFFER PARTY

A stocking stuffer party is a party where you invite guests over to snack, relax, and stuff stockings together!

The host will provide several generic stocking stuffers for communal use (quantity dependent on the number of guests). Each guest will be asked to bring 5–10 of the same item, all gifts under $10, also for communal use. In addition, everyone may bring one more personal gift to go into each specific stocking they will be stuffing.

To the tune of upbeat Christmas music, everyone will gather around the stations. The first station provides a generic stocking along with crafting materials to decorate the stockings (or guests may bring personalized stockings with them). After that there are stations to select up to ten items to go into the stockings. A wrapping station to wrap three items for each stocking.

The host will also provide fun in the form of party-themed

food and music, and finally a box for each person to lay their stockings in to take them home.

Enjoy stuffing the stockings together!

Suggested Details
Music: upbeat Christmas tunes
Decorations: general holiday décor!
Alcoholic Beverage: Driven Snow (white chocolate liqueur, white rum, ginger liqueur, finely crushed candy canes for the rim)
Nonalcoholic Beverage: white hot chocolate with a candy cane
Food: appetizers and finger foods for all to enjoy as they wish during the party
caprese bites
beer brat bites
pigs in a blanket wreath
German meatballs with mustard gravy
sweet potato bites
French dip sliders
assorted fruit tray with sweet dip
marzipan shaped into Christmas stockings
chocolate and almond petit fours
Parting Gifts: Everyone makes a stocking for one person at the party (draw names ahead of time).
Great Options for Stuffers:
For Adults
sleep mask
lip balm, lotion, hand sanitizer
gloves or socks
pocket planner
bookmark
personalized pencil set
stain stick
tissues

multitool or pocketknife
lotion or other toiletries
small organizers
wallet
bath bombs
seasonal nail wraps
For Kids
small toys
car or pocket sized games
small crafts
fidgets
small instrument (like a harmonica)
For Fun
temporary tattoo pack
Mad Libs
tie-dyed sneaker laces
Traditional
orange
a bag of gold (or chocolate wrapped in gold foil) coins
Food Items
individually wrapped chocolates
candy canes
local treats or candies
candied nuts
novelty mints (snowman poop)
novelty chocolates (lumps of coal)

TOY DRIVE PARTY

A toy drive party is a party where everyone invited brings a handful of brand-new, unopened toys and items to donate to families in need. While enjoying each other's company, great food provided by the host, and holiday tunes, everyone will wrap the gifts and label them appropriately by age/gender (if needed), or other designations.

These can be generic gifts that will be dropped off in conjunction with a larger organization's toy drive. OR, there are many ways and organizations through which to adopt one or more families. Make sure if you adopt a family, that you inform guests of the family's specific needs, so that the items purchased and brought will meet those requests.

Suggested Details
Music: upbeat Christmas tunes
Decorations: general holiday décor! OR . . . consider putting out toy-like decorations like nutcrackers and stuffed animals.
Alcoholic Beverage: The Nutcracker (vanilla vodka, Frangelico, almond milk, whipped cream, nutmeg, cinnamon)
Nonalcoholic Beverage: hot apple cider
Food: You don't want to risk getting the toys or wrapping dirty, so we suggest snacky foods that are easy to eat away from the wrapping room. Have everyone bring a holiday-themed dish with that in mind!
Parting Gifts: No parting gifts. This party is about the family/families you'll be lending a helping hand to this holiday season.

CHRISTMAS MOVIE PARTY

Get your nearest and dearest together to enjoy a holiday movie (or a movie marathon) and theme your party around your selection(s)!!!

Suggested Details
Music: songs from the movie you're watching or from any/all the holiday movies listed below, but only while the movie isn't on

Decorations: You could have fun with the decorations, bringing in the movie theme alongside your usual holiday décor. Things like stringing popcorn on your tree, or something that matches the movie you'll be watching could be fun! Or go to a party store and get movie-themed decorations!

Alcoholic Beverage: Have fun and theme a specialized alcoholic beverage to the movie (or one of the movies) you'll be watching. A few examples might be:

Ovaltine chocolate martini (*A Christmas Story*)

Cousin Eddie's Eggnog (*Christmas Vacation*)

Check out a few more Christmas movie and beverage pairings: https://www.thrillist.com/drink/christmas-movie-cocktail-pairings

Nonalcoholic Beverage: Try to do a version of any of the above without the alcohol. The eggnog is a good one for that!

Food: Be sure to theme your food around the movie(s) you select to watch! Here are some fun examples:

Gourmet popcorn of different kinds

Snowballs

Elf inspired hot chocolate charcuterie board

Kevin McAllister's ice cream sundae bar

Ralphie's Oh Fudge

Santa hat strawberries

Rudolph the Red-Nosed Reindeer brownies

Charlie Brown marshmallow pops

Grinch Rice Krispies treats (green with Red Hot candy heart in the center)

Parting Gifts: a small movie-themed gift would be great. A popcorn bucket with bags of microwaveable popcorn and boxes of candy would hit the spot!

Suggested Movies:
For the Family
A Charlie Brown Christmas
The Grinch Who Stole Christmas
A Christmas Carol (various versions, but I like the Scrooge
   McDuck one!)
Jingle All the Way
Rise of the Guardians
Babes in Toyland
Rudolph the Red-Nosed Reindeer
Frosty the Snowman
Classics
Christmas in Connecticut
It's a Wonderful Life
Miracle on 34th Street
A Christmas Story
White Christmas
Funny
Home Alone
Scrooged
Christmas Vacation
Elf
The Santa Clause
Bad Moms
Romantic
The Holiday
Last Christmas
Love Actually
Holidate
Hallmark Holiday Movie Marathon!
A Little Different
The Nightmare Before Christmas
Die Hard

ICE-SKATING PARTY

Gather up a group and take them to your nearest ice-skating rink or frozen pond, if you live somewhere cool like that. Texas does not have those anywhere. Bring your food and beverages with you, skates and gear too if you're going somewhere that doesn't rent out equipment, and have a great time. Don't forget to bundle up!!!

Suggested Details
Music: provided by the rink, or the sounds of nature
Decorations: no decorations needed as you'll be away from
home.
Alcoholic Beverage: Ice-skating could be hazardous without
adding alcohol to the mix. Consider skipping the alcohol
for this one!
Nonalcoholic Beverage: a hot chocolate station including
personalized mixers (like flavored syrups) and toppings
(think marshmallows, whipped cream, sprinkles, chocolate chips, and more . . .)
Food: Think about fun foods that can easily travel with you
(to a rink or local pond), can be picked up (including
with gloves on), and are easy to clean up. By the way,
nothing with toothpicks—don't want someone falling and
poking an eye out. Also, foods that are warm will be a
hit, just make sure you bring a way to keep them warm.
Here are a few ideas:
Bavarian pretzels (can include dips!)
churros
pigs-in-blankets
taquitos
pinwheel sandwiches
egg rolls (either traditional or stuffed with other things like
Philly cheesesteak, pulled pork, etc.)
sugar cookies (shape them like ice-skates!)
Parting Gifts: an ice-skate shaped ornament for the tree!

CAROLING PARTY

Why don't we carol as much as we used to? Gather up some people for a good time and go find a neighborhood or a busy set of shops to go sing to and watch the people around you light up with enjoyment.

A few tips . . . If going into a neighborhood, pick ones with houses closer together to save some walking. Think about only approaching those with Christmas lights so that you aren't singing Christmas tunes to someone who doesn't celebrate the holiday. Don't sing more than one or two songs per house. They don't want to stand there that long!

A master organizer might bring a truck pulling a flatbed (think hayrides) to cart you and your goodies all around. Or at least a wagon to bring the food, booze, plates, and cups with you.

Even more fun . . . try to get everyone to dress up in a theme. You could go traditional Victorian Christmas carolers, or Santa's elves, or everyone wears Santa hats, or have fun with it!

Suggested Details

Music: bring printed copies of the music and lyrics of the songs you'll be singing.

Decorations: no decorations needed as you'll be away from home.

Alcoholic & Nonalcoholic Beverage: "Here We Come A-Wassailing" is a Christmas caroling song, so . . . bring some wassail to drink (real apple cider, ginger, lemon, spices). Bring bourbon to mix in for anyone who wants it with a kick.

Food: You could go two ways here:

Option 1: Like the Ice-Skating Party, bring some finger foods for ease. (See that party for ideas.)

Option 2: Wait to feed everyone a meal when you finish caroling and get back to your house. You'll be hungry from all the walking, so we suggest either a more traditional meal like a roasted ham or turkey with all the sides or something warm and hearty like spaghetti. Have your guests each bring a side to help you out!

Parting Gifts: A holiday-themed picture frame. Make sure to get a group photo to send to everyone to put in their frame.

Acknowledgments

I get to do what I love surrounded by the people I love—a blessing that I thank God for every single day. Writing and publishing a book doesn't happen without the support and help from a host of incredible people.

To my fantastic romance readers: Thank you for going on these journeys with me, for your kindness, your support, and generally being awesome. Jocelyn and Ben's story. Inspired very loosely by classic Hollywood holiday rom coms like *Christmas in Connecticut*, I had so much fun writing this. I hope you fell in love with these characters and their story as much as I did. If you have a free second, please think about leaving a review. Also, I love to connect with my readers, so I hope you'll drop a line and say "Howdy" on any of my social media!

To my editor, John Scognamiglio: Thank you for your continued love of Snowball and a shared love of classic holiday movies!

To my agent, Evan Marshall: Thank you for your always kind and wise advice!

To the team at Kensington: I know how much work goes into each and every book, a ton of which authors never see. I thank you so much for making this book the best it could be!

To my support team of writing buddies, readers, reviewers, friends, and family (you know who you are), you are my happy.

Finally, to my husband, I love you so much. You are why I know what a good man is and how he acts in this world, which means I found my hero. And to our amazing kids, you are my light, my laughter, and my love.

Visit our website at
KensingtonBooks.com
to sign up for our newsletters, read
more from your favorite authors, see
books by series, view reading group
guides, and more!

Become a Part of Our
Between the Chapters Book Club
Community and Join the Conversation

Submit your book review for a chance to win exclusive
Between the Chapters swag you can't get anywhere else!
https://www.kensingtonbooks.com/pages/review/